Make U Sweat

Also by Amie Stuart

Nailed

"Kink" in *Built*

Hands On

Make U Sweat

AMIE STUART

APHRODISIA
KENSINGTON BOOKS
http://www.kensingtonbooks.com

APHRODISIA are published by

Kensington Publishing Corp.
850 Third Avenue
New York, NY 10022

All Kensington Titles, Imprints, and Distributed Lines are available at special quantity discounts for bulk purchases for sales promotions, premiums, fund-raising, and educational or institutional use.

Special book excerpts or customized printings can also be created to fit specific needs. For details, write or phone the office of the Kensington special sales manager: Kensington Publishing Corp., 850 Third Avenue, New York, NY 10022, attn: Special Sales Department, Phone: 1-800-221-2647.

Aphrodisia and the A logo Reg. U.S. Pat & TM Off.

ISBN-13: 978-0-7582-2855-0
ISBN-10: 0-7582-2855-4

First Kensington Trade Paperback Printing: September 2008

10 9 8 7 6 5 4 3 2 1

Printed in the United States of America

ACKNOWLEDGMENTS

I have to start with a huge thank-you to two of the most important people in my life: my editor, Audrey LaFehr, and my agent, Holly Root, for putting up with the craziness that is . . . uniquely *me*.

I hate authors who spend pages thanking everyone and the neighbor's cat, but, well, if it wasn't for a lot of pretty amazing folks, this one might not have gotten done. In no particular order (because we all know Cece doesn't play favorites) . . . Raine Weaver, Denise McDonald, Tanya T. Holmes, Lynn Matherly, and my NAS(ty) girls—Shelli, Feisty, and Karen—for the hugs, the laughs, the drinks, and the kicks in the ass, and my challenge buddies—Rachelle Chase, Jackie Barbosa, and Emma Petersen.

Last but not least, I have to thank Dad. No one else would get up at the crack of dawn, drive me across town, and sit in the hospital with me . . . reading. Love you . . . Me.

Contents

Move Me

1

Jack Saunders stood just inside his office doorway, his mouth open and ready to tell me how late I was and how *irritated* he was. His eyes, a gorgeous shade of chocolate brown, switched from anger to surprise, darting from my face to my chest, where they lingered, and back again.

I wasn't sure if he'd been reading the bold, red CAVANAUGH BROTHERS MOVING emblazoned on my gray T-shirt or checking out my tits, but figured it was probably a bit of both. "Mr. Saunders? I'm Reece Cavanaugh."

Frowning in confusion, he nodded and licked his lips as if he was still trying to get the words "You're a woman" out of his mouth. He failed miserably.

"We're here to move you." Considering what he'd probably been thinking all of ten seconds ago, I couldn't resist a smile at my little quip, and neither could he. At least he had a sense of humor.

Chuckling, he tilted his head, stepped out of the way, and motioned me inside. "I didn't realize—"

"Most people don't." I waved it off. Even though Cavanaugh

Brothers was sort of a Galveston institution, most people *didn't* realize it was now run by women until it was too late, until moving day was on them and they were so desperate to move that no way would they turn us away.

We weren't all women, mind you, but the ones who counted, who ran two of the crews, paid the bills, and signed the paychecks were. Unfortunately, being the boss didn't get any of us out of doing manual labor. Especially in the summertime and *especially* when we were shorthanded.

"Here it is," he said, waving a hand at the office. Other than a few end tables and lamps, matching leather chair and sofa, and one oversized desk that made my back ache just looking at it, the room held about twenty boxes.

Against the far wall was an empty set of built-in bookshelves, and I could only imagine how many of the boxes at my feet contained the books those shelves had once held. "You read a lot."

I'm sure I'd said stupider things in my life, but Jack either missed my statement of the obvious or chose to ignore it.

"Some for pleasure; mostly for work." He crossed the room and opened the blinds, letting in some of the mid-morning sunshine.

The sign outside his office door only said JACK SAUNDERS, but considering we were on the second floor of a medical complex, it wasn't too hard to figure out his line of work. I stopped dreading the late-afternoon backache I'd have long enough to ask, "What do you do?"

He gave me what could only be called an embarrassed smile, as if he knew all the horrible things I'd like to do to his precious books, and shrugged. "Psychologist."

Just then Carla showed up with a dolly, her back-support belt, a very nonsexy corset that accentuated her own chest firmly in place. For a minute there it seemed as if old Jack might pop out of his jeans.

"You forgot this." Carla held out my belt.

Clamping the clipboard between my knees, I took it and strapped myself in. "Where's Robbie?"

"She's backing the truck in."

"So, uh, do you ladies need some help?" Jack stared back and forth between Carla and me, as if he really couldn't believe we were going to move his stuff. As if it was all some joke and any second now we'd whip out a portable CD player and start stripping.

"No, sir. For insurance purposes. You understand." Grinning, I retrieved my clipboard and quickly finished counting boxes.

That impending backache was worth the disappointment on his face when the CD player never materialized.

"So what happened to the Cavanaugh Brothers?" Jack asked, once we had all his books and furniture stored in his newly renovated home office. All that was left was for him to sign off on the work order.

From somewhere behind me, my sister, Robbie snorted, "They had daughters, dude."

"Robbie Jo." I gave Jack an exasperated look, one he'd understand if he had siblings. Or children. "I'll meet you in the truck."

Carla was already down there, chomping at the bit to call it quits for the day and hightail it home so she could get dressed up and spend the evening in Houston.

"Fine," Robbie drawled. She spun her dolly around and headed out the front door, the wheels banging on the stairs on her way down.

She's only twenty-five, I silently reminded myself. Her age

didn't negate the occasional overwhelming desire to smack her upside her head. I'd given up a weekend with my daughter for this, and we still had one more move today.

Not that Chloe cared.

She was probably tickled shitless to miss the lectures about her excessive partying and poor performance in her first year of college.

"Is she always so . . ." Jack licked his lips, trying to hide a smile.

"—mouthy? You better believe it. But she's my baby sister—"

"—and you love her anyway," he finished for me, his voice gentle in understanding.

"You have siblings?" I asked.

"Nope."

"Oh, right, the shrink thing."

He shrugged, as if to say, "Whatever" and handed me the clipboard, a contemplative expression on his face. "I guess with a name like Reece it's pretty easy to fool people."

I stopped scribbling long enough to give him a stern look. "We don't *try* to fool people." Frankly, he'd be astounded at the amount of referral business we had. And we'd all been helping in the family business since we were old enough to drive, or add, or whatever our dads could put us to work doing.

"I didn't mean to insinuate that you did. I was just saying . . ."

"It's okay." I gave him a reassuring smile, reminding myself to ease up and not take it so personally. "Really." I ripped off his copy of the paperwork, letting him know we'd charge the final amount on his credit card, then stuck out my hand. "My friends call me Reecie, by the way."

"Reecie." His lips, surrounded by a sprinkling of stubble, curved into a small smile as he gingerly folded the receipt and tucked it in his shirt pocket. "I like that. So, Reecie, what do you do for fun?"

"Work, work, and more work," sprang to my lips, but I didn't say it. That, the headache that was a daughter in college, and the occasional date was the extent of my life. I guess the sigh that escaped me was answer enough.

"That bad, huh?"

I shrugged and sighed again, licking my lips as I took another hard look at Jack. His casual clothing looked expensive, if the little logo on his green polo shirt was anything to go by. He was about six feet tall, well built, at least my age, with a body that promised he worked out regularly but enjoyed a good meal. And those eyes, those luscious brown eyes. *I'm a sucker for pretty eyes.* "I don't get out much," I confessed. "Do you actually see people here in your home?" I asked, taking in the oversized desk set in front of an equally oversized window, and almost as many bookshelves as there had been in the office we'd moved the books *from.*

"I'm . . . actually taking a break, regrouping. And you just changed the subject."

"Sorry. Bad habit." From downstairs came the sound of the horn blowing, a sign of Carla's impatience. "I guess it must get pretty stressful, listening to other people's problems all the time." I followed him out of the room, and we meandered down the narrow hallway toward the front door.

"Yeah, well," he sighed, "I recently got divorced . . . again, and I felt kind of hypocritical counseling people about their families . . ."

I nodded in understanding, then proceeded to stick my foot in my mouth. "Can I ask you something?"

He turned and smiled down at me. His knowing grin left little creases in the side of his face, giving the impression he smiled a lot. He looked a lot more happy-go-lucky than he sounded, and I could see why people would want to pour out their troubles to him. He might not have kids, but he could have passed for any one of the dozens of football dads I'd met during Chloe's cheer-leading days—easygoing, with broad shoulders to lean on. "Shoot."

"Never mind."

"This one's on the house. Since you didn't complain about the books."

I bit my tongue, while wondering what in the hell had possessed me to even think about dumping my troubles on a poor stranger. A client, no less. Other than the bartender at the Tiki Lounge, who was also my oldest friend, I didn't exactly have a lot of sympathetic ears to bend. "I'll pass."

"Maybe you'd reconsider over drinks tonight?"

"Drinks?" I couldn't seem to take my eyes off his lips as he continued speaking.

"Yeah, you know. Cocktails . . . moonlight . . . us."

Jack got major points for asking a hot, sweaty, chubby woman who looked less than her best out. For obvious reasons (namely Chloe and the death of my Uncle Joe), it had been almost a year since I'd been on a date. And besides, the guy was a shrink, he got paid to listen to other people's problems, which, in my book, equated with *probably harmless.* "Sure."

Outside I squeezed into the cab of the truck, content to let Carla drive while the chilly A/C dried the sweat on my shirt.

"What took you so long?" Carla hurriedly pulled the truck out, turning so hard she narrowly missed a bike some kid had left laying too close to the street.

"Carla, damn!" Robbie fell against me, struggling to right herself.

"Quit'cher bitchin'."

"Me bitching? Oh my God, that's so rich! You've done nothing but—"

"Ladies," I sighed, leaning my head back against the seat. "Shut the fuck up." Silence caressed my ears for all of two minutes and forty-seven seconds . . . or something like that.

"So, Sis, why were you in there for so long?"

"He—"

"Did'ja get his number?" Robbie gently dug an elbow in my side.

"If she did, she'd only ask him to tell his friends about Cavanaugh Brothers Moving!" Carla waggled her finger in the air for emphasis, but there was no humor in her words, only sarcasm. Which, I suppose, was a form of humor, but Carla had been a first-class bitch lately, and it was getting old.

I ignored them both, turning my attention instead outside the truck's window to the sunny summer day that was nowhere near ending despite the fact it was now late afternoon.

"Damn, I'm ready for a beer," Robbie Jo muttered, nudging me again. "Go with me?"

"To the Tiki Lounge? Not tonight. Think I'll catch up on some paperwork and then grab some dinner on my way home." I'd just lied to my sister and had no clue why.

"I could bring you something."

"That's okay, Sis." Some broiled shrimp and scallops and a glass of wine on the back deck, after a nice hot shower, sounded like heaven, but I'd agreed to a date. With Jack Saunders. My own smile was reflected back at me in the passenger-side window as I reminded myself it was just a drink.

A quick call to Jack once I got back to the shop and we agreed to meet at a bar he knew, far away from Robbie Jo and the Tiki Lounge. I hit the house, quickly searching the Internet for directions. If their website was anything to go by, jeans were out for tonight. Sighing, I headed for my closet, where there wasn't much to choose from. My workday wardrobe was jeans and T-shirts, and only jeans and T-shirts. And other than the dress I'd worn to Chloe's graduation, I didn't have much to choose from, or any time to go shopping. Truth be told, I'd rather see the dentist than shop anyway. In the back of my closet I found a slinky black number that probably hadn't seen the light of day in years. You can't go wrong with black, but I made a note to expand my dating wardrobe soon.

The parking lot of the Blue Note looked like a high-end car dealership with the Mercedeses and BMWs and the like, but I didn't see Jack's as I got out and valeted my Murano. Jack stood waiting just inside the front door, freshly shaved and dressed in khakis and a crisp green shirt.

"Hope you like jazz." He pulled me to him for a quick hug, the smell of his aftershave filling my nose, and I relaxed against him, enjoying the brief intimate contact. His arm rested possessively at the base of my spine as he led me deeper into the club, to a tiny table close to the stage and the dance floor.

"What'll you have?" he asked as he moved his chair close to mine and sat.

"Scotch on the rocks, please." I knotted my fingers in my lap and took a deep breath, letting out a flutter of nerves as I glanced around the club. Even though there was no band on-stage, jazz music played softly. The couples around us chatted and laughed and nibbled on appetizers.

"I didn't take you for a Scotch-and-soda lady."

I shrugged. "I'm just full of surprises."

"I bet you are." He gave the waitress our order and his credit card to run a tab, then turned his attention back to me. In the bar's dim light his warm, intense gaze, the way he seemed so able to give me his undivided attention, reminded me of his profession, and I cursed myself. Now was not the time to be thinking of work—his or mine. "Do you dance?"

"Not since high school," I ruefully confessed.

"I doubt it's changed much." He motioned to the few couples swaying gently on the floor.

I lifted the glass the waitress had discreetly slipped in front of me and said, "Let me get a few of these down first."

His expression cooled slightly and he nodded. He accepted his own drink with a soft "thanks." "So how long have you been in the moving business?"

"Do you really want to talk about my work?"

He gave me a once-over that warmed my skin. "I want to know everything about you."

"Why?" immediately sprang to my lips, but I didn't say it. "Twenty years."

"*Twenty?*"

"I went to work for my dad at sixteen. Do the math." I sipped at my Scotch, letting the chilly drink course through me. My foot started tapping as the familiar strains of an old TLC song came on.

Jack glanced under the table, then quirked an eyebrow, a silent invitation to dance. I hadn't had near enough to drink, but I nervously pushed myself to my feet anyway and put my hand in his, the music too heady to resist. He was a good dancer, making it easy for me to relax, and we quickly went from a slow grinding sway to something much more suggestive that left us both breathless and laughing. We stayed for some old LL Cool J, moving back into each other's arms while he sang about making hot sweet love to someone else's woman. I snuggled close, burying my head in the crook of Jack's neck, while he and the music gently seduced me. His hands slid down the dip in my back to caress my hips, nibbling away at my resolve to

11

just have a drink and flirt a little with Jack. His business-casual demeanor hid the soul of a man who knew women, knew how to seduce them, and probably love them, but there'd be no loving for Jack Saunders tonight. At least not the type that required the removal of clothes.

Smiling, I snuggled a little closer.

We stood outside holding hands, waiting for the valet to bring our cars around. The evening breeze made the night an unusually cool one, causing me to shiver.

"If I had a jacket, I'd give it to you." His voice was low and husky, seductive, as he wrapped his arms around me.

"Thanks."

"How about a nightcap at my place?"

"Jack—" I turned so I could look up at him, wishing I was a different type of woman. "I had a really nice time tonight."

"But no nightcap." He smiled ruefully.

"Rain check," I offered as the valet came to a stop in front of us and hopped out of Jack's blue BMW.

"How about a drive down the beach? I'll put the top down?"

Shaking my head, I leaned in to press a kiss to his chin. He shifted his head and our lips met lightly and tentatively, exploring as we tested each other's limits.

The jingle of keys reminded us that we had at least one attendant waiting for his tip so he could move on to the next customer.

"I'll call you." Jack kissed me one last time and pressed some bills into the attendant's hand before circling his car and sliding behind the wheel.

I stood there, my tingly lower lip caught between my teeth, and watched him until the arrival of my Murano blocked my view.

2

Sunday morning I settled in with my coffee and even more paper-work, smiling smugly to myself over making it home before Robbie Jo had.

Liz, our receptionist/mother hen/bookkeeper took care of most of the day to day, but there were still time cards to check, schedules to make out, taxes, and inspections—the list went on and on. And lately most of our employees tended to be pretty transient. No sooner would the ink dry on the new-hire paper-work, then he'd be gone.

To that end, I also called a guy I'd interviewed earlier in the week and told him he could start on Robbie's crew the follow-ing Friday. At least he'd been up front about the fact that he wasn't going to be permanent. And we'd gotten applications from some pretty strong-looking college students who were home for the summer. I'd probably take at least two of them on as well. If our summer ran true to form, I'd need all the help I could get.

Help, of course, reminded me of Chloe. I'd expected her to come home this summer and help out, which I'd desperately needed, planning to put her to work in the office, but she'd informed me a few weeks ago that she was staying in Austin. She had balls, that was for damned sure, considering she'd failed two classes last semester and brought home C's in two more. C's! And the only time I ever heard from her was when she needed money. Contrary to what she believed, I hadn't managed to figure out how to pull hundred-dollar bills out of the air. Sighing, I headed for the kitchen to refill my coffee cup. At least she'd managed to get a job, even if she would probably blow most of her money.

Thank God I hadn't asked Jack for advice. The poor man probably got asked for more freebies than a hooker.

Laughing softly to myself reminded me of how his eyes had crinkled at the corners when he'd smiled. Unfortunately, standing in the kitchen aimlessly stirring my coffee and grinning like an idiot wasn't going to get my paperwork done.

Back in the office I tapped my pencil on a rubber-banded stack of time cards and tried to ignore the gorgeous day dawning outside, wooing me to come and take a walk in the salty morning air. With a frustrated scrub of my scalp, I unbound the cards and got to work. The sooner I finished, the sooner I could walk down the beach to the Hairy Elephant and get some breakfast.

I was on the homestretch when Robbie came down the stairs, dressed in oversized boxers and a faded tank top, dragging last night's conquest by the hand. The sight made me roll my eyes. I wasn't a prude and, normally, I went on plenty of dates; I just didn't feel the need to sleep with nearly anything that moved—like my sister did.

They slid past the office door and out of my view. A minute later he darted through my carefully cultivated patch of Bermuda grass and out of sight.

By the time Robbie came bouncing into the office, a satisfied grin on her face and a cup of coffee in her hand, I'd returned to work.

"Looks like you had a good time." I glanced up from the time sheets I was filling in.

"Always do." Hell, she *sounded* like she was grinning. Checking wasn't really necessary.

I flipped the card over and started on another employee's page, my pencil darting across the page until I had to stop and total the figures, my fingers flying over the adding machine with the ease of years of use. I'd been adding those damned cards up since my dad had taught me to use the ten-key machine . . . right about the time he'd had "the talk" with me (yeah, the one about puberty).

"Just be careful."

"Always am."

"I know, Robbie. I just can't help but thinking one of these days the cops are gonna wake me up in the middle of the night to tell me you flipped your car in a race or . . ."

"Jesus, Reece, chill the fuck out." She surged out of the battered red chair she'd flopped in, firing off one parting shot before she disappeared up the stairs. "No wonder Chloe won't come home."

Yowch! Talk about a direct hit. With a frustrated grunt, I tightened my ponytail and decided it was time for some fresh air and breakfast. Grabbing a twenty out of my wallet, I shoved it in my pocket and slid my feet into some Crocs before stepping outside.

Most of our neighbors were longtime Galveston residents, now retired, though the neighborhood was slowly beginning to turn over as young families moved in. More than a few of them were taking advantage of the cool early morning air to get their grass watered and flowers weeded. Many we'd known since we were in diapers—this was definitely a mixed blessing, but I wouldn't live anywhere else.

I hopped down the steps and stretched my arms over my head, desperate to clear my head as I started the half-mile walk to the Hairy Elephant. The walk down Quincy wasn't that long and other than the occasional person watering or weeding or puttering in their yard, it was just me and the rustle of palm trees. The knots between my shoulder blades slowly loosened and my leg muscles warmed up, allowing me to increase my pace until I'd covered the four blocks to Seawall Boulevard.

Five lanes and a stretch of beach were all that separated me from the Gulf of Mexico, and even though it was out of my way to cross the street, I did it anyway. I never got tired of the sight of the early-morning sun bouncing off the water, and the occasional glimpse of an oil rig far out in the Gulf. Overhead, gulls screamed, repeatedly drawing my attention to the beach as I briskly walked the last few blocks to the slightly dilapidated restaurant.

The outside was painted a sunny yellow and raspberry, with a sign done in matching colors to attract tourists to a real local eatery. Unfortunately, or fortunately depending on how you looked at it, not many strangers wanted to eat someplace called The Hairy Elephant. But that suited the regulars, like myself, just fine.

Waiting at the light to cross back to the other side, I spotted what looked like Jack's BMW convertible pulling into the restaurant's parking lot. This early in the morning it was hard to miss—a Six Series in royal blue. At least, a drooling Robbie had said it was a Six Series, and she was the car expert in the family.

It could have been a *world* series for all I knew or cared, but it was a damned pretty car.

The light changed, allowing me to cross, and I found myself practically jogging to make it to the door by the time Jack did. Then questioned myself as to why.

"Morning." I maneuvered around an old Chevy Impala covered with more than a touch of rust. One scratch and I'd probably find myself at a doc-in-the-box getting a tetanus shot.

"Morning, yourself." He pulled up short, the contemplative, almost sleepy expression on his face quickly changing to surprise. As if I'd interrupted some serious thinking.

"Are you stalking me, Mr. Saunders?" Grinning, I pushed a wisp of hair out of my eyes.

"I was about to ask you the same thing."

"I haven't seen you here before." And I came here every Sunday. I pulled the restaurant's door open, holding it for him as I stepped inside. "Oh my God," I hissed. My mouth began to water and my stomach reminded me of how empty it was.

Behind me, Jack chuckled as his hand came to rest on my shoulder. "Smells like heaven."

A heaven filled with hash, greasy eggs, ham, sizzling sausage, homemade biscuits, and redeye gravy. I could have died happy just then, even with the distraction of Jack touching me. There wasn't a thing on Jude's menu that was healthy or even remotely doctor approved, but Sunday was my no-diet day. While I scanned the restaurant for a booth, Jack's hand slid to the base of my spine, sure and strong and warm enough to leave my nipples embarrassingly hard underneath my scruffy T-shirt. My belly tightened ever so slightly in a way that acknowledged his presence as a male with protective instincts.

I liked it. It was different, warm, comforting, as if Jack were someone I could rely on. And other than my father, I didn't usually think of men as reliable.

The feeling was pleasant, but incredibly surprising.

His hand tightened enough to draw my attention as he nudged me toward the last booth in the back.

"Normally, I sit at the bar."

"Normally, I sleep late and do brunch." Jack laughed and scrubbed at his head, mussing his hair. In the morning light it was a deep chestnut with just a touch of gray at the temples to make him look distinguished. "It's been years since I've been in here."

"My dad used to bring me here as a kid," I mused, smiling to myself at the memory. Sunday-morning breakfast had been our time, when we'd drop Robbie off to play with Carla and take a few hours for some QT, as my dad had called it. Of course, most of it had revolved around business talk, but I hadn't minded.

"I used to come here with my first wife. We moved down here right after I graduated from college."

"Galveston doesn't seem like much of a place to set up shop."

"The commute to Houston's not that bad, and she loved the beach."

"What happened?" At his quirked eyebrow, I apologized. "I'm not normally so nosy."

"She decided the beaches in California were more to her liking, and I didn't want to go with her."

I shook my head in understanding. "Her and Chloe's dad. No beaches," I explained, "he just took off." After eighteen years the memory of his abandoning us barely registered on my Richter scale of emotions. It was just a fact, nothing more; nothing less. "I guess that takes care of any mutual stalking, huh?"

Laughing, he nodded, ducking his head slightly and rolling his shoulders.

"So why'd you skip brunch?"

He wet his lips, taking a moment before he replied. "Because brunch means going to the country club and running into my ex-wife."

"But—" I gave him a pointed look, thinking of his earlier comment about California.

"My third ex." No wonder he'd hesitated.

"Whoa," I said under my breath, saved from saying anything more by the arrival of our waitress with two cups of hot coffee and one menu.

Greta knew me well enough to know I always got the eggs and hash. The service left a lot to be desired, but the food made up for it. "Thanks, Greta."

"What do you recommend?" Jack asked once she was gone. He flipped the one-sided menu over and back, then looked up at me.

"Eggs and hash. It's homemade. Or the hash omelet."

"That homemade, too?" His shoulders shook with silent laughter.

"Yeah, anything with hash. Best damn thing you'll ever put in your mouth."

"I dunno about that. I've had some pretty nice . . . things . . . in my mouth." He leaned forward, his arms crossed on the tabletop, his warm, frank gaze pinning me in place. There was no apology in his eyes; he wasn't the slightest bit embarrassed at the innuendo he'd thrown down. Especially with him being fresh out of a divorce. Obviously, that didn't bother him much.

"What about your ex-wife? How long were you two together?"

Jack was a lot of things, but dumb wasn't one of them. He knew exactly what I'd just done and frankly, it'd been pretty silly of me to try and change the subject like that. But it was too late to take the question back.

"Five years. She came with a lot of money; left with a lot of money, too, and a lot of baggage." He grimaced, his shoulders rolling in a shrug as if he could shake it off. "You know how they say therapists are usually more screwed up than their patients? Guess I'm living proof."

Then again, maybe it did bother him. I'd obviously hit some sort of sore spot. I let the sound of silverware on plates, dishes crashing in the back of the restaurant, the cooks and waitresses shouting at each other, fill the silence while I mulled that over. I'd never honestly thought about it, assuming someone who made a living giving other people answers wouldn't have to go looking for answers of their own. The return of Greta for our orders also bought me a little more time.

Jack handed her his menu. "I'll have what she's having," he said, motioning in my direction. Once she was gone, he turned his attention back to me. "Does my humanity bother you?"

"I just never thought about it." I pressed my back into the worn material of the booth's cushions and crossed my legs.

"My third wife was also a drunk." He poured sugar in his coffee and stirred, his attention elsewhere. At least for a bit. "Everything was fine until I decided it was in my liver's best interest to stop trying to keep up with her." He added a little cream and took a sip before continuing. "My second wife was just plain needy. She still calls me for advice, and we've been divorced six years. The logical solution is to never get married again."

"Better you than me." I sipped my own coffee, wincing as the bitter black brew hit my tongue. After adding a dash of sugar and a bunch of cream, I tapped my spoon on the side of the cup a few times for emphasis.

"Why? Did you hate being married?"

I picked up the cup and eyeballed him over the rim. "Are you analyzing me?"

"No, but I will." He leaned forward and gave me that same unapologetic grin, but this time there was more of a challenge to it. "If you want me to."

"I was never married and I'm not sure I want to hear what you have to say about me."

He slowly ran the back of his hand across his unshaven chin a few times. Thoughtfully. I waited, hoping our breakfast would come and distract him from the business of me, but no such luck.

"You are a woman who is always in charge, in all things and at all times. Or, at least you try to be, and if you're not, it frustrates you. Quit pushing back against the booth; you're not getting your teeth cleaned."

My face burning, I released my grip on the booth's seat and slowly eased my body upright, forcing painfully stiff shoulders to relax as I adjusted my crossed legs.

"On the other hand, you're low maintenance, which I like." Grinning, he drained his cup of coffee and set it down in time for Greta's return with our breakfast. Even the smell of scrambled eggs, fried bacon, potatoes, and corned beef couldn't distract me from the fact he'd called me low maintenance.

"Why do you care if I'm low maintenance?"

A bite of his breakfast halfway to his lips, he paused. "Because I want to have an affair with you."

Okay, well, that did it. I'd officially lost my appetite. Not because Jack was unattractive or anything, just from shock. I'd had a lot of men say a lot of things to me since I'd sprouted boobs and pubes, as Robbie would say, but . . . my eyes narrowed thoughtfully. "Doesn't an affair imply one of us is married?"

"A fling, then. Call it what you want, Reecie, I want to have sex with you. Soon." And with that, he dug into his breakfast as if he'd just informed me he was going to buy a new car or paint his house. And, no, I didn't miss the fact he'd used my nickname.

I picked at my eggs and fried potatoes, nibbling at them until my appetite overcame my hang-up about eating with a man who'd shrinked me, then had the balls to tell me he wanted to sleep with me—*soon, even.* Not that I hadn't realized he was attracted to me, but his bluntness, well, amazed me.

Sighing, I grabbed the catsup bottle and liberally covered my hash, mixing some with the eggs and forking up a large bite. "Why me?" I asked once I'd chewed and swallowed.

"More coffee?" Greta appeared out of nowhere.

Nodding, I nudged my cup in the waitress's direction before taking another bite of my breakfast to cover the awkward silence. You just didn't ask a man why he wanted to sleep with you. It wasn't like I was a troll or had been celibate for eighteen years, or Jack probably wouldn't have asked me out.

Jack murmured his thanks to Greta, who slid out of sight, a smirk on her old face. "Because, one, you're low maintenance. You don't drink that much. You don't smoke. Which . . . I hate."

"How—"

"Trust me. You don't wear a lot of makeup or jewelry; you've got calluses on your hands, your hair is clean and in a ponytail, you don't dress to impress, you don't get manicures; you dress for function and comfort. I want to sleep with a woman who's laid back and easygoing. You're kind of a control freak; you need to relax, and I think I can help with that. You're not laid back, but you are low maintenance. The way I see it, we've got ourselves a win-win situation."

Under the table my unmanicured hands were curled into fists. "So you want to sleep with me because I'm a . . . Low-maintenance control freak?" *That made a lot of sense—not!*

"On the outside, you're low maintenance, and, for what it's

worth, I'll take you to dinner, too. On the inside . . . you've got issues. You need to learn to loosen up and—"

"And you're just the man to show me how." I hadn't quite decided whether to get up and leave in a huff or laugh my ass off.

"Yeah."

"And do you charge for your services?"

Laughing, he proceeded to fill his coffee cup with sugar again. "That would be unethical. And besides, I'm not a sexual surrogate."

"How do you know I'm a control freak in bed, too? Or that I'm not?" I pushed my plate out of the way, my appetite officially gone, and fixed my fresh cup of coffee. I'd never had any complaints about my performance in bed. Of course, I never stayed around long enough to find out if there were any complaints, either. I didn't like sleeping in strange places, and I didn't like sharing my sleeping space.

Shit . . . he was right. I *was* a control freak. "I don't think so, Jack, but thanks."

Sliding out of the booth, I pulled the twenty from my pocket and threw it on the table. "Nice to see you again. And thanks for the advice."

"If you change your mind . . ."

I wouldn't. As I walked out of The Hairy Elephant I knew I wouldn't.

23

3

It was Thursday, four days after my run-in with Jack at the Hairy Elephant. And all I could think of was the stress relief a nice hard fuck and a toe-curling, back-scratching orgasm would give me—damn him to hell for being right on all counts!

But some hot sweaty body-mambo was sounding better and better, and all thanks to my family.

On Tuesday Chloe had called, needing 350 dollars. Except she'd been completely unwilling to explain why. Frankly, I didn't even want to know why, but I wasn't about to turn over that kind of cash for no good reason. So we had a date for dinner this evening in Austin, which was a four-hour trip, give or take a few. Robbie Jo was late to work, which meant I was stuck getting my sister's new crew member's paperwork done.

Not that I minded; Cash seemed like a nice enough guy. Otherwise I wouldn't have hired him. I just needed to get on the road, and Carla had up and decided she needed a day of beauty to help her prepare for the arduous weekend ahead. I don't know why. Tomorrow she'd be out sweating her ass off with her crew.

Her and Robbie were going to be the death of me if I let them.

At least with three new hires this week I wouldn't have to be out leading a crew, and after the week I'd had, I deserved a weekend off. The plan was to take an overnight bag and stay in Austin so I didn't have to drive back late at night (in case this thing with Chloe took longer than I thought).

There weren't many reasons for a teenage girl to want that kind of money and none of them were good.

The sound of paper sliding across my desk brought my attention back to the here and now. I took the W-9 and the rest of the paperwork and slid it all into Cash's folder before standing up. "Let me get you a back brace and a few uniform shirts. What are you? About a medium?"

At five-foot-nine Cash McBride was only of average height, but his height was the only thing average about him, and I could only hope that Robbie Jo didn't run him off. Good help was hard to find, and even though she knew better than to (literally) screw with the help, that didn't always mean she listened to me.

In case you haven't figured it out by now, Robbie and Carla have a tendency to do what they want and leave good ole Reecie to clean up the mess.

No wonder I was a control freak.

I'd thought of nothing else since my run-in with Jack. Hell, it wasn't like I'd chosen to be one, it had just happened.

"Reece, is something wrong?"

Poor Cash was getting the short end of my attention span today. "I'm sorry." I gently closed the cabinet where I kept the uniforms. Turning, I handed him three short-sleeved polyester shirts, three gray T-shirts, and the black belt. "It's been a crazy week. But Robbie will be here tomorrow when you get here—" She'd better, or I'd know the reason why, "—and we've already

26

got three moves lined up for your crew. If it's too much for your knee, just let Robbie know."

"Is that necessary?" The solemn, softly asked question pulled me up short.

Leaning against the desk, I slowly crossed my arms over my chest and studied Cash. Honestly I hadn't looked too far past the honey-blond hair and muscles, other than to assure myself that a knee injury earlier this year wouldn't prevent him from doing his job. "Robbie really does need to know. There's a bit of a liability issue here, Cash. I want you to be able to do your job; I certainly don't want you struggling out there . . . or worse, getting hurt."

His face tightened almost imperceptibly. "I won't get hurt."

"Nobody ever *means* to get hurt." I set the clothing in the empty chair next to his.

"Tell me about it."

The four-hour drive to Austin felt more like twice that, my stomach churning and knotting up on itself with each passing mile as I prepared herself for the worst.

Pregnancy.

That thought had me stopping at a twenty-four-hour truck stop to buy a Sprite for my poor stomach.

Chloe's dad and I had been high school sweethearts planning a wedding and a future, then I'd gotten pregnant and Chad had decided that fatherhood wasn't his game. The state made sure I got my child-support checks every two weeks, but I'd seen neither hide nor hair of Chad Bastrop since our high school graduation.

I didn't want that for my daughter. I didn't want Chloe to have an abortion, either . . . or use drugs . . . or end up in jail or any of a million other things I could have—okay, *had*—obsessed about during the long drive.

I phoned Chloe the minute I pulled into the crowded parking lot of Carabba's on I-35. "Where are you?"

"At the bar waiting for you."

"Okay." I bit my tongue, choosing not to remind her that she was underage. Chloe had apparently gotten some recessive flirty girl gene—the one that had skipped me. My daughter could sweet-talk any man out of anything, and had honed her skills on her grandfather. It was scary, frightening, and a little awe-inspiring. Carla had it, too. Robbie Jo didn't, but then she didn't seem to need it.

I wedged my SUV between a Prius and Chloe's Accord and slid out, reluctant to suck in any of the hot early evening air after riding in air-conditioned comfort for so long. My poor stiff legs, however, were glad to get a stretch.

Inside, Chloe sat at the bar, wearing ripped jeans and a snug, equally worn-looking T-shirt, sipping a bright-red drink from a martini glass. With her killer bod and emerald green eyes, she was stunning the way only a young person could be, unscarred and unmarred by life. No wrinkles, no grey hairs, smooth skinned, fresh-faced and optimistic—hell, arrogant even. Arrogant enough to believe that *wanting it to be so* was enough to make her life turn out the way she planned.

"Are you hungry or are we drinking our dinner tonight?" I asked as I slid on the bar stool next to her.

"If you're buying, I'm eating."

Figured. I motioned to the bartender and ordered myself a margarita. Once it arrived, I slid off the stool and headed for a nearby table. We sat down and Chloe immediately slid a pack of cigarettes out of her purse.

I literally had to bite down on my tongue at the challenge in my daughter's eyes. Luckily I didn't have to witness her actually lighting up, as a waitress went cruising by and paused long enough to tell Chloe there was no smoking. With a roll of her pretty green eyes, Chloe shoved the cigarettes back in her purse, then met my gaze, the tilt of her chin daring me to say anything. Discretion being the better part of valor, and more importantly, my sanity, I chose to take a sip of my drink instead.

"Did you bring the money?" Chloe asked.

She didn't waste any time. I hadn't, but I'd write a check if necessary. I'd do whatever was necessary. That was my job. "You're going to have to tell me what it's for, Chloe."

She flicked at the swizzle sticks in her glass, obviously debating what to say to her mother. "Why? It's not like I've asked you for rent or help paying my bills."

"Why? *Why?* Chloe, three hundred and fifty dollars is a lot of money. It's your car payment. I'm not a—"

"—an ATM machine," she finished for me with a roll of her eyes.

"Chloe . . ." I reached out, trying to capture my daughter's hand, but falling short. "Are you pregnant?"

Chloe's face screwed up into an expression of horror (touched with a smattering of disgust either from the fact her mother had mentioned pregnancy or mentioned the occasional end result of sex, which Chloe did not want to hear about from her mother). "Do I *look* that dumb?"

"Even smart girls get pregnant." I was living proof of that, but didn't say so out loud. "If you were, would you tell me?"

"No, I'd just go have an abortion."

The thought raised questions I didn't want to ask. Questions that prevented me from finishing my drink. "Chloe."

I let my daughter's name hang there between us, the meaning perfectly clear. If she didn't tell me what she wanted the money for, she didn't stand a cupid's chance in hell of getting it.

"I'll pay you back," Chloe sighed, then took a long pull off her drink, draining half of it. Obviously, she was no stranger to happy hour.

Right at that moment, I felt incredibly old and more than a little scared. At what point had I so lost control of my daughter? Even though I didn't want it, I took a sip of my own drink and schooled my features into my best stern-mother face. "Chloe?"

"Fine!" she sighed, giving me another dreadful eye-roll. "There's these jeans—"

"Jeans?!" The knot that had once been my stomach tightened even further, but this time in anger. Here I'd been so worried that she was in trouble, was pregnant even, and all she'd wanted was a fucking pair of jeans. "Like *Levi's*?" I leaned across the table and fought the urge to smack my daughter upside her head for all the worry she'd caused me.

"Well, yeah. But they're *not* Levi's, and I'll pay you back, but there's this party next weekend and—"

"No."

"Mom!"

"No, goddamn it! I drove four fucking hours for . . . for . . . holy Jesus, Chloe, do you know what you put me through?"

"God, *chill*," Chloe muttered under her breath, glancing around, then added so I couldn't miss her, "Loosen up already. It's just a damned pair of jeans."

"Obviously it's a pair of jeans that means a lot to you. Loosen up, my ass. Maybe you should grow up. Good God, Chloe, that's more than the payment on your Accord."

"Fucking forget it, then." She drained the last of her drink and slammed the glass down.

Before I could say, "Watch your mouth," the waiter was at our table with menus.

"Would you ladies like to order now?"

"No." Chloe slid out of the booth.

"You're just going to leave?" I eased back in my seat, completely disgusted with myself, with Chloe, and with the whole situation. The fact we were fighting over a pair of jeans was ludicrous. "After I drove all this way."

"I didn't ask you to drive up here."

As she disappeared from sight, I waved the waiter off, snatched up my purse, and hustled out of the restaurant. "Chloe! Chloe!"

She never stopped walking, just hit the alarm on her little blue Accord and climbed in, backing out in such a hurry she nearly smashed into an old man in a Buick.

"Fuck it." With a sigh, I dug my keys out of my own purse and climbed in my Murano, starting it up. The thought of staying the night in a hotel had no appeal for me. Especially after things had gone so badly. The last thing I wanted to do was stay in Austin.

If I left right then, I could be home by midnight.

The long lonely ride home was better than a long lonely evening in some hotel room. I pointed my SUV back toward Galveston, wondering what Jack would say about his little control freak now. The thought almost made me laugh.

4

I sat listening to the sound of the phone ringing in my ear while I waited to see if Jack would pick up. Yes, I'd swallowed my pride and decided to call him on my lunch hour . . . or half hour. It was Saturday and we were so swamped with moves I'd ended up working, but I made sure my crews got time to eat.

"H'lo."

"Hello . . . hey, Jack." Pay attention, Reecie! "How are you?"

"Surprised to hear from you." Way to cut to the chase.

"I'm . . . sorry about Sunday. I acted childish."

"Consider yourself forgiven."

"Not so quick." Smiling, I waved José away. I knew it was nearly time to get back to work, but all I needed was five minutes.

"I'm waiting."

"I'd like to make it up to you. Buy you a drink tonight."

"It's kind of last minute."

Rolling my eyes, I crumpled up my trash and stacked the empty catsup packets. "I know," I sighed. "But I'm off tomorrow, and I'd really like to see you . . . tonight. If you're still interested."

"I didn't realize moving was such a crazy business."

"Work . . . my daughter who wanted $350 for a damned pair of jeans . . ." I sighed again, aware of how desperate I was sounding. The last thing I needed was him thinking I just wanted to meet up for advice. "First round's on me. What do you say?"

"Where?"

"Someplace low-key okay?"

"I'm game."

"Do you know where the Tiki Lounge is on Seawall?" I was well aware that meeting him there meant that we might run into Robbie Jo, but she typically went out so late that there was a good chance we'd completely miss each other.

"No, but I bet I can find it. What time?"

We chatted a few more minutes, set a time to meet, and, lucky for me, Jack never said a word about his proposition, though I had every intention of taking him up on it.

I still wasn't sure what had possessed me to call Jack. He was a lech with only one thing on his mind, but he was cute as sin and after my mind-blowingly disastrous trip to Austin, I could use a mind-numbingly good time. A bit of toe-curling, sheet-wrinkling, and sweat-dripping sex wouldn't be unwelcome, even if it meant eating a bit of crow first.

While Robbie showered for her own night out, I slipped down the stairs and out the kitchen door, only to pull up short at the sight of her Mustang blocking my Murano. With a soft growl of frustration and a roll of my eyes, I spun around on my platform sandals and headed back inside. The keys would be in Robbie's room, probably in the pocket of her jeans, which were probably buried under piles of dirty clothes.

I slid off my shoes and gingerly dashed upstairs, my ears peeled for the sound of the water being cut off. I sure as hell didn't want my sister to catch me in the middle of exercising a little revenge. In Robbie's bedroom, I kicked at piles of clothes until I found the one that jingled and shook the correct handful of soft denim free of the pile, shoving my hand in and coming out victorious. The keys clutched in my hand, I gathered up a huge armful of dirty clothes and raced back downstairs, grinning the entire time.

Laughing to myself, I stopped long enough to throw the jeans in the washer and add detergent before moving my sister's car and dropping the keys under the front seat. Once I was done, I darted back into the laundry area, pausing long enough to listen for the sound of the shower one last time. It was still running.

Good.

Giving the upper level of the old house one last glance, I started the washer and darted out the door. But not before the sound of Robbie Jo's scream of indignation over the sudden loss of hot water reached my ears.

As I settled into the leather seat of the luxurious Nissan, a thirty-fifth birthday present to myself, my nerves over seeing Jack again returned. I glanced in the rearview mirror, one eyebrow quirked as I briefly caught my own reflection. I'd arched my eyebrows, shaved my legs, my underarms, *and* my hoo-hah and put on a full ration of war paint. There was no way to fight thirty-six years of living in a sunny climate except with moisturizer, lots of it. So despite the crow's-feet and the slight creases that had appeared on my forehead in the last couple of years, I still had great skin. And I wasn't conceited, but I knew I was attractive even with a figure that was no longer in the single digits. I'd dated enough in the last seventeen years to know there was something about me that men liked— besides the great skin (which they probably didn't give a shit about) and the oversized chest (which they probably *did* give a shit about).

I blew out a heavy breath, as if I could blow the nervous flutters right out of my stomach, and ran a hand through my hair with another glance in the mirror. I needed to call my stylist and make an appointment for more highlights soon.

Three more lights and I was pulling even with the Tiki Lounge. I found a spot on the street as close as I could get to the front door, and parked.

The Tiki sat at the end of a long pier lit with multi-colored Christmas lights. The bar itself was a low-slung wooden affair. It's once cheerful pink exterior was in need of painting as badly as the interior, done in shades of rustic seaside, desperately needed the attention of a feather duster. Potted palms sat on either side of the front door, which was decorated with a dancing girl in a grass skirt. Not exactly original, but lowkey and filled with regulars, the Tiki was a place I could go and have a drink by myself. Hell, the Tiki was where I'd had my first legal drink, on my dad, no less. I'd done the same for Robbie when she'd turned twenty-one.

When I didn't immediately spot Jack, I stopped at the bar, where a few regulars had already claimed their spots for the evening.

"Hey babe!" Mikki, the bartender and one of my oldest friends, high-fived me from across the countertop. "That sister of yours was in here last night." She shook her head, a scowl on her pale, freckled face as she wiped at the bar with a damp towel.

"I don't want to hear it." I held up my hand. "So gimme a Scotch and soda and save your beef with Robbie for when she gets here."

"One more fight and—"

"I don't care." I held up both hands this time and took a tiny step backward, only to rock forward when the heel of my sandal came into contact with another foot. I spun around to apologize, only to have my throat lock up at the sight of Jack Saunders grinning down at me.

"You can make it up to me by letting me buy you a drink."

"But the first round's supposed to be on me," I muttered, my body suddenly hot and cold, and then hot again as the sight and smell of him hit me. He smelled like a man, damn it—warm and musky and spicy—and he knew how to fill out a pair of Levi's. Combined with that smile, that killer, all-knowing smile that said Jack Saunders could read my mind and knew I was thinking about what might happen after a few drinks made me want to hit him almost as much as it made me look forward to what *would* come after a few drinks.

"Outside okay with you?" he asked, pressing the ice-cold glass into my hand.

"Perfect." I sipped at my drink to cover a laugh at Mikki's frantic "hot guy" motions, and led the way outside. "Is that where you were hiding?" I threw over my shoulder.

"It's too nice out to be stuck inside." As we reached the door, his hand connected with my bare back, sending an electric tingle up my spine.

"I agree." I stepped outside, away from his touch, feeling the tiniest bit of regret at the break in contact.

"I guess you must get tired of driving all over Galveston in those moving trucks." He paused to pull out a chair for me at one of the small metal tables, and I murmured my thanks.

"Actually, most of my work is inside."

"So, I got lucky." Chuckling softly, he settled into the chair next to me, his knee resting softly against mine, worn denim rubbing worn denim. Such innocent contact, so meaningless— or meaningful. With Jack, *nothing* seemed to be meaningless. I didn't dare move my knee; didn't really want to. I knew Jack would notice and do that mind-reading thing on me again. Besides, it was just a knee. *Right?*

"You did indeed." I put my drink down and took a deep breath, settling a bit lower in my chair. My legs shifted but still, our knees touched. I could almost, but not quite, rub the back of Jack's leg with my bare foot.

For the time being we had the back deck all to ourselves. Out in the distance a half-moon glimmered off the waters of the Gulf and even from a few hundred feet away, I could hear the soft lull of waves crashing onto the rapidly darkening beach. Citronella candles on the tables lent a romantic air, though the sound of ZZ Top from the jukebox inside didn't.

"I wonder if my luck will hold," he quipped.

"Probably." I gave him a frank look he could easily interpret. If I had anything to say about it, his luck would hold and so would mine, and then some. Despite his in-your-face proposition at breakfast last week, there was something about Jack Saunders that seemed to draw me in. Something I liked. And I wasn't normally one to be easily "taken" — no puns intended. "Honestly—" I paused, waiting until he nodded before I continued, "—you were right. I am a control freak, but I like you, so here I am."

Jack nodded slowly. "I really didn't mean to offend you."

I gave him an easy smile. "The truth hurts, huh?"

"Sometimes." He toasted me with his glass and I followed suit. "Honestly—" he arched an eyebrow and I quickly nodded, wondering what he'd say now, "—I like that I can be honest with you. It's refreshing."

"I'd rather have the truth, no matter how bad it hurts, Jack." I sipped at my drink, giving us both a chance to recover from our moment of brutal honesty.

"So, tell me about your week?"

"You don't want to hear about my week," I laughed harshly, much more harshly than I'd intended, and let my gaze drift to the beach.

"Sure I do."

"Sucker," I muttered, grinning at him. "Did you *know* that jeans could cost three hundred and fifty *fucking* dollars?" I waved a hand in the air, wondering if he had any idea how completely insane I found the idea of paying that much for a piece of clothing that didn't have wedding vows attached to it.

"As a matter of fact," he said, nodding slowly, "I did. And I'm guessing you weren't shopping for yourself?"

Nodding, I bit into a piece of ice, cracking it with my teeth, and finished chewing before answering. "I am the worst mother in the world. You know, I really thought the days of hormonal hissy-fits were over, but I'll be damned if I'll let Chloe tap me out, especially after the way her first year of college ended."

"Badly?"

"That would be putting it—" I interrupted myself with a shake of my head. "—Gawd, Jack, I'm so sorry. I'm sure the last thing you want to hear about is my daughter."

He waved it off, but if the expression on his face was anything to go by, I was right. My daughter *was* the last thing he wanted to hear about. Hell, my daughter was the last thing I wanted to *talk* about.

"It's too much like work." He leaned over, his lips seductively near my ear and added, "How can I think about licking the back of your knee or sucking those luscious, cold, red lips when I feel like I'm working?"

Of their own free will, my thighs tightened and my head turned toward Jack. We stared at each other, only a few inches separating us, our lips. He leaned in until they were touching, just barely, and licked my chilly lips with his warm tongue, pulling a low moan from the back of my throat.

39

"Ewww," a young female voice broke us apart and for a minute I felt as if I'd been busted by Robbie Jo as I looked up into the dark brown eyes of Mikki's sister, Molly. "I'll be back in a minute."

"Wow."

I wasn't sure if Jack was referring to the kiss or Molly's reaction. "Indeed."

"I do have a question for you, though," he said.

"What's that?" I flashed him a tiny smile before fishing another piece of ice out of my glass.

"How did you end up with a name like Reece and your daughter ended up with such a girlie name like Chloe? Was it one of the hot names when she was born?"

"Well, Dad was hoping for a boy. I have no idea how he convinced my mom to name me Reece, but it was my grandfather's name. And I named Chloe after my maternal grandmother. My father hated her guts. Honestly, I didn't like her much, either, but I just thought Chloe Cavanaugh had a nice ring to it."

"So you weren't married to her dad?"

"Nope. So how's retirement?" I asked, switching gears on him. "Or . . . whatever."

"If you'd have told me at twenty that I'd retire at forty-one, I would have laughed at you. And honestly it's just a leave of absence while I decide what to do about my practice. Things were pretty hairy with my ex-wife for a while there."

"Do you miss your patients? Or are they clients?"

"Clients. I have a PhD, not an MD, and in a way, yes. After a while you feel like you have a vested interest in them, in their lives, in seeing them improve. I liked a lot of them . . . hell, it's hard to counsel someone you *don't* like," Jack said as Molly stuck her head out the door. "Are you related to the . . ." he asked, jabbing his thumb toward the bar.

"She's my big sister." Her smile was perky, and slightly fake, as she set fresh drinks in front of us.

"Molly, be nice," I said. "Molly went to school with Robbie Jo."

Jack chuckled, his shoulders shaking slightly.

"Sis put these on your tab." Molly collected the empty glasses. "By the way, Robbie's here. I guess she didn't see your car, but she was bitching to Mikki about the washer."

I felt smug as I stretched and ran a hand through my hair. "How much is it going to cost me to keep you and Mik quiet?"

"After the stunt Robbie pulled last night, Mikki ain't telling her shit." Spinning on her heel, Molly headed inside, her miniskirt-clad ass twitching with every step.

"I don't even know which question to ask first." Jack sipped at his drink, still waiting patiently for me to fill him in.

I sank a bit lower in the chair and crossed my legs, my drink clutched in my hand. "I have no idea what Robbie did last night, and I don't care. As for why she's mad at me, *she* had to work later than I did today, which is what she gets for not being born first." By the time I finished telling Jack what I'd done, he was wiping tears from his eyes and I was shushing him, praying Robbie Jo didn't find us, even though I knew it was inevitable.

"Can I ask you something, Reece?"

"Reecie, remember. You can ask me anything."

"Reecie," he echoed, pleasure at my gentle reminder obvious in his eyes. "You and your sister live together?"

"Yup. I swear, between Carla, Robbie, and Chloe, I can't figure out which is the bigger pain in my ass." I drained my glass again. "I'm doing it again, aren't I?"

"It must be hard to shut it off when you work with them *and* live with her. You don't ever get away from it, do you?"

"No." I sighed as the sound of my sister's voice reached me.

God, please just a few more minutes. Just a few! I just wanted to enjoy the rest of my evening and go back to Jack's place. If I could quit talking about Robbie and Carla and Chloe.

"You mentioned your dad. What about your mom?"

"Are you shrinking me?"

He nodded, his teeth gleaming in the dim light. "Go with it."

"She died when I was thirteen."

"And Robbie was—"

"Three . . . nearly four."

"So your dad had a business to run and two girls to raise. He put you in charge of the house, told you that you were the woman of the house, and you helped him raise your sister."

"Carla's mom helped until she died—" I shrugged, feeling almost apologetic, "—but she was no match for the Cavanaugh men."

"Did you ever want anything different?"

I thought about it honestly for a minute before I replied. "Not really. I love Galveston, I love the water and the sun and the beaches. I enjoy the business and when Dad died, it was so natural to just take over."

"How long has he been gone?"

"Eleven years. Now, I went with it. What was the point?" Being shrinked was acting as a total buzz-kill. Not that I *wanted* to be drunk, but, still, I'd been feeling mellow and relaxed, only occasionally stirring myself at the sound of Robbie's loud laughter drifting out to remind me that all wasn't quite as copacetic as I'd like.

"You need to learn to relax."

"I called you, didn't I?" I picked up my empty glass and shook it, rattling the ice before diving in with two fingers and fishing a piece out. "Have you always been so relaxed?"

"Pretty much, yeah." He shrugged slightly.

"Never really driven to, say, move to Houston and have a big, booming practice?"

"If I wanted a big booming practice, I would have moved to California with my first wife, where I could have shrunk the rich and neurotic . . . and probably ended up rich and neurotic myself."

The evening breeze picked up ever so slightly, raising goose bumps on my arms. "I'm trying to relax. I guess I just don't know how," I ruefully admitted. Not beyond the occasional afternoon at the hairdresser or a Sunday run on the beach and an evening at the Tiki. It had always seemed like enough to me, until Jack.

"Maybe you should try harder."

"Maybe you should be less relaxed," I countered, my mock frown quickly falling apart and morphing into a smile.

"Maybe it's something we could work on together," he said.

Just then, Robbie Jo came outside dragging Cash McBride with her, and I never got a chance to respond. Robbie was clearly drunk, and poor Cash was obviously uncomfortable. Robbie draped an arm around my neck and planted a big wet kiss on my cheek. "Thank you for Cash," she said just loud enough so that only I could hear her.

Sighing, I grimaced in Jack's direction. "Robbie Jo." I let the words hang there between us, even while I knew my sister would completely miss the point unless I pounded it in with a hammer.

"Don't worry, boss, I'll make sure she gets home safe," Cash said.

"How was your first week?" I pushed Robbie off me and leaned around her to see Cash. God help us all if they didn't leave soon. The urge to leap out of my chair and drag Robbie Jo off for a good talking-to was growing to unbearable proportions.

"Good, thanks." He gave me a short nod, and I breathed a sigh of relief. He'd be staying a while. The work wasn't too hard for him.

Damn me, I'd even been worried about *him*. Jack was right. I really needed to relax. Lurching to my feet, I grabbed my purse and held out a hand to Jack. "We were just leaving."

"Was it something I said?" Robbie drawled, her full lips twisted in a deep red grin. "Hey, aren't you—"

"No," I said, then mouthed a thank-you in Cash's direction as I pushed Jack toward the door.

"I'll go take care of my tab," Jack said.

"Well—" Robbie Jo flounced around, true testament to how drunk she probably was, because Robbie *never* flounced. "We'll go back inside and finish our game of darts."

"And then we'll go home," Cash added, allowing himself to be led inside ahead of me.

"Absolutely, honey."

A growling sigh of frustration was all I could come up with. I hurried through the bar, outside to where Jack was waiting for me. "I'm trying, Jack, but it's shit like that . . ."

"I'm very proud of you." Grinning, he cupped my face and planted a quick kiss on my lips. "Now let's get out of here. Your car or mine?"

"I have a feeling it better be yours." I smiled sheepishly in the moonlight.

"Not much of a drinker, are you, sugar?" Jack tightened his arm around my waist and led me toward his car.

"No, not really." I relaxed and let my stride match his, deciding to let poor Cash worry about Robbie tonight and let Jack worry about me for just a while. I'd worry about my car, and my sister, later.

"Stop thinking so hard." Jack came to a halt next to his car and opened the passenger door.

"Sorry," I murmured, sliding in. I closed my eyes, letting the smell of leather and man envelop me.

The ride to Jack's was short and quiet. I felt surprisingly content after leaving the bar and was happy to let the streets quietly slip past. There was nothing wrong with some good old-fashioned silence.

"You okay?" he asked at one point.

"Great," I said, adding with a husky laugh, "Better than Cash."

Jack joined in, then asked, "So, who do you think feels worse for Cash? Us or him?"

"Probably us, but he did look pretty miserable." I giggled again, looking across at Jack. He caught me staring and reached out, covering my hand with his for the rest of the drive.

Jack turned the car in to his driveway and parked before pinning me to my seat with a rather intense stare. "Are you sure you want to be here?"

"Positive."

5

Other than the occasional porch light and scattered street-lights, the neighborhood was quiet. I took Jack's hand and let him help me from the car. The door closed with a soft *thunk* of finality.

I could barely make out his features in the darkened carport as he leaned in to kiss me, at first slow and sweet, teasing, his lips firm, his mouth warm and slightly tangy from the Scotch. He pressed me against the car and cradled my head in his hands, using his lips and tongue to tease, pushing my limits, only to draw back and lightly lick and nibble at my lips.

Finally, I broke free, sucking in some of the moist night air, hoping to calm my racing heart. "Maybe we should take this upstairs."

"What's your hurry?" While he talked, he eased his fingers around my wrists and his body against the length of mine.

"Your neighbors—" I flexed my hands against his grip, testing, weighing.

"Are sleeping," he whispered against my lips before flicking his tongue out to trace them with the tip of his tongue.

I shivered as he delved lower, nudging my jaw, which rolled to the side, giving him easy access to my neck. I arched my neck at the first touch of his tongue, moaning softly, still a little worried about his neighbors. As if any of them could see inside his darkened carport. I relaxed the tiniest bit, allowing him to mold me to the curve of the car, allowing his hands to push my halter top up and free my braless breasts before I finally roused myself.

"Jack—"

He pressed his lips to my swollen ones. "Nobody can see us."

"I'd prefer a bed," I said, my voice sharper than I'd intended, my body stiffening against his.

"Don't be in such a hurry." Jack let his hands slide back up my rib cage to cup my breasts. My nipples grew achingly hard against the soft pads of his thumbs, and when he turned his attention from my chest to my lips, I had my lower lip caught between my teeth.

Jack leaned down and drew one of my nipples into his mouth, the warmth combined with the velvety texture of his tongue turning my legs to Jell-O. He moaned in obvious satisfaction, and I'd just reached the point where I didn't care if he sold tickets to his neighbors when the sound of a car taking a corner on two tires and a cacophony of dogs barking startled me. I struggled away, yanking my top down and running a hand through my hair.

"That's enough." I couldn't read Jack's expression due to the lack of light, and didn't care. I wasn't sure I wanted to know what he'd been thinking while he seduced me in his carport—though I could make a pretty good guess.

Exhibitionism wasn't my thing. Even if it was late and most of Jack's neighbors were asleep.

"You lack a certain sense of adventure," Jack whispered in my ear.

"And you lack common sense." I crossed my arms over my chest and pursed my lips, trying to figure out just what his game was.

"Race you up the stairs," he said, poking me in the belly before taking off.

"Oh my God." With a roll of my eyes, I followed. As silly and crazy as *he* was, I was still in it to win it. I trotted after him, taking the stairs two at a time, one hand skimming the railing for safety and the other cradling my breasts so they didn't bounce too much.

When I reached the top, he yanked me inside the laundry room and slammed the door, a seductive smile on his face. The tiny alcove smelled like fabric softener and detergent and was comforting in its familiarity. Jack was just all hands, lifting me onto the washer and pushing my halter up again, barely giving me time to catch my breath. I helped, yanking the top off over my head and laying it on the dryer next to me before drawing his head to my chest. The light scrape of stubble against the tender skin brought goose bumps to my arms.

Jack chuckled softly in the back of his throat as his mouth engulfed one nipple. He sucked, he teased, he nibbled, switching from one breast to the other while I sat helpless, my legs wrapped around his waist, my fingers buried in the soft, thick depths of his hair. The material of his shirt was tantalizingly rough on my skin, as rough as the stubble, and I squirmed against him like a cat, needing more friction, more of him.

"How about that bed now?" I whispered before nipping at the tender flesh of his earlobe. I struggled to slide off the washer, but Jack wasn't having it. Instead he pushed me back, kissing and licking his way lower, burying his face in my stomach, then shifting just enough to tickle my side with his tongue until I squirmed away. "Jack."

"I like the way you say my name," he said as I struggled out of his grasp, finally worming my way off the dryer, but not for long. He had me against the door, my breasts mashed against cold glass, arms pinned at my sides while he nibbled at my neck.

God, I was gonna melt if he didn't stop.

One hand deftly undid the snap and fly on my jeans and delved inside, past my panties to gently stroke my pubic hair. His hot body on one side and the chilly glass on the other was a heady combination, especially since I was already burning up with need. I rested my cheek against the cool surface and gave in, with a soft, "Oh, Jack."

"Told you we didn't need a bed."

My pants skimmed over my hips and pooled around my feet.

"Kick them off." He pressed a shiver-inducing kiss to my shoulder.

He wasn't holding me in place anymore, but I stood still, my palms pressed against the glass, just barely aware of the porch lights on across the street, of Jack kneeling at my feet and slipping my jeans and panties off until that first tiny lick at the back of my knee.

My breath caught in my throat and I tensed, fighting the natural inclination to squirm away from his tongue in such a ticklish spot, then relaxed against the glass, letting Jack work his magic on the back of my legs. When he reached the cheeks of my ass, my hips arched all on their own, begging him to slide that sweet wet tongue deeper, and he obliged, planting a wet sensual kiss deep in the crack of my ass. I moaned, my breath fogging up the glass, and adjusted my legs to give him better access. He delved deeper, rimming my asshole with his tongue. I would have squirmed away at the invasion, but it felt good, real good, and I relaxed as his tongue moved to my swollen clit and caressed the sensitive lips of my pussy.

I'd even lost the willpower to beg Jack to take me to his bedroom. I couldn't bring myself to care anymore as he settled between my thighs . . . didn't care if one of his neighbors saw my tits pressed up against the glass, didn't care if someone saw me playing with my own nipples, which I did while Jack continued to lick at me, didn't care if Jack fucked me right there in the laundry room even though it definitely qualified as trashy and low-class. Didn't even care what he'd think of me in the morning as his tongue repeatedly circled my clit until my legs shook and my juices were soaking my thighs. All I could think about was the orgasm building inside me.

My hips arched out further, seeking, and I reached down, holding my pussy lips apart for Jack, silently urging him to hurry. The spark he'd lit between my thighs finally caught hold, curling deep in my belly, giving my hips a mind of their own as I convulsed against his mouth and tongue. He didn't stop there, just kept licking and sucking and probing me with his fingers until my knees gave way and I was begging him to stop. "Jack, please."

He finally released me, catching me as I sank down beside him, then disappeared into the darkened house. I sat there drenched and shaking, my nostrils filled with the scent of my own sex, one breast still clutched in my hand. That's how Jack found me when he turned on the kitchen light. Just enough light spilled into the tiny laundry area to force me to squint. I was still so dazed I didn't even try to see myself through his eyes as he came closer, blocking out the worst of the bright glare.

I felt satisfied . . . but still hungry.

"Too bright?" He knelt in front of me, pushing my legs apart.

I shoved my hair off my face and shook my head, only able to work out a soft "sorta."

He moved closer while he talked, "I turned it on so I could see you when I fucked you."

I shivered in anticipation as he grabbed my hips, slowly sliding inside me. He cut off my moan with a kiss, sliding his tongue past my lips, to tease and tangle with mine as he repeatedly sank deep in my slick wet cunt. I braced my hands at my sides, meeting every thrust, and the wet sound of our bodies meeting and retreating filled my ears.

Jack raised up, using the back door for support, as he pumped into me faster, the sight of his cock sliding in and out of me arousing me even more than his going down on me had. My cunt clutched around his cock, and he looked in my face.

"Hey." He smiled down at me.

"Hey," I panted, barely able to speak as another raw moan ripped through me as he came, his cock pulsating deep inside me. "Fuck . . . Jack."

"Yes, you did, sweetheart."

The feel of someone pressed up against me woke me up. Well, that and the sunlight battering my eyelids. Rolling over meant coming face-to-face with the other party, but it'd get the sun out of my eyes. So I rolled.

"Morning."

I peeled one eye open just enough to ascertain that it was indeed Jack, then tried to stretch and discreetly shove him away all at the same time. I hated anyone being close to me when I slept—and blamed it on being single for so long.

Hopefully Jack wasn't a morning talker, I thought as I rolled over and sank against him. Not snuggling wasn't an option, since he was pressed against the length of my body.

This . . . this right here was why I *never* stayed the night with a man.

Jack finally got the broad hints I'd been throwing out and shifted, giving me more room while his fingers traced through my tangled hair, but I refused to open my eyes and snuggled deeper in the bed, letting the languid half-asleep feeling steal over me.

It was Sunday, after all, and I didn't have to be anywhere or do anything except this week's time cards—and that only if Robbie had remembered to bring them home. I pushed the thought out of my mind, determined to enjoy the cushy depths of Jack's king-sized mattress and the seductive feel of his hands in my hair, almost groaning in frustration when he stopped. Sprawled onto my stomach, I sank back into oblivion until the feel of someone's lips on my bare back woke me up.

"Hey, Sleeping Beauty," Jack growled." Planning on sleeping all day?"

I sighed and stretched, clearing my throat so I could form a response of some kind.

"Cause if so, I think I might join you."

The idea had merit, though I was still a little tender from our encounters the previous night. The memory of us on the laundry-room floor got me moving, in more ways than one. I rolled over, pushed my hair off my face, and smiled sleepily up at Jack. "Morning."

"I've got breakfast on the porch. Unless you'd rather wait and hit the Hairy Elephant."

"Nooo, breakfast on the patio sounds nice."

"I've even got a T-shirt you can borrow." He'd obviously been up for a while; his hair was still slightly damp and he smelled like Irish Spring.

And he'd fixed breakfast. I glanced out onto the deck, the sheer curtains at the door of Jack's bedroom fluttering in the late-morning breeze.

Man, I'd really been asleep.

His hand slid across my bare belly before he stood up and turned, crossing to the dresser and digging out said T-shirt. "Your clothes are in the chair."

Once he was gone and I was satisfied I'd have at least a few minutes of privacy, I slid from the bed and dug out my panties before yanking the soft white shirt on and darting into the bathroom. With Jack getting breakfast on the table any second now, I barely had time to shower, and my hair would just have to wait. I quickly finished up, making a mental note to thank Jack for the spare toothbrush, opening the door just as he returned from the kitchen with a carafe of coffee and a bowl of fresh fruit.

"I don't suppose you've got a pair of sweatpants I can borrow?" I wasn't ready to give in and slide my jeans back on. Dressing meant leaving soon, and I wasn't quite ready to abandon Jack. I followed him, standing just inside the doorway so none of his neighbors would see me.

"You're fine. Come on out and make yourself comfortable." He set the carafe on the table, then turned to face me, his gaze slowly traveling past my nipples protruding underneath the T-shirt that was still slightly damp from my hurried wash, to my bare legs.

A quick glance around assured me that none of Jack's neighbors were out and about and the slats of the balcony were so close together only someone with binoculars could see I was only half dressed. I yanked the T-shirt down as far as I could manage and glanced around one last time before gingerly taking a seat.

Jack had been a busy boy. There were croissants in a basket, along with honey and butter, fruit, coffee, and orange juice.

"If you're a good girl, I'll take you out and buy you lunch, too."

I "humphed," then said, "This is very sweet of you."

"Aw, shucks," he said, adding a touch of hick to his voice as he filled my cup with coffee. "Opening a can of croissants is awful hard when you're a bachelor man."

"Very funny. And thanks for the toothbrush." I paused in the middle of adding sugar to my coffee to watch Jack take my plate and fill it with food.

"Butter?" he asked, holding up a steaming croissant.

"Please . . . no honey." I took a sip of coffee and said, "You're spoiling me."

"Everyone needs a little spoiling." Flashing me a quick smile, he slid my plate in front of me. "Sleep good?"

I sighed and pushed a hank of hair over my shoulder. "Yeah." I had, better than I'd slept in a long time. Apparently last night's stress relief had been just what I needed. "Thanks."

"Don't thank me, thank your libido," he quipped, slathering his own croissants with honey and butter. "God knows I am."

I snorted softly and took another sip of my coffee. "My libido says you're welcome." Breaking off a bite of my roll, I popped it in my mouth, conscious of my half-naked ass pressed against the chair cushion. On the street below a Tahoe went cruising past and stopped at the house across the street. "Should I—"

"They can't see anything."

"Are you sure?"

Across the street an elderly couple climbed from the oversized SUV they'd parked in a carport.

"Watch, they won't even look over here."

Jack was right; they didn't. Instead, they climbed the stairs and entered their house, their arms full of grocery bags.

"They come in on Friday, and then leave late Sunday night

55

for Houston. They're so busy cramming in a weekend of relaxation, the last thing they're worried about is what's going on across the street. And besides, look at their balcony. You can't see a thing."

The house across the street was almost an exact replica of Jack's house, on stilts, with a carport almost directly under the living room and an enclosed patio directly off what I guessed was the master bedroom.

"See. Safe and sound. We could fuck out here and no one would ever know."

"Don't even think about it." I slid a piece of cantaloupe into my mouth, almost moaning as the sweetness exploded on my tongue.

He scooted his chair closer to mine, then sat down again, a feral grin on his face. "Is that good?"

Nodding, I kept chewing.

He forked up a piece of strawberry from my plate and held it out for me. "I'm thinking about it."

I tightened my crossed legs, unwilling to admit to myself just how much the idea tantalized me, and leaned over to get the strawberry off his fork. Again the fruit exploded in my mouth, sweet and tangy. "What did you put on this?"

"Honey and lime. I've got some more in the kitchen in case you want to . . ." here he paused to waggle his eyebrows at me as he slowly slid a bite of fresh peach between his lips.

I chuckled softly, unable to hold back a flirty smile. "You want to go back inside for dessert, that's fine, but not out here."

"You sure?"

"Positive."

"I won't tell if you won't."

"Jack," I warned giving him my best stern-mother face. Sex any*time* was fine, but any*place* wasn't.

"I love it when you get angry." He slid a hand up my naked thigh, raising goose bumps in his wake and making it hard for me to concentrate on my breakfast. Impossible for me to think about getting out of there and getting home to finish my work. It'd be there when I got home and besides, I'd much rather be here with him than adding up time cards or doing one of a million other chores I should have been doing.

"Behave." I knocked his hand away, but he caught my fingers in his, sliding them up his leg toward the erection tenting under his sweats. Smiling, I cupped it in my hand, giving it a firm squeeze.

"What if I went down on you, right here?"

I glanced across the street before I could stop myself, then felt my cheeks warm as I met his gaze. He knew exactly what I was thinking as he took my hand and dragged me onto his lap . . . that I didn't want his neighbors to see us. So, okay, I let him drag me. But I had no intention of having sex outside with him. *Honest.*

He tucked me up against him, his erection pressing insistently against my hip, and gently sank his teeth into the top of my shoulder. My knee jumped, banging the underside of the table and making the silverware jangle as I squirmed away from the electric sensation that shot through me.

"You did that last night, too."

"Tender spot." Leaning over, I rubbed my aching knee and struggled to catch my breath, my panties already growing wet, urging me to just relax and push his hand inside to relieve the ache he'd caused. In the process, I managed to bend over just enough to give Jack access to the back of my T-shirt, which he quickly lifted upward. His hands were warm and smooth on my skin, one slipping around to pull my legs open, the other caressing my spine.

"Jack." I sat up, my back ramrod stiff, but my legs had turned leaden and refused to move. Refused to close themselves, which was just as well seeing as how Jack was cupping my pussy through my cotton panties, his gentle touch turning my insides to liquid.

"Jack," I bit off sharply, my head not quite as willing as my body was to give in to getting naked on his patio. I struggled off his lap and danced around his chair, tugging my shirt down. "Inside?"

God, please let him say "yes."

"Is that your final offer?"

Nodding, I reached for his hand, almost jumping for joy when he stood up, only to have him push me down in his chair.

6

He pressed his lips to my thigh, all while never taking his eyes off my face. "Tell me you don't want me to go down on you and I won't."

My leg muscles twitched under the caress of his chin, under the caress of soft cotton against the insides of my thighs, under his intense scrutiny. I sat there, staring down at him, trying to form the right words, trying to say no. The air around us was seductively quiet, marked only by the occasional rustle of palm trees. It was almost as if the entire world had stopped for just this moment. I raised my hips for him to remove my panties and licked my lips, "Do it."

Jack hooked his fingers in my panties and slid them off, tossing them in the bedroom. "Scoot up."

I did, practically shaking in anticipation as he slowly lowered his head between my thighs, pushing them apart. "Oh my God." My fingers curled into fists at my sides and I couldn't seem to take my eyes off Jack, who slid one of my legs over his shoulder, his lips against my skin as he whispered things I couldn't hear, secret mysterious things I wanted to know. My breath caught in the back of my throat and my leg muscles tightened at the first light touch of his fingers, one sliding deep inside my pussy, gliding, exploring.

He spread me wide, exposing every inch of me, then looked up at me, his eyes so dark they were almost black. "Do you have any idea how beautiful you are?"

"Please," I breathed, nearly dying from the anticipation.

"Relax. We've got all day."

At that point I realized I'd been holding the armrests in a vise grip, my entire body wound tight in anticipation. I forced my fingers to let go and my legs to relax.

"Breath, Reecie. Just breathe," he coaxed, his fingers still holding my pussy open for all the world to see. "Don't talk, don't think; just close your eyes."

I stared down at him for a few heavy heartbeats, then finally closed my eyes as he'd instructed.

"Can you hear me?"

I nodded, then moaned.

"Put your hands in my hair."

Reaching out, tentatively, I found his head and cupped it with my hands. I moaned, louder this time, almost a sob, as I waited for whatever came next. His head slowly lowered as he kept whispering to me to relax, then his lips and tongue were on my clit, exquisitely soft and excruciatingly tender. He lightly sucked and teased, tormenting me inch by inch as I finally relaxed against the cushions, caressing his hair, moaning and panting and completely uncaring if his neighbors decided to come watch. If they heard me. If I shocked them.

All I cared about was Jack's tongue, making my clit swell and ache with every sweet stroke and his fingers gliding in and out of my pussy, fucking me, tormenting me, pushing me until it was all a hot blur. Until I came, feet braced on the wooden deck, hips pushed as high as I could manage, Jack's hair clutched in tight fistfuls as I moaned and fucked his face until I was completely spent.

A silent Jack rested his head on my stomach. I forced myself to let go of his poor abused hair, hoping I hadn't caused too much damage. I felt drunk . . . satiated . . . embarrassed . . . and hungry, but not for breakfast.

I squirmed out of Jack's embrace and stood on shaky legs, fixing my shirt. He stared up at me, unable to hide the worry in his eyes, worry that he'd pushed me too hard, gone too far. But he didn't have to worry. "Come on."

I stepped around the chair and through the curtains, stripping off my T-shirt and tossing it aside before glancing over my shoulder. Jack stood at the door, watching me. "Don't you want me?"

"More than you can imagine." He stepped closer, nudging me toward the bed.

"Condom," I reminded him, regretfully, almost unwilling to let him go.

"Got it."

I curled up on the edge of the bed, waiting for his speedy return from the bathroom. He threw a couple packets on the bed next to me before handing me an open one. I deftly rolled the condom on, unable to take my eyes off him. "My way this time?"

He nodded, and I rolled over, grabbing a pillow for my head and pushing my ass in the air.

From somewhere behind me, Jack chuckled. "You do know what you want, huh?"

"Usually." I glanced over my shoulder, wondering what he was waiting for. "Not half as much as you, apparently."

One finger deftly slid down the crack of my ass to my wet, swollen pussy.

"I like a woman who knows her mind," he said huskily as he

positioned himself between my legs. My cunt clenched in antic-ipation as I pushed my hips higher, as if that would make him hurry.

"God, honey, my mind and the rest of me wants you to fuck us."

Chuckling, Jack replaced the finger that had been teasing me with his cock and slid inside. He covered my body, practically pinning me in place, and began a slow bump and grind that had me moaning into the pillow. After our encounter on the porch, I'd been hoping for something fast and hard and sweaty, not a big tease. But that seemed par for the course with Jack, so I went with it.

With most men I didn't care if I came off bossy in bed. I knew what I liked . . . knew what got me off, but Jack . . . hell, Jack was five steps ahead of me.

Jack pulled his BMW in behind my Murano and put the car in park. "So what are you doing Wednesday afternoon?"

"Dunno." I unsnapped my seat belt and reached for the door handle, then turned to face him, unsure of what to say. "I had a really good time, Jack."

His lips twitched as if he wanted to laugh. "We'll have to do it again sometime."

"Sure." I clutched the door handle, still not quite ready to get out of the car and return to the real world.

"Wednesday," he coaxed softly. "I'll borrow a friend's sail-boat."

"Where are . . . where are we going, Jack?"

"Sailing." He grinned at me, completely aware he was being obtuse.

"That's not what I meant."

"I know. So relax and just go with it. Okay, Reecie?"

"Okay."

* * *

It was well into the afternoon and there was no sneaking into the house even if I wanted to. Robbie Jo, who, by the way, looked like absolute hell, sat rocking back and forth in my office chair. "Nice of you to finally decide to come home."

"Don't, Robbie. Just *don't*. Lord knows after the way you were behaving last night at the Tiki, you've got no right."

"Funny how you conveniently forgot to tell me you were dating one of our customers."

"Did you fuck poor Cash last night? Am I gonna have to replace him, too?" I let it hang there between us, a reminder of the few employees I'd had to replace over the years thanks to her sexual shenanigans.

"No." She lurched to her feet and circled the desk, muttering as she stalked past me, "I didn't fuck him." And apparently that was a huge problem for her. Robbie Jo usually got what she wanted through sheer force of will, and other things I didn't even want to know about, but it looked as if Cash had left her with her ass in a twist.

I stared out the bay window behind my desk at the beautiful day outside and blew out a heavy breath. As far as I could tell, Cash was still an employee of Cavanaugh Brothers Moving; I'd leave Robbie Jo to deal with her own man problems.

Turning, I headed for the kitchen, and my recipe box, leaving the paperwork for another day.

7

I was in my office Tuesday morning, putting together the schedule for the upcoming week, when Carla stuck her head in.

"Busy?"

"I can take a break." Smiling, I eased back in my chair and adjusted the foot tucked underneath me. "How was your weekend?"

"Okay . . . Good. You know." Carla took a seat in the battered old faux-leather chair all of us had once sat in to do our homework. She seemed to have a hard time finding a comfortable position, though. "Where's Robbie? I thought she'd be here by now."

"She had a dentist appointment. Why?" I took a long hard look at her. He normally pale cheeks were slightly pink and she kept fiddling with the curls at the nape of her neck. "What's going on, Carla?"

"It can wait." She slid from the chair, but so did I, circling the desk and catching the edge of her T-shirt.

"No. It can't. Come on." I pushed the door firmly shut, then pushed Carla back into the chair she'd vacated before sitting beside her in its twin. "I'm not blind. I know something's up. I've known for a long time that something wasn't right with you, so you might as well spill it." Only a blind person could fail to see how little time Carla spent around the shop, how little she helped out beyond running her crew every weekend, how often she headed up to Houston, and even how little time she spent with Robbie and me outside work. Up until her father's death a few months ago, Carla and Robbie had been like best friends, and Carla had always treated me like a big sister, but now . . .

Carla slumped lower in her seat, and nibbled on one ragged thumbnail. My botched confrontation with Chloe in the front of my mind, I steeled myself for anything, vowing not to give Carla a hard time if it was something as silly as Chloe's request for jeans. "Sweetie, whatever it is—"

"I want out." She finally sat up straight and turned so she could look me square in the eye.

"Out of . . ." I let her words trail off, not quite sure what Carla was saying.

"I want out of the business, Reece. I've already talked to a lawyer—"

"What?" I shot out of my chair, my stomach pitching and rolling, my hands shaking from the adrenaline rush my immediate panic caused. "Whoa, *what the hell*? How? Why?" "*What the hell?*" kept playing on an endless loop in my head, jamming up anything resembling a coherent thought as I stared at Carla.

Now that she'd actually said the words out loud, a much calmer Carla continued, "I'll give you first option to buy, and a fair price, but I never intended to spend my whole life as a *mover*, Reece. Do you honestly think I like hauling other people's shit around? Let's be frank here. I fucking hate manual labor, I hate these nasty T-shirts—" Sneering, she plucked at her shirt, "—I hate sweating like a man, and I don't want to do it anymore. I'm not *going* to do it anymore. So I'm selling. The appraiser—"

"Jesus Christ, Carla, couldn't you have come and talked to me before you walked in here and yanked the fucking rug out from under me?" Oh my God, I needed to sit down in the worst way; I needed a drink; I needed to puke.

"I'm giving you first shot at my half." She said it as if that made it all right. She stood up and circled around the chair, putting as much distance between us as she could. "But I can't do this anymore." At the door she stopped and turned to face me one last time her voice soft. "By the way, the appraiser will be here tomorrow with my lawyer. He'll need to go over the books and . . . everything. Sorry, Reecie."

Sorry, Reecie . . . *Sorry, Reecie! What the hell?*

I leaned against my desk in stunned silence, eyes glued to the door Carla had just walked through as if I could will her to return. Instead, all I heard was the steady thump of Carla's sandals on the concrete floor and the slam of the heavy metal door.

I crossed to the window that backed up to my desk and watched as Carla slipped into her Eclipse and sped away without a backward glance. Not even a flicker of her taillights as she passed Robbie's Mustang. On shaky legs, I sank into my chair to wait for Robbie's arrival, completely at a loss for words. Jesus, we could lose everything our fathers had built, all because Carla had an aversion to sweat.

Even while I thought it, I knew that I was being unfair. Sure, Carla had been raised in the business, but she's also had a mom until she was nineteen, someone to temper Joe Cavanaugh's desire to immerse his daughter in the family business.

Robbie Jo and I had never stood a chance. Not with *our* dad. Not that we'd minded.

A hint, a clue, a little warning from Carla would have been

nice. After all, she'd had nine months since her father's death to think about this . . . and act on it.

At the sound of my office door opening, I looked up to find Liz, the bookkeeper, standing in the doorway, her normally pale complexion a horrible shade of white. Concern for the older woman had me on my feet, scurrying to help her sit down, then to fetch a glass of water. By the time Robbie joined us, everything appeared normal—at least on the outside. On the inside, I felt as sick as Liz looked.

"You okay?" I asked.

The older woman nodded and sipped her water, clutching the plastic cup with shaky hands. "Your father and your Uncle Joe would be appalled. But, then, she was always a bit on the selfish side," she said, referring to Carla.

The sound of the door opening and closing announced the arrival of Robbie, who came breezing in the office on a flutter of paperwork.

"Look, ma, no cavities." Robbie looked from me to Liz and back again. "What's going on? Where's Carla going? I thought we were supposed to do oil changes on the trucks today?"

"You . . . we are." Once again, I sank against the edge of my desk, motioning for Robbie to take a seat. How the hell was I going to fix this? How the hell could I buy Carla out? Every spare dime I had was earmarked for Chloe's college. I couldn't take away my daughter's future, but at the same time, if I had no future, what kind of a future could I guarantee for Chloe? "But first, you need to sit down."

"What did Carla do? Quit?" Robbie pulled back the extra chair to give herself some legroom, and sat, legs crossed at the ankles.

Boy, had she quit. "In a manner of speaking, yeah." Tears filled my eyes and my nose began to water at the thought of losing the business. I didn't know how to do anything else, and I absolutely had to buy Carla out.

The thought of working with an outsider just made me want to hurl.

I ran my hands through my hair, and sucked in a deep breath, willing myself to stay in control just a little longer. "She wants out."

"Out . . . of . . ." The expression on Robbie's face was a cross between curiosity and dawning horror. She rubbed at her temple with her fingers, then pinched the bridge of her nose as reality set in.

"The business," I said solemnly, and slowly let my eyes drift to where Liz sat. "She wants to sell her half of the business."

"You and your sister get first shot at it." Liz reached out, wrapping her fingers around Robbie's. "I'm sure your sister will figure something out." She stood up, ready to give us some much-needed privacy, her gait slow as she crossed the tiny space because of the arthritis that racked her hips.

I took my cue from Liz, her confidence in me pushing me past shock and into action. "We'll figure something out. Don't worry."

"Reecie." Robbie stood up, glancing at the door, then back at me, dropping her voice. "How can you say 'don't worry'? This is . . . this is . . ."

Our life. I thought it, but I couldn't bring myself to say it. "I'll figure something out." God help me, I had no clue how, but I would. "Now, let's get the oil changed in those trucks."

Robbie Jo didn't move, and honestly, didn't look like she *wanted* to move. "Did she say why?"

"She doesn't want to be in the business anymore," I sighed. "But she'll give me first shot at buying her out."

"*You*? What about *us*?"

"Of course I mean *us*. I just have to figure out where to get the money from, Robbie Jo." I stepped around the desk, putting off those oil changes a little longer, and collapsed in the over-sized leather chair that had once been our dad's.

"That's awfully damned generous of her . . . and I can help, you know," Robbie said.

I tightened my ponytail, then grabbed my purse off the credenza behind my desk and slung it over my shoulder. I took my time, forcing myself to put on a calm face for Robbie before I turned around, hoping that if I could convince *her* that everything would be fine, I could convince myself as well. "We'll figure something out."

"What are we going to do now?"

"Change the oil in those trucks." And as soon as we were done I had a hot date with my PJs and a tub of Cherry Garcia. "Tomorrow the appraiser comes and I don't want to be here, so let's get moving."

"Reecie." Robbie Jo sounded closer to five than twenty-five.

I ignored the pleading in her eyes. "We'll. Be. Fine! Now let's go." I headed out my office door, praying Robbie would follow and I wouldn't have to go back and drag her out.

We each grabbed a set of truck keys from the rack on the wall, then headed out the door with a wave to Liz. Outside, eight twenty-four-foot trucks stood at attention, four of them needing oil changes. I kept them on a rotating schedule to save me the headache of doing maintenance on all of them at once.

On the drive to the dealership, I called Jack, thankful Robbie was following and couldn't hear me talking. The last thing I needed right now was more grief from her.

"Hey, I think I need to cancel tomorrow."

"You think?"

"Yeah . . . something's come up."

"Everything okay?"

"Of course. I just need to deal with something." Figures I couldn't get one past the therapist.

"You just sound funny."

"I'm in the truck. It's oil-change day."

"No, you sound . . . *funny*."

Tears clogged my throat. "Look, I just need to cancel tomorrow. Something's come up."

"How about Friday, then?"

"I have to work. What about Sunday?" Anything to get him off the phone before I turned into a big old bawl-baby.

"I need to make a call, but sailboat or not, I'll see you Sunday night."

The downside to doing the oil changes was the waiting. Never mind that we had appointments, we still had to wait. And waiting meant Robbie Jo had a chance to pump me for information I didn't have. After about five minutes, I snapped.

"How the hell can I figure out what to do with you badgering me? I don't know anything other than what Carla said and I told you, word for word, twice! I don't know what's going to happen, other than I'm going home as soon as we're done so I get sloppy drunk and cry and eat ice cream." Damn, did I just say that out loud? The girl at the counter was smirking at me, probably thinking I'd just been dumped by my boyfriend. I didn't need much of an excuse to get up, walk across the room, and slap her. I said, "Don't push your luck, sister."

That, combined with hard stares from both me and Robbie Jo, got the errant clerk to go back to work. Robbie stood and kicked at my foot, motioning me outside. I reluctantly followed and we found a spot on a wrought-iron bench painted a sloppy white. Next to us sat an ashtray overflowing with butts and trash and reminding me of Chloe's nasty new habit.

"Why is she doing this?" Robbie slumped forward, elbows propped on her knees, head bowed.

"I honestly don't know. Other than she said she wanted out." I scooted closer so we were leg to leg and draped an arm over her shoulders. It was the best I could do as hugs went. "Want to help me kill some ice cream tonight?"

"Sure."

"You could call her," I suggested. "I mean, y'all are close. Maybe she'll talk to you."

"We *were* close. We haven't hung out or even talked much in a while."

"Since when?"

"Since—" Robbie sat up and gave me a sharp look over the edge of her sunglasses, "—since Uncle Joe died."

I slowly nodded my head in understanding. "Which means she's been planning this since day one."

"You think she feels bad?"

Carla never was one for confrontations, which explained a lot about our earlier encounter and how she'd just run off afterward. It also explained a lot about how she'd been acting the last nine months. I'd cut her a bit of slack—I knew how hard it was to lose a parent—but in hindsight, it almost seemed as if guilt over what she'd been planning had made her the bitch she'd become the last few months. "Yeah," I sighed, running both hands through my hair and slumping forward to lean on Robbie Jo. "Yeah, I think she does. Now, how about that ice cream tonight?"

Robbie, her mouth slightly agape and still looking a little shell-shocked, nodded. "Sure . . . whatever. Just get me some of that stuff with the Heath bars in it."

"You go by the liquor store, I'll get the food."

* * *

Once we were done with the trucks, I left Robbie to close up the shop by herself and took off. My first stop was Carla's apartment, a two-bedroom in a high-rise on the far end of Seawall Boulevard. I could completely understand why Carla sold her parents' house. Too many memories, too much history. But she'd traded off nearly 2,500 square feet for less than 1,000.

Giving the tiny elevator a hard look before stepping inside, I silently dared it to fail me, then jabbed at the button for the fifth floor, my stomach heaving slightly as the box began to move. I wasn't normally claustrophobic, but this elevator had always bothered me. It was probably perfectly safe; it just didn't feel safe.

I stepped off the elevator, taking a deep breath of fresh sea air as my slightly turbulent stomach settled back into place, and turned toward Carla's door. Even from twenty feet away there was no mistaking the sound of Kenny Chesney. I bet Carla's neighbors just loved her for abusing their ears, Chesney fans or no. Then again, most of them were probably at work or seasonal residents. With one last eye-roll, I rapped on the door, standing to the left of the peephole so she couldn't see me.

"Who is it?" Carla shouted over the music.

"Building maintenance. We've had complaints about your music."

The door flew open, a red-faced Carla dressed in designer jeans, high heels, and a skimpy top, obviously ready to do battle for her right to offend other people's ears. If her open mouth was anything to judge by, anyway.

Carla never stood a chance. I was older, stronger, and outweighed her by at least thirty pounds. I shoved my way inside and stalked across to the stereo, punching buttons until the volume wasn't so offensive. "We need to talk."

"I'm not changing my mind, Reece." Carla stood in the middle of her pristine living room, arms crossed over her chest.

I ignored her, choosing to examine the pricey glass knick-knacks on the media cabinet's extra shelves before turning and running my hand along the back of the saddle-leather couch. The newness hadn't even worn off the condo yet. "You going to sell this place, too?"

"Maybe . . . probably," she sighed.

"You know, Carla—" I stepped to the balcony, taking in the view of the Gulf, "—you could have handled this better. You could have come to me and sat down—"

"I did. Today. There's nothing more to say. Now you need to go. I've got plans and I need to get going." As if to drive her point home, Carla picked up an expensive-looking purse and snatched her keys off the counter.

"Fine. But keep in mind, that even after this is all over, we're still family." I crossed to the front door, pausing with my hand on the knob. "Matter of fact, last time I checked, Robbie Jo and I are the only family you've got."

"You think?"

"Just don't forget that old saying about shitting where you eat."

I needed a plan! I needed to think . . . in the worst way possible, and I did my best thinking when I cooked. It was late and I was supposed to meet Robbie Jo at the house soon, so I'd have to settle for something easy. I hit the grocery store, picking up all the fixings for meat loaf, homemade mashed potatoes, the required ice cream, and a few other things before heading back to the house, where Jack's BMW was parked out front.

Circling my SUV, I got the ice cream from the back and waited for him to join me. "What are you doing here?"

He grabbed four bags and leaned down, brushing his lips on my cheek. "I was worried."

Swallowing the lump that materialized in my throat, I headed for the kitchen door. "Robbie Jo will kill me if this ice cream melts."

Jack silently followed me inside, emptying his bags on the counter while I put the ice cream away. I finally pulled my face out of the freezer and turned to face him; he was standing against the kitchen island, arms crossed over his broad chest. I followed suit, leaning against the fridge.

"Whatever it is, it can't be that bad."

"Ohhhhh, yes, it can, sugar." Laughing, I swiped at an escaping tear with the back of my hand.

"Tell me."

"I need to get the rest of the groceries first."

Once we were done, I started talking and cooking, unable to stop doing either, as I peeled potatoes and told him about Carla. Finally, I stopped, a half-peeled potato clutched in my shaking hand. "I'm scared, Jack."

He took the peeler and the potato from me and wrapped his arms around me. "I've got some—"

"No," I choked out around my tears. "This one I've got to solve myself."

"Fine, but that doesn't mean I can't listen or that you can't lean on me." He tightened his grip on me and held me while I cried. Finally, he handed me a clean, damp paper towel and I wiped my face, blowing my nose. Embarrassed to the core, I could barely bring myself to look at him. "Ready to listen?" he asked, pushing my hair off my face.

"Sure." I nodded, even though I knew there was no way I could take money from Jack.

"I have a couple of friends who are bankers. I could put in a good word for you with both of them, but Randy is probably your better choice."

"Why?"

"'Cause I'll never play poker with him again if he turns you down for a loan."

A hand pressed to my forehead, I laughed, then sighed with relief as my head slowly began to clear. "What if I can't do this?"

"You *can* do this. You know you can; I know you can."

"Jack—" I held out my hands, at a loss for words.

"You can thank me tomorrow."

"The appraiser—"

"You don't have to be there, do you?"

"I . . . I don't *want* to be there." But I probably needed to be. Just the thought of it made me ill.

"Then don't. Come sailing with me. I think you could use a day away."

"You want to stay for dinner?" I offered as the back door opened.

Robbie Jo's eyes widened at the sight of the both of us. "Well! Hey there."

"You uh . . . you know Jack."

"I remember Jack." She set down two paper bags and hung up her keys. "You staying for dinner?"

"Nope. I'm taking a rain check."

"Thanks, Jack." "For everything" went unsaid, but I knew he understood.

"Sooo," Robbie Jo drawled once he left, "It wasn't my drunken imagination."

"No. It wasn't. Now finish peeling the potatoes for me, please."

While Robbie Jo silently peeled, I washed and chopped bell peppers and onions, proud when my eyes didn't water a lick, then finished assembling the meat loaf and put it in the oven.

"You're awful quiet," Robbie put the potatoes on the stove and turned on the burner.

"Just thinking."

"Did you come up with a plan yet?"

"It's not that difficult. We've got to buy her out." The bigger question was, how to finance the buyout. "I went to see her, by the way."

"Are you nuts?

"No. She might have lost her mind, but she's still family." I tested the potatoes to see if they were tender even though it was way too soon. "Maybe you two—"

"—Fuck no. I'm too mad."

I stopped, pot holders clutched in both hands, and hugged her.

"Gawd, I fucking *hate* her!" Robbie Jo scrubbed at her face, her skin all blotchy and red from unshed tears as she pushed away from me.

"It's gonna be okay."

"That's not the point. The point is she's an underhanded, sneaky-ass bitch." Robbie Jo pulled some brownie mix out of the cabinet and got back to work.

Carla was, but she was also young. I could think of a million other excuses to give on her behalf, but I was too busy worrying about how to keep us from losing our livelihood—even with Jack's offer of assistance.

"We may have to use the house for collateral." The house was in both our names and mortgage free. Other than my car, taxes, and one credit card, my only big debt was Chloe's college, and if I was careful, I could cover all four years. Now I wished I'd been more insistent about her going to a junior college and living at home, but that was water under the bridge.

I paid myself a small salary—enough to cover my living expenses and sock some away for a rainy day—but I had no idea what the appraiser would come up with and I had a feeling that, as rainy days went, buying Carla out ranked somewhere around a hurricane.

"You're thinking too hard." The sound of Robbie Jo's voice sent the cucumber I'd been peeling slip-sliding into the sink and the knife tumbling from my fingers. I danced out of the way just as it hit the floor and bounced, the sharp blade missing my toes by inches.

"Shit . . . sorry."

"You were having some pretty deep thoughts there." Robbie Jo picked up the cucumber and rinsed it off, handing it back to me. "Want to eat out back?"

"Sounds good." Our backyard was small, most of the house's lot being taken up by . . . well, the house, which was long and lean and two stories high. I hadn't been able to maintain the small garden Mom had planted, but I'd tried. It was just a patch of grass now, with bougainvillea on the fence and a few hearty rosebushes along the border. At least the pretty purple flowers made it seem homey.

While I finished the salad, Robbie Jo whipped up a batch of brownies, then made a pitcher of tea. Once the meat loaf was out, the brownies went in, and the kitchen smelled as comforting as the food I was cooking.

Two bottles of wine and two plates of meat loaf and mashed potatoes later, we had enough of a buzz that tomorrow's visit from the appraiser was a mellow thought to be chased with ice cream . . . like our dinner.

"Damn, that was good. How come you never taught me to cook like that?" Robbie Jo kicked at me underneath the table.

"Because then you'd have no use for me. You'd put me out to pasture like an old dog."

"You mean an old horse." Robbie cut a piece of brownie in

half and slid the oversized bite into her mouth. "Mmmmm-mmm, damn that's good."

"You're welcome." I drained the last of my wine and carried our empty plates inside, piling them in the sink.

"So how are things going with what's-his-name?" Robbie Jo followed me inside, the pan of brownies clutched in one hand, her wineglass in the other. She set her glass down and fished out the second half of the brownie she'd cut. It disappeared much the same way the last one had.

"You know, eventually all those brownies are going to catch up with you." I nodded toward her waistline.

"Not for a long time." Robbie licked her fingers, drained her wineglass, and rinsed it off, sliding it in the dishwasher. She nudged me out of the way and started scrubbing.

"In the meantime, eat 'em while you got 'em." I dug out the ice cream, then broke off a piece of brownie to nibble on while I cleaned the counters off.

Once the dishwasher was full and the kitchen put to rights, Robbie shut off the water and turned to face me, pale-faced. "Sis?"

I crossed to where she stood and wrapped my arms around her. "It's gonna be okay." We'd been through worse.

"What if it's not?"

"It will be."

The Right Moves

1

Where am I?

I rolled over and slowly stretched my limbs, trying to determine if there was another body in bed with me. Neither my arms nor legs collided with any body parts, but it didn't _feel_ like my bed. _Mine_ was a queen and the sheets were much softer and smelled like Downy, and every morning when I woke up it smelled like coffee, because Reece always set the coffee timer. _She's good like that._

The urging of my bladder forced me to move, forced my eyes open, which I immediately regretted. I guess I forgot to mention the headache I'd woken up with. A headache brought on by a night at the Tiki Lounge. At least I hadn't gotten into a fight . . . hhmmm.

I searched my hazy, booze-soaked memory, trying to assure myself that I _really_ hadn't gotten into another fight. Otherwise, my favorite bartender would have my ass, and I'd be banned from the Tiki Lounge for life. And at twenty-five, I had a lot of life left. My bladder struggled to get my attention again, and I finally sat up, looking around through painfully gritty, hung-over eyes.

Just outside the bedroom door was a hallway, a tiny one, with two doors, and it seemed to open up into a living area. Ignoring the indignant cries of my long-lost modesty, I hopped out of bed and stuck my head in the first one, coming out a winner. Once I'd relieved myself of most of last night's tequila and beer, I washed my hands and face, avoiding my own reflection in the mirror as I scrubbed off the last of the previous night's makeup, then headed back to the bedroom to take stock.

There was only one set of clothes on the floor—mine—and the bedroom was sparsely finished—just a double bed and dresser, devoid of personal items and homey touches. The bathroom hadn't been much better, with a shower curtain that looked like it had come from the Dollar Store, a few bare necessities, and a bottle of Hugo Boss.

Since the apartment was still quiet, I slipped into my panties and went exploring some more, the rumble of an ancient air conditioner covering my footsteps.

I found him on the living room couch, one arm thrown over his head, his face turned toward the cushions, but there was no disguising Cash McBride and his angelic face. His bare chest was liberally peppered with scars, including a thick, rather ugly white one that ran for about six inches along the curve of his ribs.

"Well, good morning to you, too." The sound of his voice, thick with sleep, made my cheeks burn. As if he'd known exactly where my eyes were heading.

"Morning." I glanced up at his face, expecting to see a smile.

Instead, he was frowning in that sort of disapproving way he had that, even after a twenty-four-hour acquaintance, annoyed me. Thanks to the chilly air, my nipples were rock hard, but I got the feeling, Cash was anything but turned on. I jabbed my thumb toward his tiny kitchen. "I was just going to make some coffee."

"I don't have a coffeemaker, but there's a Starbucks two blocks down, or a gas station across the street."

"You don't seem to have much of anything." Other than the couch, the living room was empty. Not even a television! And *who* the *hell* didn't have a TV?

"Go get yourself some coffee, and then I'll drive you back to your car."

He acted like he wanted to get up, but he didn't move. Neither did I, choosing instead to stand there in nothing but my panties. Color me perverse, but I could tell by the way his eyes would drift down to my chin, then stop, that he was having a hell of a time talking to me.

"I guess I should get dressed before I go get coffee." I stood there a few seconds longer, trying to, God forgive me, get a rise out of him, before backtracking to the bedroom and sliding into last night's clothes.

"That might be a good idea," he called out after me.

In the bathroom, I used Cash's toothbrush—hell, it looked brand-new—and finger combed my hair, gathering it into a scrunchie I'd dug out of my purse. By the time I hit the living room, Cash had slipped his jeans on, or maybe he'd slept in them. I hadn't noticed any on the floor though. "You could drive me across the street and then back to my car and get rid of me that much faster."

"I still need to get my shoes on."

I shrugged and glanced at his feet. "I'm not in that much of a hurry."

"Suit yourself." He headed down the hall toward the bedroom, leaving me alone.

"Can I ask you something?" I shouted while I circled the deserted living room. Not that there was far to go.

"What?"

Besides the bed and dresser, the couch and some moving boxes were all he had. The boxes sat between the couch and the bay windows; big ones sealed tight with lots of tape and pre-printed shipping labels. I leaned against the front door, the knob clutched in my hand, and stared at them, wondering what was inside them, why he hadn't unpacked them. Why it looked like a woman's writing on the outside, where it said, "Cash's Stuff" in big red letters. And who was she?

"How come you didn't sleep with me?" I shouted, my eyes on the boxes.

"You're my boss, Robbie Jo."

Oh, yeah. My sister had hired him this week and put him on my moving crew. After we'd finished up late Saturday after-noon, I'd sort of well . . . tricked Cash into meeting me at the Tiki Lounge by telling him that everyone from work was going to be there. In truth, I'd just wanted him to come have a couple drinks with me because he was hot, and I had high hopes of getting him into bed. Apparently, *he'd* gotten *me* into bed in-stead—and not in a good way.

Well, not in a *sexual* way.

He came limping out of the bedroom, wearing a faded blue T-shirt. He palmed his keys off the counter and headed toward me, still looking vaguely unhappy.

"You okay?" I asked wondering why he was limping. The last thing we needed was a Workman's Comp claim. Reece would kill me.

"Fine, boss. Why?" He stopped right in front of me, close enough for me to smell the toothpaste on his breath.

My cheeks heated up again at the thought of him knowing that I'd used his toothbrush. It'd been a long time since a man had left me this flustered. I'd gotten over being shy around boys at about age fourteen, when I'd let Matty Green reach up under my shirt—in exchange for him dropping his drawers so I could see his penis. It hadn't impressed me much, but he'd made it up to me at the junior prom.

"Don't call me 'boss.'" The way he rumbled out "boss" almost sounded condescending, but I knew it was just me. I was just another peon, my sister was the real boss. "And you're limping."

"Old age."

"Ha." I turned and opened the door, wincing as the morning sunlight bitch-slapped me. "What are you? Thirty?"

"Thirty-six."

"Wow. You're like, *super*-old." I got so tickled I started to snort and even the sun didn't bother me so much anymore. "So which one of these beauties is yours?" I asked, motioning to the assortment of sort-of-new to barely functioning cars and trucks in the parking lot. To my surprise, the newest car in the lot was his . . . well, truck. It was one of those big, black, gas-guzzling dualies with four wheels on the back instead of two, dark tinted windows and a bucking bronco painted in silver on the door. "Wow, ain't you fancy-schmancy?"

"Anyone ever tell you what a smart-ass you are?" He hit the alarm and circled around to the driver's side, ignoring my laughter.

I really needed to stop being so mean, but as last night came back in bits and pieces, I kept remembering how he'd thwarted every attempt at seduction. I'd even worn my best bra and panties and my most expensive perfume.

I climbed into the truck, thinking what a waste of perfume he'd been, until I turned to look at him. He stuck the keys in the ignition, one hand wrapped around the steering wheel as he started the truck up, his eyes unfocused, the sunlight caressing thick gold-tipped lashes and highlighting the freckles that were barely visible under his tan.

In a word, Cash McBride was breathtaking.

"What?" He turned those startlingly blue eyes my way and totally busted me.

"*What*, what?"

"You were staring." He glanced at me out of the corner of his eye before snapping on his seat belt. "Something wrong?"

I forced my stiff fingers to follow suit. God, if he quit, Reece was going to beat me within an inch of my life. "Nothing some coffee won't cure."

He turned his attention back to the road and put the truck in gear. The damned truck rumbled like a semi, nearly drowning out the sound of Chris Cagle coming from the speakers. "Then let's get you some coffee."

Across the street at the Quick Trip I paused, the door open, preventing another car from pulling into the parking spot next to us. "You want anything?"

"Some more sleep."

Okay, then! He was a tough one. *Real* tough. I climbed out of the truck, nearly needing a ladder despite being five-foot-seven, and slammed the door. The logo circling the bucking bronco came into focus despite the dirt covering it—ROCKIN' D RODEO COMPANY 2005—ALL-AROUND CHAMPION. I read it again for good measure, then looked at Cash through the tinted window, trying to picture it. To my horror, the window slid down and I realize I'd actually been staring—again.

"Do you need money?"

Fuck! Every cell in my brain short-circuited, leaving my tongue lying limp as five-day-old turkey.

"Uhhh—" I shoved a hand into my pocket and my fingers curled around what felt like dollar bills. Last night I'd shoved money in my pocket and locked my purse in my car, "—no. Where are my car keys?"

"In my pocket," he spoke slowly, giving me a look that said "hurry up or hitchhike."

I practically high-fived myself as I stepped inside the busy gas station and headed for the coffee counter. I found a ten and a twenty in my pocket. But last night I'd taken forty with me, which meant Cash had bought my drinks. And driven my drunk ass home and . . . wow.

Back in the truck I asked the question that had hit me while I was standing in line waiting to pay for my coffee. "Why didn't you just take me home?"

"Your sister left the bar with some guy, and I was afraid you might get sick. You know, throw up and choke on it or something."

The sip of hot coffee I'd just taken nearly ended up on my jeans. I didn't know whether to laugh or cry. He'd been worried about me? No one but Reece ever worried about me. Of course, I wasn't exactly the steady-boyfriend kind of girl, either. "I'd hate for you to have my death on your conscience."

"Me, too."

The sound of AC/DC made up for our lack of conversation as Cash drove across town, the scenery slowly improving until we reached the Tiki Bar. Even the tourists were still asleep, the streets deserted, most of the shops still closed. My bright yellow Mustang was the only car parked on the street. Reece called it Obnoxious Yellow and it was, complete with a wide black racing stripe across the top, low-profile tires and many, many ponies under the hood.

Cash pulled a U-turn in the road and parked behind my car. He reached in his pocket, pulling out my keychain. The two little dice dangled happily, clicking against each other and the assortment of keys.

I really did appreciate the fact he'd taken care of me when he totally didn't have to. I reached out to take my keys from him, a thank-you on my lips, when he tossed them to me.

"See you Thursday."

"Okay." Clutching my keys in my fist, with my coffee, I slid out. "Thanks again, Cash. I really do appreciate it."

"Don't mention it, Boss Lady." His gaze was as lazy as you could ask for on a Sunday morning, but the fingers tapping the steering wheel were all business.

I slammed the truck's door before I could say something I'd regret. And if he called me Boss Lady again I just might have to kick his ass.

2

After my dentist's appointment on Tuesday, I headed for the shop. Technically, our workweek didn't start until Thursday, but I usually stopped by earlier in the week to see if Reecie needed any help with paperwork, scheduling, and the occasional walk-through, though those were usually reserved for bigger jobs. And this week was a maintenance week, which meant changing the oil in four of the eight trucks.

I flew down Airport Road, the windows down, singing along with the Dixie Chicks at the top of my lungs, tapping my brakes when my cousin Carla went shooting past in her little red Eclipse without even a wave. *Bitch.*

Lowering the volume and shifting gears, I turned in to the moving company's lot and parking next to Reece's Murano. It was cute for a Mom-mobile, but now that Chloe was in college, Reece really needed to invest in a nice sports car—preferably in Come Fuck Me Red.

I found Reece leaning against her desk, Liz sitting in a chair, both of them way too quiet for words. "Look, ma, no cavities!" I smiled, showing off my newly cleaned teeth.

Reece gave me a halfhearted smile that registered somewhere around my toes. Something was wrong, *bad wrong*, like our Dad dying wrong.

"What's going on? Where's Carla going? I thought we were supposed to do oil changes on the trucks today?" Of their own accord, my feet moved backward and my hand tightened its grip on the gunmetal-gray doorframe. I wasn't sure I wanted to hear what was coming.

"You . . . we are," Reece said, her voice huskier than normal, her gaze anywhere but on me. "But first, you need to sit down."

"What did Carla do? Quit?" That minty-fresh feeling in my mouth was making me queasy as I forced my feet to shuffle around the extra club chair and sit, stretching my legs out in front of me as casually as I could and crossing my arms over my chest.

"In a manner of speaking, yeah." Tears filled Reece's eyes and her nose turned a bright shade of red. "She wants out."

"Out . . . of . . ." I prompted.

"The business," she sort of growled, then cleared her throat, speaking loud and clear so there was no mistaking her. "She wants to sell her half of the business." Reece was white-knuckling her desk. Even though I knew she was trying to look all calm and shit, she was as scared as me, maybe even more so. She tended to take stuff pretty hard.

"You and your sister get first shot at it." Liz reached out, wrapping her gnarled fingers around mine. "I'm sure your sister will figure something out." She left, giving us some much-needed privacy.

Reece took her cue from Liz, but did a crash and burn on trying to sound all bright and chirpy. "We'll figure something out. Don't worry."

"Reece—" I glanced at the door to make sure Liz was

nowhere to be seen. "How can you stand there saying everything's going to be fine? This is . . . this is . . . ."

"I'll figure something out. Now, let's get the oil changed in
those trucks." Reece had officially lost her mind. I was sure of
it as I sat there staring at her; some hysterical corner of my brain
suggested that maybe I should slap her. She'd just dropped a
bomb and expected me to blithely follow orders to go service
trucks we might not own much longer? Uh-uh.

"Did she say why?" Carla wanting out hadn't quite registered, but it explained why she'd been such a royal-ass bitch
lately.

"She doesn't want to be in the business anymore," Reece
sighed. "But she'll give me first shot at buying her out."

"*You*? What about *us*?"

"Of course I mean *us*. I just have to figure out where to get
the money from, Robbie Jo." She pushed away from the desk
and stepped around it, sinking into the oversized leather chair
that had once been our dad's. If I tried real hard, I could still
smell his cigars. He'd only smoked them up here, never at
home. Funny, I'd never asked why.

"That's awfully damned generous of her . . . and I can help,
you know," I said.

She tightened her ponytail, then grabbed her purse, calmly
smiling at me, trying to silently reassure me that everything was
going to be fine. Like I was a kid or something. "We'll figure
something out."

Deep down I knew that meant *Reece* was going to try and
figure something out, and it burned my gut almost more than
Carla up and wanting to sell the business without any warning.
I guess, in hindsight, I should have seen it coming. Ever since
her dad had died, she'd been progressively less interested in the
day-to-day running of the business and occasionally downright

nasty about having to work a moving crew, but she'd *always* worked a crew.

Hell, we all had.

At sixteen Reece had started working with Dad on the weekends and then gone fulltime after Chloe was born. Reece had paid her dues and even though I occasionally resented her for getting most weekends off, I never begrudged her the right to sit behind Daddy's desk and all that went with it.

"What are we gonna do now?"

"Change the oil in those trucks." She eased to her feet, looking older in the blink of an eye. "Tomorrow the appraiser comes. And I don't want to be here, so let's get moving."

Me neither.

I was up early Thursday morning, gassing up all the trucks so Reece didn't have to. Normally, I would have done it on Wednesday, but under the circumstances, we'd given ourselves a day off. Neither of us had wanted to be there with Carla and the appraiser. We probably would have skipped the oil changes if we could have, but without those trucks, we didn't have anything, so taking care of them was essential.

To my surprise, as I pulled back into the lot with the third truck, I spotted Cash turning in behind me.

"Can I help?" he asked.

So much had happened in the last two days that last Sunday seemed like such a long time ago. "You're not on the insurance yet, but you can make sure they all have drop cloths and dollies in them." I pointed to the four trucks I'd already gassed up.

"Good enough. What time's our first job?"

"Not for an hour, I think. Why are you here so early?"

"Didn't have anything else to do."

We stood there staring at each other, me thinking about those boxes in his apartment, him thinking about whatever cowboys thought about at seven in the morning at the beginning of a ten-hour workday. The crunch of more tires on gravel announced Reece's arrival. "And it's a good way to get brownie points with the boss," I quipped as Reece stepped inside, her key jangling in her hand.

Whatever she'd done yesterday with Jack, she'd had a good time and gotten some sun. God knows she needed it. The sun *and* the good time. She hadn't even come home last night. At some point, we'd have to discuss the appraiser's visit, what it meant, and what our next move was, but at least Jack had recommended a banker for Reecie to contact about a business loan.

"Cash doesn't need to finagle brownie points, but you sure do."

I whirled around and stuck my tongue out at her. "Excuse me, Miss Bitch, who made you brownies the other night?"

"You did, and they were damned good. Too bad you don't make them more often."

"You cook?" Cash asked, a hint of laughter in his voice.

"No," I confessed, "*Reece* cooks. *I* bake brownies and stuff like that." Too bad I didn't cook. I could have made him dinner. Yeah, I know I'm shameless, but I still wanted to get him into bed.

He was dressed in work boots, a different pair of jeans with faded creases in them, and a T-shirt that had little creases in the sleeves. He'd ironed his T-shirt, for fuck's sake.

"What about you? You cook?" I waggled an eyebrow at him and tucked the keys to the next truck in my hand.

"Spaghetti." Cheeks flushed, he quickly turned away from me, heading toward the lot to check the trucks.

Before I could take off to gas up the last four trucks, Reece called me into her office. "Did you see this?" She held up a sheaf of papers.

"No, I don't snoop in your office."

"Well—" She shook them at me, "—*this* is Carla informing us she's not working anymore. And *this*—" she shook another thick wad at me, "—is the appraisal." She dropped them on her desk and shoved past me, heading to the coffeepot just outside her door. I sank into the chair and waited for her to return, knowing better than to hurry her along. "You'll be glad to know we're worth nearly eight hundred thousand dollars." She smiled brightly above me, the coffee clutched in her hand, a tic in her jaw playing a lively tune.

"So—" I grinned, praying like hell she didn't throw her coffee at me, "—all we need is four hundred grand. No problemo!"

"I'll make an appointment with Randy at the bank. And Robbie Jo, I love you but—"

"But what?"

"Leave *him* alone." She motioned out the window with her coffee cup.

"But he's cute."

"But he works for us."

"But he's cute as a bug, Sis." I gave her my best pleading look. "And he's got the nicest—"

"Robbie. *Jo.*" One eyebrow arched insistently.

"Reecie Piecy." I pushed one of my own eyebrows skyward in response. "He's a grown man. If he doesn't want to sleep with me, he can say no." Hell, he *had* said no, not that I'd remembered him saying no; he'd just said he couldn't sleep with me because I was his boss. I could push the bounds of logic and have him put on Julio's crew, or Evan's, or even Reece's, but I knew he wouldn't sleep with me as long as my last name was Cavanaugh, and that was kind of hard to change at this stage of the game. Through Reece's office windows, I watched him wheel a dolly outside to one of the trucks.

Cash McBride was a man with principles, which meant getting him into bed was going to be a bitch.

With one move successfully under our belt for the day, I called a lunch break early in the afternoon and parked the truck next to a Burger Barn well off the beaten path. "Suit y'all?"

"Works for me," James said. James was a tall, gregarious redhead whose constant chatter and jokes covered the strained silence between me and Cash. James worked a second job at one of the local hotels doing maintenance and spent his lunch hours on the phone catching up with his wife, who was stuck at home with two kids. It was tough, he said, but he didn't want her to have to work and the second job was only thirty hours a week.

What a price to pay. I'm not sure I could ever do it. Stay home and let some man support me or, for that matter, be married. Of course, the only married couple I knew much about, besides a few friends from school, had been Carla's parents. My own mom had died when I was three, and I barely remembered her.

I got a double cheeseburger and fries and settled at one of the round tables outside, soaking up the afternoon sunshine. Trust me, I'd earned it, and it would probably be years before my eating habits caught up with me—if ever. Tray in hand and a cell phone jammed in his ear, James took a seat a few tables over, then Cash stepped outside. From behind my sunglasses, I could feel him trying to decide whether to sit with me or James. Instead of calling him over, I methodically swished some fries in catsup and ate them, chewing slowly and wiping my fingers on a napkin. I wouldn't have been surprised if he'd chosen to sit with James. Actually, I would have been *less* surprised if he'd sat with James than I was when his shadow fell over my table.

"That seat taken?"

"Yeah." Glancing up at him over the rim of my sunglasses, I licked some catsup and salt off my fingers, then grinned at him.

He shrugged and made to turn away.

"I was kidding, Cash."

"You never know." He rejoined me, the laughter in his voice evident as he took the seat across from mine. "I thought maybe you had an invisible friend."

I grinned over at him, pleased to see him display some sense of humor. "Maybe." We ate in comfortable silence for a few minutes before I spoke again. "You okay?"

"Why do you ask?"

"If you're not used to all the physical labor, it can be tough the first couple of weeks."

"I'm good."

"I guess rodeo is tough physical labor too—" I watched him intently, "—is that what you did? Rodeo?"

"Yeah." His shoulders stiffened and he took a huge bite of his burger, licking some mayo off the side of his finger. He had great hands, with strong capable fingers. Sue me; I had a hand fetish—sort of. And after spending the previous weekend working with him, it was obvious he wasn't afraid of hard work. *So what was his deal?*

"You quit?"

"Quit what?"

"Rodeo?"

"You always ask so many questions?" he countered between bites. "How long do we get for lunch anyway, Boss Lady?"

Swear to God he said it because he knew it lit my ass up. I chewed on a couple of greasy fries, then studied my watch, making him wait for my response. "About thirty more minutes. Why? What'cha got in mind?" Smiling innocently, I sipped at my iced tea and watched the wind ruffle Cash's hair.

He smoothed his fingers down his clean-shaven chin, and

shrugged, turning his attention back to his lunch. "Nothing much. How come a nice girl like you isn't married? What are you doing out here . . . moving?"

"Settling down with one man," I sighed, "I just don't know if I'm cut out for that, and for what it's worth, I love my job." The silence that fell between us was much easier this time. Once he stood up to throw his trash away, I tried again. "So what's for dinner, Boss?"

He ignored me, making me wait until he'd returned and sat back down, his own expression hard to read from behind his sunglasses. "Graciela's."

I whistled appreciatively. Graciela's was the best Mexican food in Galveston.

"Interested?"

"You mean, like a date?" I stood up, piling my own trash on my tray.

"No." A tiny smile tickled his lips. "I just don't like eating alone. And you're the only person I know around here besides Reece."

"And James." Giggling, I pointed to where he sat, still talking on the phone. Then I left Cash stewing while I threw my own trash away. "Sure." It was my turn to shrug. "And if you want, afterward, we can hit the Tiki for a beer." Grinning insanely, I walked past him and tapped James on the shoulder, signaling that it was time to go.

3

So what exactly do you wear for a date that isn't a date when you have seduction on your mind?

Damn, I was tired. Like mind-numbingly tired. Maybe I'd just get Cash to come back to the house for some nice, non-threatening snuggling. We had tons of movies to watch and like six billion, nine hundred and eighty-four thousand cable channels to choose from.

Clad in only a towel, I was standing in front of the closet, water sliding down my legs as I debated which outfit to wear, when Reece rapped on the door and stuck her head in. "Yeah."

"You going out?"

"Just dinner . . . with a friend."

"Robbie Jo?" There went that eyebrow again.

"It's just dinner!" And anything else I could get out of Cash. He didn't have a steady woman. And I seriously doubted that rodeoing made having a steady diet of women possible. Then again, as fine as Cash was, I doubt he had problems getting laid . . . a thought I found incredibly depressing. I'd just be an optimist and believe that he was horny as hell—even if he wouldn't admit it. "What about you and Jack? You gonna see him tonight?"

Her eyes slid away from mine and she stepped into the room, leaning down to pick up some of my dirty clothes in an attempt to avoid my question.

"Leave them."

She stood there, lips pursed, my jeans dangling from her fingers. "You're a pig, Robbie Jo."

"We should hire a housekeeper and, hey, it's okay to date. You're a grown woman and your daughter's in college. You can have wild monkey sex if you want."

"We can't afford a housekeeper. Not when we're about to sink our asses into a lifetime of debt."

Just so little Miss Carla could go on her merry way, carefree and irresponsible as ever. "Love the great attitude."

"Bite me. And I am well aware it's okay for me to date." "And have sex" was left unsaid. *I swear, sometimes Reecie is such a prude.*

"You act like you've got something to hide."

"I'm not hiding anything." She folded her arms over her chest, my jeans still clutched in her fingers. Even under her tan, I could see the hint of a blush. And Reecie wasn't one to blush—normally. Jack must really be working her over. Go Jack!

Chuckling softly at my naughty silent pun, I crossed the room and took my jeans from her, stuffing them in the empty clothes hamper, then gently grabbed her by the shoulders and steered her toward the door. "Enjoy your date."

I closed the door, then got back to the business of deciding what to wear to seduce a man when you weren't really on a date with him. I settled on a lemon-yellow satin bra and matching thong, grinning at myself in the mirror. Other than the tattoo around my belly button, nothing marked the tanned expanse of my belly. Turning to the side, I gave my ass a little smack, pleased to see it didn't jiggle. I figured that with Cash I better keep it simple. Despite the sexy undergarments, I settled on my best low-cut jeans and a sheer orange top that set off my tan and the bra underneath. The hair and makeup were simple; even for him, I wasn't going overboard.

That wasn't my style.

I slid my feet into a pair of wedge sandals and sprayed on some Happy before heading out to seduce Cash McBride.

Graciela's was nowhere near the beach, but with food like they served, they didn't need a view to draw in the customers. Even on a Thursday evening, the place was crowded, and Cash and I decided to sit outside. Or rather, I talked Cash into sitting outside. The patio had its own bar and a more relaxed atmosphere, since most of the families stayed inside. Frankly, too many high-pitched voices made me want to rip out my eardrums.

I reluctantly waved to a pretty blonde watching us from a few tables away. She was running to fat and if she wasn't careful she'd soon catch up with the portly bald man sitting next to her. "We went to high school together," I explained to Cash, dropping my voice. "She was *such* a slut. She's still a slut. Her husband's in real estate and loaded."

"So is it a crime to marry a rich man?" Cash grinned at me, those gorgeous blue eyes twinkling.

"No. I suppose not. But he's kind of old," I discreetly motioned in their direction.

"Some folks might say I'm kind of old." Cash held my chair for me, and while I was tempted to remind him this wasn't a date, I refrained. I didn't want to piss him off. I wanted to fuck him. And besides, his manners were kind of endearing.

"You're not old, just . . . older." I gave him my wide-eyed innocent look and fluttered my lashes for good effect.

"Can I get you two something to drink?" The waitress deposited chips and some of Graciela's famous homemade salsa on the table between us.

"Margarita, please." I smiled innocently at Cash, who leaned back in his chair and tucked his sunglasses in his breast pocket.

"I'm not driving you home again."

"You won't have to. He'll have a Miller Light."

She glanced at Cash, who nodded a confirmation, then said she'd be back with our water and drinks.

I reached for the salt, all set to soak the picante sauce with it, then glanced at Cash. "You mind?"

"Knock yourself out." He grabbed a chip, dipped it in the hot stuff, and popped it into his mouth before I could warn him that the salsa was famous for a reason—it was hotter than hell.

"You might regret not waiting for that water." I nibbled at a naked chip, flicking off a bit of the salt with my tongue and letting it melt.

"Damn, that was hot." Laughing, he fanned at his mouth.

"Told ya so."

Lucky for him, the waitress returned with his water and our drinks posthaste. I took a long sip of my margarita before braving the very hot salsa and finally glanced at the menu. Behind us, chairs scraped and the rustle of people leaving grated on my ears before a hand came to rest on my shoulder.

"Roberta Jo, how are you, honey?" Marietta Young's voice was as syrupy as the rest of her carefully cultivated Southern-belle demeanor.

I glanced at her hand, tipped by icy pink nails, and then smiled at her, glad I still had my sunglasses on. She wasn't just a slut, but a royal bitch, too. "Fine, and you?" I slid my sunglasses off, eyes on her husband, as I spoke again, "How's your dad . . . and mom?" *Yeah, I'm mean, so what?* Beside me, Cash cleared his throat. He'd obviously caught my inference.

"They're good. How's the moving business?"

"Great . . . great . . ." I drawled, praying she'd leave soon.

"I just don't know how you handle all that manual labor." She shuddered and clutched her designer purse a little closer to her stomach.

"It's a great way to stay in shape," I said, taking in the spread of her ever-widening hips. "You two must have a passel of rug rats at home!"

"No, we haven't been blessed."

"Oh . . . I thought . . ." I let my word and the pointed look I gave her stomach speak volumes. Marietta heard me loud and clear, too, hustling her husband off before I could take any more shots at him.

Once they were out of earshot, Cash spoke up from behind his beer bottle, "Remind me to never piss you off."

"Was it that obvious?" I did my own Southern belle imitation, smiling coyly and fluttering my eyelashes at him.

"You're about as subtle as a Category Five hurricane, babe." With that, he turned his attention to his menu, lifting it high enough to block my view of him.

"No smirking, Cowboy." I glanced at my own menu, assuring myself they hadn't changed it.

"I wouldn't dare, Boss Lady." The way he said "Boss Lady" sent shivers up my spine.

He glanced at me over the top and wiggled his menu to get my attention; I couldn't believe he actually thought he had to *work* to get my attention. "What's good?"

"Me. Though I think 'amazing' is somehow more fitting. Good is so—" here I paused and wrinkled my nose for effect, "—middle of the road."

Cash gave me a narrow-eyed grimace as if to say, stop being a smart-ass. "I meant on the menu."

"Everything, but I highly recommend the pulled-pork enchiladas."

"I think someone wants you." Cash nodded toward the patio gate.

Against my better judgment, I looked, then wished I hadn't.

"Robbie Joooo!" Dressed in baggy jeans and an equally oversized T-shirt, Dean Remington stepped through the gate, followed by his brother Sam.

They waved and I halfheartedly waved back, reluctant to have them join us, but unable to find a way around it. They were just *those* kinds of guys, nice but bulldozing their way in before you had a chance to tell them to get lost.

Dean squeezed my shoulder and took a seat next to me while Sam claimed the one on Cash's other side, waving to the waitress as Dean dug in to the chips.

"You coming out tonight?" Dean shoved a chip full of salsa past his lips.

"Guys." Giving them both a pointed look, I nodded in Cash's direction.

Sam blinked in surprised as if he'd just noticed Cash. "He fuzz?"

"Dude." Dean punched him in the arm and made to stand up. "She's on a date."

"I don't care if they join us." Cash leaned back with a smile for both of them. "It's not like we're on a real date."

Fuck me.

Cash, Dean, and Sam were having a splendid time on my "not-a-date," but I was miserable.

Luckily, I had a second margarita—this one mango—to keep me company.

"Can you imagine Cash here racing that big old truck of his?" Dean laughed and drained the last of his second beer, motioning to the waitress for another while Sam made loud truck noises like a little kid. For a second I wished they'd both go drink some hot sauce.

Cash's broad shoulders shook with repressed laughter as he finished chewing a bite of tamale covered in chili. He'd gotten the Mexican platter only because it had a little of everything, and apparently Cash loved Mexican food. Not that he'd bothered to tell me that. No, he'd told Dean and Sam, extolling the virtues and vices of every Mexican restaurant from Georgia to California.

"No races tonight. I have to work tomorrow." I took another large sip of my margarita and winced as minor brainfreeze set in.

"That never stopped you before," Dean said.

"Yeah. It's not like you have to get up early or something." Sam shoveled a chip full of salsa into his mouth and smiled around it, shrugging as if he knew how much his presence was irritating me. "You could just come watch."

"I don't feel like it. I've got a lot on my mind." With Reece's admonishment to not say anything about Carla or the buyout echoing in my head, I felt like slapping myself.

"Where do y'all race?" Cash asked, neatly avoiding my booboo.

"We never know where they are until about thirty minutes before." Feeling more than a little pouty and put out, I drained some more of my margarita.

"So you mean your Mustang has a secret NOS button somewhere?"

"No, but Robbie Jo does." Dean smirked in my direction.

My face heated up, and I knew there was no hiding my embarrassment or my red cheeks, but right that moment I seriously wanted to cry. "Go fuck yourself, Dean."

One mistake and they never let you forget it. I'd slept with

Dean almost two years ago and even though we were still friends, he had a way of remembering our . . . entanglement . . . at the most inopportune times.

Like now.

"I'd rather—"

"Anyone else care for another drink?" The waitress set a fresh beer in front of him, then came around and picked up my unfinished dinner. She reached for it, glanced at me, and I nodded.

"No. I'd like my check, please." Despite that second margarita, I was more than ready to write tonight off as a bust and just head on home.

"Me, too," Cash said, pushing his own plate away. He'd barely eaten half.

"You can get the rest of that to go." I pointed at Cash's dinner. I glanced at him and then the plate, wondering what his game was. Maybe he was ready to call it a night. God knows I was, even if it meant sleeping alone.

"We can go back to Robbie Jo's and play Quarters."

Rolling my eyes in his direction, I said, "I quit playing Quarters in high school, Sammy."

"Besides," Dean said, "If Reece isn't there, I don't want to go."

Not only had Dean slept with me, he'd told me he had a crush on my sister. The man was as irritating as earwax. "Reece is on a date. She's *seeing someone.*"

Before I could stop him, Cash had picked up both the checks and slipped some bills into the little wallet, handing it back to our waitress before she could get away. "Keep the change." He stood up, running a hand down one leg and massaging just above his knee.

I took one last sip of my margarita, savoring the salt and tequila and wishing I could have had one more. "Later, guys."

"Have fun," they chorused. Assholes. Okay, so I loved them,

sorta, but they were assholes sometimes. Like brothers, but not related to me.

Anyway . . . "I thought this wasn't a date." I said as we stepped outside the gate.

"It's not, but I didn't feel like waiting for the waitress to bring the charge slip back for you to sign."

"How'd you know I'd charge it?"

"Guessed." He rested his hand at the base of my spine as we walked, his touch burning a hole through the thin material of my shirt. "And you looked like you really needed to get out of there."

"Thank you." I paused to let a huge black Chevy rumble past, then crossed to my Mustang, Cash at my side. I stopped at the door and turned to face him. "I'm really sorry about them. *Really.*"

"It's my fault for being a smart-ass and letting them join us. I figured picking up the tab was the least I could do."

True that, but I didn't say it out loud. Not when tonight was starting to look salvageable and he'd been such a champ about getting me out of there. "How about dessert?" I asked brightly.

"I said no sex, Robbie Jo—and is it Robbie or Roberta?"

"If you want to die a slow painful death, it's Roberta. I meant, I have ice cream and brownies at the house." God, please let Reece not have eaten all the ice cream . . . or brought Jack home.

"No hanky-panky?" He slid his sunglasses back on, that stern mask of his firmly back in place.

"None, I swear."

Behind my back, my fingers were *so* crossed.

I kicked off my shoes in the laundry room, fully aware of Cash on my heels, of him watching me, of the heat of his body so close to mine . . .

"Are we gonna stand out here all night?"

"Of course not." Sighing, I stepped into the kitchen and flicked the light switch, ducking into the freezer for ice cream and a face-cooling. I'd spent the entire drive home trying to figure out how to seduce Cash, and fantasies of getting him naked, finally, had left me tingly all over.

"Where's your, uh, facilities?"

I closed the freezer door enough to point him in the right direction. "Out the door, down the hall, and under the stairs. It's small, so you might have to duck."

At his mumbled thanks, I stuck my head back in the freezer and grabbed the vanilla ice cream, then fished the brownies out of the fridge, quickly assembling our desserts. By the time I was done, Cash had rejoined me. "Want to sit outside or on the couch?"

"With you, I'm not sure which is safer. Where's Reece?"

"Out on a date. Remember?"

"I thought you just said that to irk what's-his- name."

"Nope, she's really on a date." I handed him his bowl, unable to hold back a huge grin at my next question. "What's it gonna be, Cowboy? Inside our out?"

"Only you could make that sound . . . perverted." His own lips twisted into a tiny grin. "Inside is fine by me."

I dug down in my bowl, filling the spoon with brownie, icing, and ice cream and sliding it into my mouth with a moan. "Heavenly," I said around my bite as I led the way into the living room. "Come on. I'll even put in a movie for you."

"Nothing over PG-13 for me."

"Damn, guess that means no porn, then, huh?"

"I guess so, unless you have some PG-13 porn."

"Very funny, Cowboy."

"Don't call me that. I'm just Cash."

"Cash McBride, ma'am," I dropped my voice a few octaves. Giggling, I set my bowl on a coaster and grabbed the remote. Cash, however, didn't look amused. "I was just teasing, sugar."

His eyes sort of drifted away from mine, the way Reece's did when she was lying. I'd apparently hit a nerve, teasing the cowboy about being a cowboy.

"You want to watch *Flubber*?" I said by way of a peace offering.

He sat on the couch and put his bowl next to mine, then propped his elbows on his knees. "I'm sorry, I'm just—"

"You don't have to explain."

He gave me a serious, hangdog look. "I'm just not a Disney kind of guy."

"No porn, no Disney. You're killing me here. *Friday the Thirteenth*, then? Or would you prefer an action flick?"

"I'm surprised you don't want to watch one of those girly kissy-kissy movies."

"You said no porn, remember?"

He leaned forward and spooned up a bite of his dessert. "You choose. Whatever you want to watch is fine with me."

"Okay, but just so you know, we've got to call it an early night. I need my beauty sleep." From behind me came the distinctive sound of him snorting in disbelief. I bit my lip to keep from laughing and scanned the DVDs for a minute, then slid a case from the shelf and loaded the disc into the player. "Hope you like blood and guts."

"What the hell did you put in?"

"*Men in Black*." Smiling smugly to myself, I settled on the couch next to him and proceeded to plow through some of my desert before it turned into a big blob.

Beside me, Cash seemed content to mix his together and nibble at it, letting it melt as the movie played.

"You gonna eat that or play with it?" I finally asked.

"I'm eating." He glanced at my half-eaten bowl, then at me, but didn't say a word, just shielded his with his hands.

"You're a good man, Cash McBride."

"And you're a brat, Robbie Jo Cavanaugh."

I leaned into him as close as I could get and said, "Smoochie, smoochie!" laughing as he moved out of reach and nudged me with his elbow.

"Behave." His eyes were on the television, where Will Smith was shooting up a room.

"Or you'll take your toys and go?" I settled back on the couch, my feet on the table, my body pressed against Cash's. He didn't seem to mind, though, and I took it as a good sign.

"Yeah, and I want to watch this."

"You've seen this."

"Nope. I haven't." He took another bite of chocolate-covered ice cream.

Filing that little tidbit away, I quieted down so he could watch the movie—still unable to believe he hadn't seen it. It was one of my favorites and I'd watched it dozens of times. I practically knew all the dialogue, though I refrained from talking along, like I did when Reece watched it with me.

Once I was done with my dessert, I switched off the living room lights, rejoining him on the couch, sitting as close as I dared, which was pretty much arm to arm. Cash didn't say a word and didn't shift away when he reached for his drink, just settled back next to me. I propped my bare feet on the table and leaned against him, all the food and booze and a day's worth of hard work making me sleepy.

When I woke up, the screen was black. Cash, who was snoring softly beside me, had his feet on the table next to mine. He had a tiny hole near the toe of one sock. My head was on his chest and his hand was draped over my waist. It felt so good, I closed my eyes again and let myself drift off for a few more minutes. Then my mind sort of wandered to the proximity of Cash's belt and everything underneath it and the fact his chest was so firm and comfy. Then I got this visual of me riding his cock right here on the couch.

Reece would have a fit and despite the fact I was getting turned on, I didn't want to wake Cash up. I was afraid if I did, he'd leave or, worse, stay and things would be all awkward between us afterward.

He continued to snore very softly, his breathing slowly pushing my head up and down.

I continued to contemplate the rightness or wrongness of waking him with a blow job or whatever other seductive measure I could scrape up.

Underneath me, he groaned slightly and shifted before settling back down. I eyed the snaps on his shirt, finally daring to undo them one by one and slip my hand inside. His skin was warm under my fingers. Occasionally they'd scrape across a scar and I remembered the old one I'd seen along his ribs. I reached for it, tracing the puckered skin as lightly as possible with my fingertips while my head slowly inched downward, my lips prepared to press themselves into that spot where his chest met his rib cage.

The hand that had been on my back, curved around my side, drifted upward and caressed my hair as I finally gave in to temptation and pressed my lips to his skin, letting my tongue lick at him, unable to hold back a little moan of satisfaction. His belly quivered slightly under my tongue, while my fingers continued to trace that scar. His hand in my hair picked up the pace, stroking it a little faster, a little rougher, the lower I got. I gave in to even more temptation and went for his belt buckle, a simple affair. As I sat up and undid it, I couldn't bring myself to look at him, afraid I'd break the spell.

My tongue got as far as his belly button before his hips lifted off the couch, moaning and pushing his cock in my direction. My worries about distracting him while attempting to free his cock were apparently unnecessary. As the thick member slid free of his tighty-whities, he sighed, a harsh sound that filled the living room. I wet my lips, then slowly flicked my tongue across the soft head, melting a bit at the feel of him in my mouth.

"Fuck," he hissed. "I'm gonna regret this."

"Want me to stop?" I whispered, my lips against his cock. Closing my eyes, I inhaled the musky scent of his sex.

"Hell, no."

Smiling to myself, I wet my lips again and dove in. He pulsated with life at every stroke of my tongue, his hand keeping rhythm with my mouth while I sucked his cock and stroked him with my hand at the same time. His free hand was balled into a fist against his thigh, his knuckles showing white against his skin while his other hand tightened in my hair. His cock stiffened and swelled and leaked the tiniest bit of cum in my mouth. He was smooth and savory against my tongue, and I closed my eyes, losing myself in the moment, in the smell of his sex, in the rhythm we created together, until he pulled me off and sat me up, yanking at my blouse all in one motion.

"You know we shouldn't do this." His hands shook as he fumbled with my bra, then caressed my face, rough and anxious.

"Shut up, Cash."

"Please tell me you have condoms," he said, his expression pained.

"Upstairs."

"Go get 'em."

"I've got a bed up there, too." I pressed my lips to his jaw, the slight stubble tickling my tongue."

"Just go get 'em." He pushed me off his lap and off the couch, then yanked off his shirt, stopping with one arm out. "What are you waiting for?"

I didn't need to be told twice, but dashed upstairs for condoms, pillows, and a blanket. Reece would kill me if I left cum stains on the couch. I also took off my jeans, rejoining Cash in nothing but my yellow lingerie.

"You look like sunshine." He held his arms out to me, and I dropped everything beside the couch to straddle his lap. I tipped his chin up and kissed him, sliding my tongue past his lips to taste him and tease him and make him as hot as he made me. His hands slid down my back to cup the curve of my ass, and I moaned against his lips, pressing myself against his cock.

I came up for air long enough to nip at his ear. "I want you so bad."

His fingers were under the elastic band of my panties, pushing them down, and I stood up long enough to slide them off and grab the condoms before straddling Cash's lap again. He had my bra off in no time. I was buck naked but he still had his jeans on—mostly. "Want to get comfy?"

"I'm *very* comfy," he hissed, his lips pressed to the curve of my breast, his hands wrapped around both of them, squeezing and kneading them, tweaking my nipples until I was grinding against him, hot and aching.

I could have happily died right there pressed up against him with his hands on me, and his dick in my fist. My toes curled, digging into his calves, pushing against the denim of his jeans as I buried my face in his neck. He sighed again and turned his head away, giving me access. I traced my tongue up his neck, pausing to suck at the pulse.

"God, we shouldn't be doing this," he breathed, his hands sliding down my back to rest at my hips, leaving a shivery trail in their wake.

"Yes, we should." I stopped what I was doing and pushed his hands lower, between my thighs.

"You certainly know what you want."

"I sure as hell do," I replied with a laugh. I wanted him and he was all mine. I'd worry about tomorrow . . . tomorrow.

His fingers gently probed the slippery folds of my pussy, stroking me, spreading my juices around, and teasing my clit slowly, methodically until I could barely remember to breathe. Shaky with excitement, I leaned in and pressed my lips against his; his chest hairs tickled my nipples and sent icy shivers up my spine. "You feel *so* good."

"So do you."

His voice made me shiver; our eyes met. I wasn't so lost to my own need that I missed the bit of sadness in his eyes—or the hunger. "Are you sure about this?"

I had no idea where that bit of conscience had come from, but there it was, raising up like a three-headed beast. "We can stop if you want." I pressed another soft kiss to his lips, unable to contain a loud sharp moan when his finger curled deep inside me, rubbing the walls of my pussy.

"*No.* I'm good." He groaned and fisted his free hand in my hair, pulling me in, his mouth opening under mine and his tongue meeting me in a hot, heady tangle that ended with both of us reaching for the condoms.

"You want on top?" I asked, ripping the package open and slipping it on him.

Shaking his head, he gave me a sleepy smile of reassurance, and stretched briefly beneath me. His cock bobbed slightly against his belly as he caught his lower lip between his teeth. "Hurry."

He didn't have to tell me twice. I positioned myself over his thick, stiff cock and slid him inside me. My pussy automatically clenched around him, welcoming. A moan tumbled from my lips and I struggled for air as I wrapped my arms around his neck and buried my face in his hair. It was soft against my cheek, and he held me tight while I rode him, slipping up and down on his cock. Underneath me, his legs shifted, the table moved, and a glass fell, but I wasn't about to stop. I'd clean up the mess later.

Cash shifted some more, sliding lower beneath me, making it more difficult for me to hold him.

"Want to lie down?"

"No, just don't stop," he panted, struggling, for control I guess. His fingers dug into my hips and he groaned again, louder this time, his eyes squeezed tightly shut. That's when I finally realized that he needed this and it wasn't just because he'd been without for a while. I curled against him, pressing soft kisses across his forehead and stroking his hair, hoping I could stave off my own orgasm until he came.

Underneath me, he bucked, meeting me thrust for thrust, harder, faster until it was a frenzied fucking and I softly urged him on, urged him to come inside me and he finally did, his shout of pleasure absorbed by my skin.

I held him tighter, his own grip almost leaving me breathless as I came with a few more strokes, my clit hungrily rubbing against him.

He'd needed this. He'd needed me and probably meant to have me all along.

Instead of doing the seducing, I had a feeling I'd been seduced, and I couldn't say I minded.

4

I woke up alone.

Sighing, I blew some hair off my face. At least Cash had covered me up before he snuck out, but damn it, I hadn't even *heard* him leave. After round two (again on the couch), I'd crashed out, hard, too satiated to move. All I remembered was him lying next to me, stroking my forehead until I'd drifted off.

Stretching and wiggling my toes, I thought about how different it was from waking up in his apartment last weekend. If I'd learned nothing else about Cash, I'd learned he was a difficult one to figure out . . . that didn't make up for waking up alone, with no explanations, though.

"Well, good morning, naked bunny."

I glanced up at Reece, freeing a finger to shoot her the bird and hoping she didn't say anything about the coffee table littered with condom wrappers, remotes, and sticky dessert bowls.

"Are we going to be short a mover today?" Arms crossed over her chest, she arched an eyebrow my way.

I searched through my memory banks for a few seconds, then gave her my best shit-eating grin, glad I had a sister who didn't pry too deeply. "Don't think so. He didn't complain, anyway."

"Jesus, Robbie Jo." Shaking her head, she circled the couch, headed for the stairs. "Your timing really stinks."

"Well excuse the fuck out of me!"

"You are *not* fucking excused! I've got enough on my plate right now with Carla. I don't need to be worrying about how to fill a fucking crew because you screwed the help—*again*!"

"You're not the only one worried about Carla, you know." I struggled to a sitting position. "And he's not the help, he's *Cash*."

"Oh my God!" She came trotting back down the stairs to stare at me, her mouth slightly agape. "You really like him."

I sat up as much as I dared, the blanket clutched to my chest. I don't know why. It's not like I needed to be modest with Reece; she'd seen me naked enough times, but still . . . I felt weird. "Shut up. Of course I like him. I don't sleep with men I don't like, Reece. What would be the point?"

With another "Oh my God" and a roll of her eyes, she turned and headed back upstairs. "You better hope he shows up today! And get your ass dressed. The trucks need gas, and Carla's not coming in today, which means I've got to take her crew."

The trucks always needed gas.

Cash came strolling in around nine, dressed in snug faded jeans and his work T-shirt, his blond hair still damp from a shower. Smothering a fit of excited nerves that left me jittery, I poked my head in Reece's office long enough to stick my tongue out at her and grab our schedule. "You better not have given me any shitty moves."

"Would I do that?"

"Yes, you would, bitch." *She's my sister. I can call her that.*

She damn well might do it in retaliation for me sleeping with Cash.

Grinning to myself, I handed out all the clipboards, made sure everyone understood their schedules, and then motioned to Cash and James to head for our truck. Since Cash was the shorter of the two men, he got to sit in the middle. James needed the legroom.

Cash climbed in next to me, an oversized cup of soda clutched in his hand.

"Tired?" If James hadn't been hard on his heels, I'd have said something witty about waking up alone.

He shrugged a bit, barely glancing at me out of the corner of his eye as he hooked his seat belt. "Sorta, yeah."

"No, I'm not tired, thanks for asking." Laughing, James climbed in and slammed the door.

I started the truck, praying it wasn't going to be a long day and that Cash wouldn't be a puss about last night.

Well he wasn't a complete puss, but there were definitely some uncomfortable moments on that first move. During lunch, I cornered him for five, curious about why he'd left, but unwilling to push too hard.

"You okay?" I finally muttered.

"I'm fine." He had his sunglasses on, so I wasn't completely convinced he was telling the truth.

"You know, if you want on another crew, I can have Reece put you on hers."

"How come Reece is taking Carla's crew?"

We'd gotten our lunch and parked across from the beach, electing to sit on one of the stone benches and enjoy the sunny day. James stayed near the truck doing his usual thing.

"Carla's sick." *In the head.*

"Is that why she's never around?"

"No." I turned my attention to my chicken tenders.

"That was vague." He snitched a fry and dabbed it in catsup.

"What do you want me to say?"

"I'm sorry. I shouldn't be so nosy." He made to stand up, but my apology halted him halfway out of his seat.

"It's complicated." I nibbled a little more at my tender, wondering how much I should say. "Lately she's been . . . her dad died late last year."

He sank back down, nodding in understanding.

"Why did you leave?" I asked, hoping to catch him off guard by switching gears.

"Leave?"

Surely he wasn't that dense! "Last night."

"Now you know why I didn't want to sleep with you." He stood up again, for real this time, sighed, and wadded up his burger wrapper, pitching it in a nearby trash can.

I followed, unwilling to let him run away so easily. "I'm not one of those clingy women, you know?"

"Aren't you?" He turned to face me, arms crossed over his chest, his face unreadable.

"I've never clung to any man in my life!"

"You cling to this place."

"There's a huge difference—" I paused, frowning, "—what does this have to do with last night?"

"I'm not staying here, and you're not leaving here, which means what happened last night can't happen again."

"All I'm saying is a good-bye would have been nice."

As soon as I got off work, I cleaned up and headed to Carla's ugly-ass condo, pushing my troubles with Cash out of my mind. *For now, anyway.*

I knew Reece had already seen her, but Carla's leaving us in the lurch like this didn't sit well with me and there was still the small matter of coming up with the money to buy her out.

Luckily, she didn't live in one of those buildings where she had to let me up or I never would have gotten in. As it was, I barely made it through her front door.

Carla had a full regalia of makeup on and her hair in rollers. "Going somewhere?"

"It's none of your business what I do, Robbie Jo." She shut the door and headed for her bedroom, her back and shoulders stiff. I followed, unwilling to let her shake me that easily.

"It doesn't have to be . . . this . . . Carla." My voice trailed off as I stopped dead in my tracks, taking in the queen-sized bed covered with designer clothes. Bags from Nordstrom were scattered all over the floor and intermingled with shoe boxes with names on them I couldn't even pronounce. "Jesus Che-rist, Carla Renée, what the hell have you been doing?"

"Shopping."

"This looks more like a raid than a shopping trip." My heart slowed to a heavy beat before a jolt of adrenaline coursed through me and I curled my shaking hands into fists at my sides.

"You wouldn't understand." She snatched a slinky white number off the bed and stepped into it, turning her back to me. "But as long as you're here, make yourself useful."

I talked while I zipped. "Look, things have been really weird the last couple months. But after this is over, we're still family."

"I know."

"And we're all we've got."

"I *know*, Robbie Jo."

"After the way you've acted the last couple months, I do wonder." Her shoulders stiffened and she turned around, mouth open. I held up a hand to stop her. "Hear me out before you get all huffy. I respect the fact you want out—sort of—I

123

don't really agree with it, but if it's what you want, then fine. I just . . . well . . . you're still my cousin and—" I sighed, digging deep, "—we used to be close. I just wish, you know, you'd given me some sort of warning, said something. But you've just—"

She crossed her arms over her chest. "I've what?"

"You—" I waved a hand in her general direction, "—I don't even know you anymore." I sat on the bed, not caring about the cost of whatever I was sitting on.

"Is it a crime to want more out of life than manual labor?" She stepped into the bathroom where I couldn't see her, but could hear the sound of her rollers hitting the sink. "I want a great job, a husband and kids, and a *nice* life." She stuck her head out, her springy curls bobbing around her tiny face. "A nice life where I don't have to get all grubby and work like a dog. I want more, Robbie Jo. That life's fine for you—"

"That life? *That life* put you through college and raised you and fed you." Here I pushed to my feet and crossed to where she stood, getting as close as I dared (but not so close I could smack her like I really wanted to). "Do you think your parents—"

"My parents are gone! And this is *my life*, goddamn it. Now get the fuck out."

"Carla—"

"Get out!" She turned back toward the bathroom. "I have a date and he'll be here soon."

"Can you really know what you want, where you're going, if you're ashamed of where you came from?"

"Fuck you."

When I got home, Reece was in the kitchen, pounding chicken breasts to stuff.

"Figured you'd be too tired to cook." I hung up my keys and poured myself a glass of orange juice. "Or is this for Jack?"

"This is for us." She scooped stuffing from a bowl, filled the breast till it was overflowing, then pinned it together with a toothpick.

"Bad day?"

Reece was a stress cooker, and a bit of a stress eater. But then, I was definitely up for being her guinea pig. I got some tea bags from the cupboard and started some tea on the stove. "Anything else I can do?"

"No."

"I could run and get more ice cream."

"Why don't you run to the store and get four hundred grand while you're at it?" She grabbed another breast, split it, and started pounding it.

"Was that Carla's head you just gutted?" I asked with a giggle.

That at least got a snort out of her. "Maybe we should have Carla over for dinner tomorrow, and talk." After my talk with her earlier, that didn't seem like the greatest idea in the world, but something had to give.

"I dunno. She seems pretty . . . I don't *even* know," I concluded lamely.

"Did you finally go see her?" Reece turned to face me, a knife clutched in her hands.

"Unfortunately. When did she get to be such a fucking snob?" I dug the tea pitcher out of the cabinet, slamming it on the counter hard enough to make Reece jump. "Sorry, Sis. So what else is on the menu? Steamed Carla?"

She shook her head, one stuffing-covered hand waving in the air. "Ha-ha. Tear a salad. And don't worry about the money. I'll figure something out."

"You know, I can help." I dug around in the fridge, getting out the salad fixings, then palmed a cantaloupe, setting it on the counter to cut up for dessert.

"Robbie," she groaned.

"*Reecie.*" I piled everything on the counter and reached around her for another knife and the other cutting board. "It's my business, too."

"I know it's your business!" Her face was red and her hands were shaking.

"It's *our* business, so stop acting like you have to do it all yourself!" We worked in strained silence for a while, me cutting and chopping and tearing, and her slicing and stuffing. Once she had the chicken in the oven, she finally spoke again.

"You know, Jack says the same thing."

"What? That you don't have to do everything yourself? Maybe you should listen to him." I covered the salad with Saran Wrap and threw all my garbage away before turning to face her, my arms crossed over my chest. "I have money, Reecie."

"I know you don't have four hundred thousand dollars, Robbie Jo."

"I've got fifty grand in a CD. We could use that for collateral. Or . . . whatever." So I knew absolutely nothing about buying a business, but I figured I wasn't the first person to just wing it. Finances weren't my forte, but I wasn't a complete goob.

"Where the hell did you get fifty grand?" she practically shouted, hands propped on her hips.

"What? I can't save money?" Other than my car and half the bills on the house, which didn't amount to much, I didn't have much to spend my money on, and I'd always been a saver. "It's rainy-day money, Reecie." I crossed the kitchen and hugged her, only to end up with her sobbing on my shoulder. "And I'd say this definitely qualifies as a rainy day. Have you even called Chloe about this?"

Reece took so much to heart, took so much on herself. Hell, she'd raised me, more than Dad had, and raised Chloe, and she had a tendency to let things weigh her down, whereas I rarely let things get to me.

Normally.

Right now, Carla and Cash were definitely getting to me.

"Why the hell would I call Chloe?" Sagging against the counter, she wiped at her face, dampening a paper towel to blot the tears away.

"Because she's family."

"Chloe wouldn't care." She started sniffling again. "All she cares about is herself, just like Carla."

"She's a teenager. Of course all she cares about is herself. At her age, all I cared about was myself. She's a good kid. She'll come around, but she needs to know about this." I hugged Reece again. "You know, she probably won't want any part of the business once she's grown."

"Is it even worth hanging on to, then?" Reece sighed and pushed away to baste the chicken breasts with butter. "Should we even bother?"

"What the hell do we do without it? I'm not up for getting a real job. I'm too damned old."

"Ha-ha. You think *you're* too old!" She waved her hands in capitulation. "I say we keep it. What if you have kids some-day?"

For her trouble, she got an eye-roll. Not that kids weren't great. They just weren't real high on my priority list right now. "I guess hell could freeze over."

She gave me a once-over I didn't understand and couldn't read.

"What was that?"

"Nothing . . . so we're in?"

"We're in. Together . . . a hundred percent." I stuck out my hand for her to shake. "Partner."

"We split it fifty-fifty this time. And as much as it pains me, mortgage the house."

"Or use it as collateral. Did you call Jack's banker friend?"

"He said he'd get back to me by Monday with a decision." She slipped her hand in mine and we shook, smiling like major idiots at each other.

Our dinner turned out to be a celebration dinner.

"Everything's gonna be fine, Reecie." I refilled our wineglasses.

"I know." She propped her legs up on the empty chair and sipped her wine. "I almost wish Jack were here."

"You like him, don't you?"

"Yeah, I do." She smiled at me. "He's a good guy."

I raised my own wineglass, thinking about Cash. "To good guys."

"And to our future."

5

Despite our brief entanglement, I didn't have a problem working with Cash, but apparently he had a problem working with me. Via Reece I learned he'd be working on her crew on Saturday, so other than when he clocked in and out, I didn't see him. Hell, he was gone by the time I got back to the shop with my crew. We all crawled out of the truck grimy, sweaty, and tired as hell.

Reece was in the office compiling the day's paperwork to leave for Liz on Monday.

"Cash gone?" Hands stuffed in my pockets, I leaned against the doorjamb. My mouth tasted like dirt and every inch of me was gritty; inside my steel-toed boots, my feet were hot and achy, and all I wanted was to get horizontal, right after a long, hot shower.

"Yeah," she drawled.

"Did he say anything about me?" And why did I care? Why the hell *should* I care? The questions didn't really matter, because the bottom line was I *did* care.

"Robbie Jo, it's nearly eight o'clock at night. I don't have time for this. I want to finish this paperwork, grab a burger, and head home."

"Fine. How about I order us some dinner and pick it up on the way home?"

"Sure, fine." She waved me off, then added, "I want fish!"

While the guys closed up the shop for us, I used the phone in Liz's office and ordered dinner from Casey's. I'd picked it up and was nearly home when my phone buzzed.

AT TIKI. DRNKNG W/CASH. YR MISSING ALL THE FUN.

It was from Sam.

"Oh my God." Tossing my cell phone in the seat beside me, I pulled onto our street, slowing as my headlights bounced off a dog weaving on and off the road, his nose to the ground. He turned briefly and looked at me as if he were upset I'd interrupted him, and went back to sniffing out whatever he was hunting.

I sat in my driveway talking to myself until the smell of shrimp and grilled fish got me moving. No way, nohow was I going to that bar. Sam, Dean, and Cash could just drink without me. I was too tired and my feet were killing me. I carried our dinner inside and left it on the counter, heading for the stairs and a shower.

In my room, I undressed and started the shower, almost missing the buzz of my cell phone from the depths of my purse. Against my better judgment, I punched the ON button and barked, "What?"

"You coming down here, or what?" It sounded like Dean.

"No."

Hanging up, I climbed in the shower, standing under the warm spray, letting it beat the soreness out of my back and shoulders. How the hell had Cash gotten to the bar so fast?

I didn't care. I was going to eat my dinner and go to bed. And that was that.

Once I was done, I threw on my favorite sweats and an old T-shirt, then headed for the kitchen, where Reece was kicking off her shoes, her slumped shoulders testament to how tired she was.

"Did you leave me any hot water?"

"Of course I did." A little; I hoped. I didn't want her doing laundry while I was in the shower again.

I'd just peeled the top off the foil container and taken a bite of fried shrimp when the house phone rang. I didn't even have to look at the caller ID to know who it was.

Holy Fried Calamari. Throwing down my fork, which bounced off the counter and clattered to the floor, I lifted the handset. "Dean, damnitalltohell!"

"It's not Dean, darlin'."

Gawd, it wasn't Dean; it was Cash and if his slurred speech was any indication, he was well on his way to shit-faced.

"You gonna come down here and drink with us?"

I could barely hear him over the music and laughter. Dean . . . or Sam . . . shouted something that made Cash laugh, but I'm not sure what it was. And I wasn't sure I wanted to know.

I sagged against the counter. "Dude, no."

"Oh, come on. I don't like drinking alone."

"You're not alone." I jabbed the plastic fork into the shrimp and rice, ready to take another bite. "You've got Sam and Dean to drink with. I'm tired."

"There's a race."

"Not even a race can tempt me tonight."

"So what can tempt you?" His question was followed by male laughter. Assholes! All of them.

I hung up and headed out onto the patio with my rapidly cooling dinner. Away from the house phone and my cell, which I'd left upstairs in my room. It was the type of summer night I lived for: warm, breezy and with only the crickets and my dinner for company. Until I heard Reece's bedroom window slide open.

"Hey, your cell phone keeps ringing."

"Ignore it!"

"You going out?"

My "No!" was interrupted by the house phone . . . again.

The bar was about half-full, which was good, since I'd worn my oldest, most tattered jeans, an AC/DC T-shirt, and flip-flops in protest of being dragged out. And the only reason I'd *allowed* myself to be dragged was because the guys said they were leaving Cash to head out to a race. As for poor Cash, he wasn't just three sheets to the wind, he was more like the whole comforter set.

"We warmed him up for you. Now he's all yours." Sam patted me on the shoulder and they both disappeared through the murky bar, leaving me alone with Cash.

"Want anything?" Molly the waitress asked from behind me.

"Nope. I'm good." I'd just officially become Cash's designated driver. Changing my mind, I added before she could get away, "Coke."

"You got it. What about him?" She motioned to Cash.

He peered up at us through slightly bleary eyes, a drunken smile on his pretty mouth. "Hey, Boss Lady."

I barely heard his greeting over the sound of Blue Oyster Cult, but the intent was there. "Hey, yourself."

"Glad you decided to—" he paused to look around, "Where'd Sam and Dean go?"

"They left. You want some coffee?" I sank into the chair next to his, a part of me softening—a little.

"No." He eased back in his chair and stretched his legs out

in front of him, crossing them at the ankles. He looked thoughtful as he crossed his arms over his chest. "I will take another beer, and a shot of Scotch."

Molly arched one delicate brow, meeting my eyes. All I could do was shrug. He was grown. If he wanted to get shitfaced, so be it. I wasn't so heartless that I'd desert him and, after he'd driven me home last time, the least I could do was return the favor. With a nod, Molly took off to fill our order.

"You're gonna feel like shit tomorrow, Cash."

"Naw." He shook his head a tiny bit, and gave me this seductive, half-lidded glance that made me melt. At the same time, I knew there was no sleeping with him tonight. I wasn't above shacking up with a Saturday Night Special, but Cash wasn't a SNS, and I knew he'd have serious regrets if he found me in his bed tomorrow morning, to go along with his serious hangover. "I'm no lightweight, baby. I've been drinking since you were in junior high."

Holy . . . ! "Damn, Cash! You're not that much older than me."

"Ha. What are you, twenty-two? Twenty-three?"

"I'm twenty-five."

"And I'm the same age as your sister."

"So what's your point?" I asked as Molly returned with our drinks.

"Want these on his tab?" she asked as she unloaded her tray.

Figuring that buying me a Coke was the least that Cash could do, I nodded, then turned my attention back to him once she was gone. "What's your point, Cash?"

"You're just a baby. You haven't even lived." He sipped at the shot of Scotch, made a funny face, and then slugged it down.

"I haven't lived? How the hell would you know? You don't know jack shit about me!"

"When's the last time you left Galveston?"

"I don't see what it matters, but when we took my niece up to Austin for college . . . I think."

"It matters."

"It *doesn't* matter." I was beginning to feel frustrated at what was a very pointless conversation with a drunk. "Just drink your beer."

"I have been in forty of the fifty states, and Canada."

"Good for you."

"I have slept with women in damn near all forty of those states too . . . *and* Canada."

Wincing, I said, "I'm proud of you." *Thanks for telling me something I really didn't want to know.* "Is that what you wanted to hear? Good for you. Now, go fuck women in the other ten states."

"You're jealous." He leaned over and smiled up at me, nearly falling out of his chair in the process.

"No, I'm not." I pushed him upright, letting my hand linger on his bicep. "And if you can't sit up and drink your beer like a good boy, then I think it's time for us to leave."

"I can drink my beer just fine." As if to prove his point, he picked up the bottle and took a long pull.

I couldn't believe I was sitting here watching him get even more plowed.

"Life is tough," Cash said, interrupting my thoughts. "Life is *real* tough, Boss Lady."

Holy shit on a stick with sprinkles. "You arrogant ass," was all I could manage. I waved at Molly and motioned her over. "I need to close his tab and get him the hell out of here."

She glanced down at him, then nodded in understanding. "Be right back."

"You think I don't know about tough? That just goes to show how little you know me."

134

He shrugged and took another sip of his beer. "You ever been married, Boss Lady?"

"No." I scowled in his direction, and he laughed.

"You don't have a taste for wedded bliss?"

"Not at this time, no. What about you?"

"I loved being married." He clinked his beer bottle against my glass of Coke, his shoulders shaking with laughter.

"I just don't see what's so funny." I thought of the boxes in his living room, wondering if they were from his wife. If she'd dumped him and if that was how he'd ended up in Galveston.

"It's funny 'cause I'd like to do it again." He leaned forward, his arms folded on the table. "I liked being married. I liked having some sweet thing to come home to. But she hated me being gone all the time."

"Well I guess that's better than leaving you for another woman," I said, tongue firmly planted in my cheek.

"Shit, if she'da done that, she could have just invited me along." The grin he gave me was heart-stoppingly, shamelessly, adorably full of mischief. "I wouldn't have minded."

"She might have," I muttered as Molly slipped me his charge slip. I scribbled his name on it, adding a generous tip for her. He'd thank me later, I thought as I stood up. "Come on, cowboy. I'm taking you home."

"I'm not done with my beer." There went that smile again.

I snatched it out of his hand and drained the last third, belching behind my palm and setting it on the table. It swayed precariously, then settled in place. "Now you are."

Burping again, I tugged at the sleeve of his T-shirt. "Come on."

"That was rude." He didn't budge.

Armed with my sexiest "come hither" voice, I wrapped my arms around his neck, my breasts pressed against his arm, fingers sliding through his silky hair, and I leaned in as close to his ear as I could get. "Come on, baby. Let's go home."

Before I could even get out of his way, he was on his feet, one arm wrapped around my waist, pulling me to him in a surprisingly firm grip. He lowered his head, closing the distance between our lips. I closed my eyes, too, unwilling to watch and unable to interpret the words he whispered against my lips as he kissed me. His own lips were cold and tasted like beer as he sealed our mouths in the heavenliest kiss ever. The liquid seduction touched me to the core and melted my bones as well as my anger. Unfortunately, getting carried away in the middle of the Tiki Lounge was out of the question. Against my better judgment, I pulled away, gently squirming out of his grasp.

"Let's get out of here."

"Take me home." Something about the way he said "home" dug at me. Maybe it was the boxes; maybe it was the ex-wife. Maybe it was the booze.

Halfway home Cash informed me that he was going to be sick. I pulled over on the gulf side of Seawall Boulevard and helped him out. It was too late for a lot of traffic, but not so late we didn't run the risk of attracting the police. He swayed on his feet, leaning so close to me for support his chin bumped the top of my head. "Let's take a walk."

I led him down the steps to the beach, figuring that, if he didn't fall, it was better to hurl in the sand than on the sidewalk where the cops might pass by and see us. And arrest us. And I sure didn't feel like going to jail . . . or bailing him out for public intoxication.

The beach was dark, all the tourists safely tucked away in their hotel rooms, or out sampling what passed for nightlife in Galveston. We were all alone with the sand and the water and a nearly full moon that played peek-a-boo with the clouds, occasionally spilling a silvery path on the water.

Cash collapsed on a small dune and tucked his hands behind his head.

"Feel better?" I sank down next to him, arms wrapped around my knees, and watched him.

He blew out a heavy breath before answering. "Yeah, a little. Think I just got kinda motion sick."

Aided and abetted by a bunch of booze. "Do this often?" I asked, unable to keep the laughter out of my voice.

"No, thank God. I learned my lesson a long time ago about drinking. The last thing you want to ever do is climb on a bull with a hangover."

Ouch! "I can imagine. But then, climbing on one without a hangover seems pretty crazy, too."

Cash looked so peaceful, almost like he was sleeping. I stretched out beside him, even though it meant I'd be covered in sand, and turned to face him. The moon was briefly hidden in the shadows and made it so dark I couldn't even tell if his eyes were open or closed. "When did you quit?"

He waited so long to answer me, I was afraid he'd passed out. Neither leaving him here nor spending the night on the beach were options. "About six months ago." He sat up abruptly and climbed to his feet, swaying as he held out a hand to help me up. "You know I've been here nearly a month and haven't even walked on the beach."

I put my hand in his and let him help me to my feet. "Sure you're up for this?"

He nodded, swaying just a bit as he brushed sand off his jeans.

"Well, let's go." I stopped long enough to kick off my sandals. Cash followed suit, and we left them behind to mark our spot.

The sand under my feet was still warm from the summer sun, but I knew it'd be a bit colder down by the water. Hand in hand, we walked closer to the Gulf until the slightly chilly water lapped at our feet.

"You ever think about leaving?"

"Galveston?" I practically shuddered at the thought. I couldn't imagine living anywhere else. "No way."

He sighed, a heavy sound that filled my ears.

I leaned against him, squeezing his hand. "Where you from, Cowboy?"

He laughed, harshly. "I'm not even sure. It's been so long since I've been home."

"Where were you born, then?"

"New Mexico." He shivered slightly. The cool sea air coming off the Gulf seemed to help sober him up.

"Is that where your ex-wife is?" My feet sloshed through slippery wet sand that shifted under my feet as we walked and talked. Our hands clasped together, swinging gently.

"No."

"Family?" I asked, thinking of Carla and her desertion.

"Some."

"So you went from bull rider to mover."

"Quite a stretch, huh?" He laughed softly, his head dipping in the dark so I couldn't see his face, and shaking from side to side as if he couldn't believe it himself. His voice was deep and thick with sadness when he spoke again. "Rodeoing isn't something you can do forever."

I stayed quiet after that, leaving him to his thoughts for a while and sinking a bit deeper in mine. Thinking about Carla and Reece and the business; thinking about the changes coming hard and fast at me and Reece, and about how more than anything, I didn't want to lose my cousin and best friend over a business transaction. "Nothing lasts forever," I said, finally.

"How long did it take you to figure that out, kiddo?"

"I'm not a kid, Cash, and not that long. I think I always knew it; I just sort of forgot it." We took a few more silent steps before I spoke again, and my words surprised even me. "You know my mom died when I was three. I don't even remember her. All I remember is Reece and Dad. And Carla and her family. They've always been there—"

"You're lucky."

"My dad passed when I was thirteen and Reece took over his half of the business. Uncle Joe, that's Carla's dad, he wasn't completely thrilled, but she knew as much about the business as he did, so it wasn't like he could run her off. Then he died nine months ago and now Carla wants to sell his half of the business, so yeah, I'm no stranger to change. No one is, Cash."

6

After our walk, I took Cash back to his place and undressed him as he sank into an oblivion brought on by booze and a melancholy that I didn't quite understand. Once again my eyes were drawn to the deep scar under his ribs. I sank down on the side of the bed and traced it with my finger, keeping an eye on Cash, who didn't stir.

Just before he'd fallen asleep (or passed out—take your pick) he'd muttered something about leaving him in his jeans. Surely not for modesty's sake, and besides, that just couldn't be comfortable. His stomach slowly rose and fell, a testament to how deeply asleep he was.

I swear, my intentions were completely honorable as I slipped that button from its hole and unzipped his jeans. Another check assured me he wasn't moving, so I eased them off his hips, past his tighty-whities, then moved to the end of the bed so I could finish the job. I got them as far as his knees and stopped, my eyes glued to a long, ragged, red scar on his left thigh.

I leaned closer for a better look, crawling up on the bed. Just above his left knee the scar was no thicker than a pencil lead, then ran up his thigh in a ragged arc for about eight inches, growing thicker and then roughly tapering off again, the edges pulled tight, the hair around it pale and sparse. A glance at Cash's face assured me he was still out, his stomach still slowly rising and falling; he was lost in the sleep of the obliviously drunk. He groaned, kicking off his jeans and rolling on his side to reveal another scar as ugly as the first.

This was bad, very bad, I thought as I backed off the bed. My throat thick with unshed tears, I gently covered him up, tucking the blankets and comforter around him, and flicked off the light. No wonder he'd quit the rodeo. He'd been hurt; that much was clear.

In the living room, I slid out of my own jeans and grabbed the comforter, stretching out on the couch where Cash had slept just a week ago. The role reversal might have struck me as ironically funny if not for those damned scars. And I wasn't even sure why they bothered me so much. I guess, for Cash, they represented a change he hadn't been prepared for. With one last sigh, I forced my gaze off the ceiling and told my brain to focus on sleep, but it was a long time coming and when it finally did arrive it wasn't restful.

The sun had barely managed to peek through the blinds when I woke up. I checked on Cash, who was still out like a light, snoring softly under the blanket, his ruffled blond hair peeking out, begging to be played with. Sighing, I headed for the kitchen to make coffee, only to remember he didn't have a coffeemaker.

The tiny kitchen was worse than bare. It was just sad. I opened the refrigerator, not at all surprised to find nothing but a few bags from Jack in the Box, take-out containers, packets of ketchup, and a half-empty bottle of orange juice. After slipping back into my jeans, I borrowed Cash's toothbrush again, making a note to buy myself one, and headed for Wally World.

A glance at the clock on my cell phone revealed it wasn't quite seven. I texted Reece, then quietly slipped out of the apartment, with one last glance at the boxes behind the couch. I assured myself that when I got back, I'd give them a thorough once-over.

Even if I couldn't open them, there was nothing to stop me from looking and stuff, was there?

I sped through the grocery section, picking up milk, eggs, bacon, coffee, and any other basics I could think of, then grabbed myself a toothbrush and some Crest (I hated Cash's toothpaste), and a coffeepot. Back at his apartment, I unloaded everything and put it up, then checked on him. He hadn't moved. I made a beeline for the boxes. My reward.

They were nothing more than ordinary boxes, all three large enough to fill the entire space behind the couch and leave me no room to maneuver around, so I leaned over the back to get a better look at them. One had been opened and then the tape stuck back on; the other two were still taped shut.

Of its own free will . . . okay that's bullshit . . . *I* reached out and peeled back the tape on the one open box, fully expecting to find some sort of Dear John letter on top, but there was nothing. A cough from the bedroom and the suck and gurgle of the coffeepot brought my snooping to a halt.

No way did I want to get caught.

With shaky hands I put the tape back in place and forced myself to take the time to fold the afghan I'd used last night before heading for the kitchen. In a cabinet beside the stove, I found a very battered frying pan. I stood holding it in my hands, wondering how the hell anyone managed to cook anything on its pitted and scarred surface. Which made me think of Cash and his poor mangled leg. Ugh. It explained a lot, including why he'd left me the night we had sex. Well, probably. It sounded good, anyway, even if it seemed a bit lame.

"You gonna cook with it or just stand there staring at it?"

I jumped and squealed, losing my grip on the frying pan. My fumbling attempts to catch it were almost comical, but the pained expression on Cash's face once the pan landed on the linoleum, with a ton of clattering, was not. "Sorry." I bent over, picked it up and blew on it, like there was some five-second rule for frying pans, then set it on the slowly reddening burner. "Hungry?"

He scrubbed at his face and ran his hands through his hair, making the baby-fine mess even worse, though I have to admit he actually looked cute with bed head. A thought that made me kind of nauseous. Not because he looked cute, but because I'd actually thought it. "Not really."

"Well, go take a shower. You'll feel better." Cup in hand, I moved where I could get a better look at him, anxious to see if he'd put jeans on. He had, despite knowing I must have seen his scar.

He gave the cup I was holding a hard stare, then gave the kitchen an equally hard look. "What the hell do you think you're doing?"

"Cooking." I sipped at my coffee, willing myself not to offer him any. He'd just say no, anyway. "You know, preparing food. Kitchens are usually good places to do that."

"I know what it is, Miss Smart Ass." The smile he gave me was tiny, to say the least, but he didn't seem angry, just tired and, of course, hungover. Maybe he just didn't feel like fussing about it. "*Why?*"

"Figured you'd be hungry and this is so much easier and cheaper than going out." Well, not really, not after buying the coffeepot and stuff, but oh well.

"Hope you know I only have one plate," he said, shuffling off while I stood there with my mouth gaping open, my vocal cords unable to form a reply.

Damn, I should have bought paper plates. Probably should have bought plastic forks and spoons, too, if the few utensils I'd found were anything to go by. Guess that'd teach me to do a good deed.

"How do you want your eggs?" I yelled, digging out the lone plate—and a bowl, damn it!

He stuck his head out of the bathroom door, the toothbrush I'd bought in one hand. "Purple's not my color."

"That's mine." I quirked an eyebrow at the sudden slightly panicked expression he failed to hide. Failed in a big way! "Don't worry. I'm taking it home with me."

I hadn't actually *planned* on taking it home with me, but I figured it sounded good. And it'd keep him from completely freaking out and throwing me, the coffeepot, and my eggs and bacon out the door.

"And the toothpaste, too?" He didn't wait for an answer, and he didn't see the grin on my face as I turned back to the kitchen, smiling as he slammed the bathroom door.

"Thought you said you weren't hungry?"

"I'm not." He scooped up the last of his eggs—over easy, and nice and runny—and piled them on some toast I'd baked under the broiler (since he didn't have a toaster, either), shoving the oversized bite in his mouth and wiping a bit of yolk off his lip. He licked it off his fingers, his eyes on mine.

Inside the apartment, it was quiet as I struggled to make small talk; outside, the apartment complex was coming alive, with doors slamming and cars coming and going.

"Want to hit the beach with me today?"

"No, thanks."

"Why not? You said last night you hadn't been. I thought you might like to see it in the daylight."

145

"I'm not a beach sort of guy." He stood, carrying his plate to the kitchen.

He didn't come right back. Instead, he started the dishes, the sound of running water and dishwashing effectively cutting off any conversation we might have. I popped the last bite of bacon into my mouth, prepared to join him, but unsure what to say. I couldn't tell him I knew about his knee; I didn't even feel comfortable asking him about it, afraid he'd completely freak out.

I set my bowl next to the sink, then put the food away, wrapping up the leftover bacon and storing it in a Ziploc baggie.

"It wouldn't hurt you to get a little sun." From my spot at the edge of the counter I took in his sweats, riding low on his hips and the muscular planes of his back.

"I said no, Robbie Jo."

Damn, his tone was frosty.

Grinning, and completely unwilling to give up, I asked, "How about Schlitterbahn?"

He didn't turn around, just kept washing and stacking his few pathetic dishes in the drainer by the sink. His shoulders were shaking and laughter filled his voice as he asked, "Do I look like a water-park kind of guy?"

"Well, why not?" I joined him at the sink. He looked like a grouch, but he wasn't going to get rid of me that easily, damn it. "It's got to be better than hanging out here all day, unless you were planning to unpack."

"Nothing to unpack." He snatched a dish towel from the drawer it was hanging on and handed it to me, a silent cue to dry.

I picked up the warm clean silverware and started wiping. "Except those boxes." Ignoring his sigh, I pushed on. "It wouldn't hurt you to make this place a little homier."

He flipped off the water, the pulse in his jaw ticing as he turned to face me, arms crossed over his chest. "Why?"

"It's not exactly . . . inviting," I said, motioning around the sparse kitchen.

"Well, I don't plan on being here that long." He stared down at me, silently daring me to say something, anything. And I'll be damned if I'd turn down a challenge.

"Why not?"

"Jesus Christ, Robbie Jo!"

"Jesus Christ, on you, Cash! Get over yourself already!" Turning, I threw the dry silverware in the drawer, some part of my brain registering he didn't even have anything to keep it sorted.

"Get out."

"What are you waiting for? Inspiration? Answers? A clue? Well here's your clue. I really like you. I like spending time with you . . . sue me. I respect the fact you might not be here forever. *Obviously*—" I waved my arms around indicating the apartment's poor decor, "—you don't plan on being here forever. But lighten the fuck up already. The world doesn't stop because you got hurt."

I threw the dish towel at him and gathered up my purse and keys. I was heading for the door when his voice stopped me. "I'm sorry."

"I think you need some time alone." Even though I felt like crying, I forced myself to keep moving. "I'll see you Thursday."

On the way home, I stopped along Seawall Boulevard, close to where we'd been last night, and kicked off my shoes, leaving them in the car. Climbing out, I walked to the top of the seawall and took in the view, so different from last night. The beach was teeming with people, screaming birds, screaming kids, harried mothers and fathers even at this early hour, their kids wound up after eating a sugar-filled breakfast from Denny's or IHOP and ready to cut loose. I walked for a bit, digging my toes in the chilly dense sand, but staying out of the water. The warm sun baked into my skin, seeped into my bones and deeper, slowly unworking the knot in my stomach until I felt like my breakfast might actually stay down.

I headed back to the Mustang and drove the rest of the way home. I'd just parked in the driveway when Reece came out, keys and purse in hand.

"Cash called."

"And?" I slid out and shut the door, crossing my arms over my chest.

"You left your phone, and he needs a ride to his truck."

"I'll go."

"Why don't you let me?"

"I'll go."

"Want to talk about it?"

"Not really, sorta. We sorta had a fight and I yelled at him." I briefly considered seeing him, but admitted I wasn't ready. "Maybe you should go."

"Maybe I should." She hugged me, then we stopped in the kitchen long enough for me to write down directions to Cash's. "If you want to talk when I get back, we can."

"Thanks, sis."

While Reece was gone, I took a quick shower, wondering if Cash would send my toothbrush and toothpaste back. Rather than waste time, and hot water, I hurriedly lathered and rinsed my hair and body and climbed out, barely stopping to dress before climbing under my comforter with a towel still wrapped around my wet hair. I was in a semi-doze when Reece finally joined me.

"How is he?"

"Well, he looked like shit."

"And?"

"He didn't say much. Just something about you yelling at him for having a pity party." She nudged me and I moved over so she could stretch out beside me. "How are you?"

"I'm okay." I sighed, wondering what I should or could say.

"You know he's not gonna be here forever."

"I *know*. The question is how'd you know?"

"I hired him, remember?" She grinned at me. "I just don't want to see you get your heart broken."

"I'm a big girl."

"I shouldn't tell you this—"

"—but you're going to anyway." I grinned over at her, and she laughed.

"I am. He was hurt. Did some rehab in Houston, that's how he ended up down here. I kinda got the feeling he didn't know what to do with himself and needed some time to figure it out. That's why he got the job."

"I saw his scars," I confessed. "Last night, when I undressed him, and he still wouldn't talk about it. I mean, he had to know I saw them!"

"Well did you really expect him to talk about it?" She propped her head on her hand, her fingers sunk deep into her hair.

"Not really, but, yeah. It was just weird. Honestly, I don't see what the big deal is."

"I think he's just confused and I'm sure a relationship wasn't in his plans."

"I didn't ask for a commitment, just a fucking day at the beach." I sat up and started toweling my hair, feeling marginally better after hashing some of it out with Reece.

"Give him some time."

"What else can I do?"

149

7

"Think we'll get enough for a new sign?"

"What the hell do you want a new sign for?" Reece asked, pushing the bank's door open. A blast of frigid air slapped us both in the face.

"CAVANAUGH SISTERS MOVING."

We both laughed as the door silently swooshed closed behind us, and more than one bank patron turned to give us a dirty look. As if banking was such serious business. Beside me, Reece winced silently.

"Stuffed shirts," I muttered.

She laughed quietly, jabbing me in the side with her elbow. "Behave, and let's get this over with."

"I brought the blood." We'd cracked more than one joke on the way over about us signing the contracts for the loan in blood.

"You ready for this?"

I took a deep breath and slowly blew it out. "Yup."

Once the papers were signed, the funds would be transferred, then it was off to the lawyer's office. Right after lunch, which Reece had insisted we use as a celebration.

We headed across the marble floor, past the tellers, to Randy's office, where his secretary ushered us in.

"Morning, ladies." He reached for a thick file and waved to two chairs in front of his desk.

"Coffee anyone?" the secretary asked.

"No thanks," we echoed, Reece handing him the bill of sale.

Despite my resolve, despite knowing this was a good thing we were doing, something about borrowing such an ungodly amount of money made my palms sweat. Hell, even my car was only financed for four more years. This was the biggest commitment to date in my life, and the thought actually made me want to giggle. I guess I gave myself away to Reece, who shot me a dirty look as Randy started passing out papers. Bright little stickers that read "sign here" were already in place.

We signed and signed *and signed*, until we were all making jokes about signing, and then we stopped making jokes, ready to have it all over with.

Once we were done, Reece and I just sorta stared at each other, as dazed and confused as if we been in a car accident. We'd just signed our lives away for four hundred thousand dollars.

At least no one could call us cheap dates.

We stood on the sidewalk kind of staring at each other yet again. Reece clutched her purse tightly to her side, and I giggled some more.

"Jesus."

"Indeed." She headed for her Murano, and I followed. Other than the slight breeze that teased our hair, the sunny summer day barely registered.

"Did you talk to Chloe?"

"Yeah, I filled her in." She hit the alarm and unlocked the SUV's doors as we covered the last few steps. "She wasn't very happy with her Aunt Carla."

"Wonder why not?" Despite my many efforts over the last few days, Carla hadn't returned my calls, hadn't come to work or talked to either one of us. Her lawyer had even called us to firm up today's meeting time. "I tried to talk to her again."

"So did I. We'll worry about it later. Let's go eat."

Even though Gaido's was crowded with the lunch-hour rush, there were still plenty of tables, and we didn't have to wait. And what they lacked in ambience, they made up for in crab cakes and shrimp fettuccini, which is exactly what I had. We bypassed wine for tea, both of us wanting a clear head at the meeting with the lawyer.

"Did you notice anything weird last time you were at Carla's?" Picking the last of the shrimp out of the bowl, I popped it in my mouth and chewed while I waited for her response. I was almost afraid to say something, afraid Carla's shopping wasn't the problem I thought it might be, afraid her shopping had nothing to do with anything.

"She lives in an ugly apartment, what's not to be weird?" We laughed, then Reece sipped her tea, clearing her throat. "She did say she might move to Houston."

"Well her ass better stop shopping, then. It'll cost her a fortune to move all that shit she's bought."

"What's up?" Frowning, Reece forked some of her crab-stuffed tilapia and waited on me to respond.

"She had all these bags from Nordstrom and clothes with the tags still on and boxes and boxes of expensive shoes. Designer stuff with names you can never pronounce and price tags that'd make an accountant cry."

"Like . . . how pricey?"

"Like Jimmy Shoo pricey."

153

"It's chew, like chewing your food." At my wrinkle-nosed frown, she added, "Choo like 'choo-choo train.'"

"Whatever. It's expensive." I leaned closer, a part of me still afraid I was overreacting. "I looked some of those up online, and they go for like six and seven hundred *a pair*."

"You think she's selling out to cover some debt?"

"It's possible. To be honest, I'm not sure. Maybe we can get there early and try to talk to her one last time."

"It's too late. The papers are signed." Reece accepted the check from our waitress and fished some cash out of her purse.

"She's still our cousin, Reecie."

"I know. We'll deal with it. Now say good-bye to your last meal out for a while."

"Good-bye last meal."

The lawyer's office was located in an older converted house close to the courthouse. The tiny parking lot held a Jag, two Audis, and Carla's Eclipse.

"Let's get this over with." Reece killed the engine and we climbed out, a wind gust blowing hair in my face. I pushed it out of my way, stumbling as I missed the curb and saving myself by grabbing the Jag.

"No suing," a male voice called out.

I righted myself and looked up, smiling at Carla's lawyer. All jokes aside Josh Winters was *hot*, lawyer or *not*. And I wasn't exactly the type to favor men in suits, but Josh made the whole suit-and-tie thing look good. The hot bod and killer smile helped, and he was nice. He'd been really good through the whole process, keeping it so we all managed to stay fairly civil.

He grasped my elbow, helping me up the curb. "You okay?"

"Good, thanks. Except for my toe. How much you think I can get?" I held out my foot, pointing to the scraped toe peeking out of my sandal.

He threw back his head and laughed, then reached in his pocket. "I think I got a twenty in here."

"I'll take it." I reached for the bill, but Reece's admonishment stopped me. "As much as he's got to be charging Carla, he can afford it," I laughed, nudging him in the side. Hell, I wonder if he was getting a commission on the sale, even? Food for thought, though he definitely didn't come off as a shark. I wondered briefly if they taught that in law school: *How Not To Come Off as a Shark 101.* Coughing to cover my laugh, I let Josh lead me up the walk and into the house with Reece trailing behind.

Dressed in an expensive-looking red suit, Carla sat in the plush reception area, thumbing through *Architectural Digest.* Her eyes widened briefly at the sight of my arm wrapped in Josh's, or maybe it was just the three of us laughing and happy that spooked her.

"Having fun?" I asked as the door swung shut behind us.

"Robbie Jo," Reece softly warned.

"I just asked if she was having fun."

"I swear you Cavanaugh women have given me more gray hairs in the last few weeks than—"

"You don't have any gray hairs, Josh." Carla smiled sweetly up at him.

"How would you know?" I asked, finishing with a smirk. Scowling, she opened her mouth, but I beat her, Josh, and Reece to the punch. "Let's get this over with."

Nodding, Josh lead the way past a vacant conference room, down the empty hallway, to the last door. His office looked out on a well-tended garden, the greenery and landscaping, combined with floor-to-ceiling windows, making it almost like being outside—except for the frigid air and the carpet.

I let Reece pass me, choosing to linger near the door while I debated where to sit. Looking very ladylike in her black pantsuit,

Reece sank into one of the cushy wingback chairs. "Carla, I was wondering if you'd like to come over for dinner tonight."

"Can't. Got plans." She sank into a seat strategically positioned closest to Josh's desk and facing outward, and crossed her legs without another word.

"Let's get started, shall we?" Josh guided me forward, nudging me toward the other wingback. I'm sure the last thing he wanted was a three-way catfight, but if Carla didn't shape up, she sure as hell was gonna get it.

"Can I say something?" I sat, crossing my legs as primly as she and Reece had.

Poor Josh's Adam's apple bobbed and weaved like a prizefighter as he took a seat behind his desk and slid his glasses on.

"I'm *not* changing my mind, Roberta Jo." Out of nowhere, Carla's face was nearly as red as her suit.

"She wasn't going to ask you to change your mind, Carla Renée."

"*Renée.*" Josh's lips twitched as he glanced at the three of us, before turning his attention to the thick file on his desk. "You ladies take care of business as you see fit, but I charge by the hour."

"That's on Carla, not us, tiger." He and I grinned at each other briefly, then he seemed to struggle at working his face into something more serious and lawyer-like.

"Carla—"

"Reece, you are not my mother!"

"I never said I was."

"So quit being a bitch, and let her talk, you hag!" If she didn't stop, I was going to grab one of Josh's very expensive knickknacks and throw it at her.

"Carla, relax! Robbie Jo, you, too!" Reece ran her hands through her hair and leaned forward. "We'd like for you to come and have a celebration dinner at the house tonight. Just the three of us. This is ... new ... for all of us, and we just want you to know that we understand you want to go on with your life and—" she waved a hand in the air, "—do whatever you want to do, but we want you to know that we're still your family and we're still here for you. We love you, Carla Renée."

"Yeah," I echoed half-heartedly.

"Robbie Jo," Reece warned again, glaring at me.

"It was a sincere yeah, thank you very much."

"Carla—" Reece gave her a gentle un-Reece-like smile, "—Will you come have dinner with us tonight? If nothing else, for old times' sake."

Carla's eyes darted from me, to Reece to Josh, who sat industriously sorting papers. Maybe a little *too* industriously. And the way Carla's face softened when she looked at him spoke volumes. Something smelled a wee bit romantic in Denmark.

I glanced at Reece, wondering if she'd noticed, but she either hadn't or was avoiding looking at me.

"What's it gonna be, Carla?" I shot a glance in Josh's direction, then met her gaze head-on, letting her know as best I could that her case of the hots for her lawyer was no secret ... at least not from me.

"I really do have plans. Sorry, guys." She actually did look sorry, too.

"Well what about tomorrow?" I suggested.

"Tomorrow's ..." She gulped, glancing at Josh again. "Tomorrow's good."

My curiosity was definitely piqued. I couldn't wait to get the hell out of there and hash out every naughty detail with Reece. Unfortunately, signing the paperwork was even drearier and more drawn out than our visit to the bank had been, though Josh's occasional jokes about tree consumption did help— some.

157

Finally, it was over.

Carla was free, and Reece and I officially entered a new phase of our lives. I suppose Carla was entering a new phase in hers, too. I glanced at Josh again; he seemed oblivious to the undercurrent between me and Carla. Must be another lawyer trick.

I stood up, taking a moment to stretch stiff muscles. "So we'll see you tomorrow about six?"

"Do you want me to bring anything?" she asked, just as sweet as you please. As if she hadn't spent the last few weeks completely disrupting everyone's life for reasons she hadn't even bothered to explain.

Okay, I'll get over myself now.

8

I was sleeping the sleep of the new business owner—or rather, not at all. Reece and I had gorged ourselves on leftovers and had collapsed in front of the television, dozing, when the phone rang. We sat up and stared at each other, wide-eyed, thinking the same thing.

No good news comes at one in the morning.

I followed Reece off the couch and across the hall to her office, praying Chloe was okay. My heart still pounding from the mad rush to the phone, I stood watching her talk, relaxing the tiniest bit as her shoulder sagged and she told the caller that she'd take care of it.

Once she hung up, she turned to face me, her hands still shaking. "It's Cash."

I sank down in the nearest chair, my knees giving out as I waited for the bad news.

"He was in a car accident."

"Is he—" I choked out, unable to finish my sentence as tears pricked my eyes.

"No, babe." She knelt at my feet and squeezed my hand. "He's at Mercy."

"Do I even want to know what happened?" Reece's shaking became mine. It traveled up my hands to my shoulders, down my back and through my legs, rattling me to my core.

"He and Dean were running from a busted race. They wrecked. Dean's fine. Cash has a concussion and a dislocated shoulder. I need to call his next of kin and let them know." Easing to her feet, she squeezed my still-shaking shoulder. "*You* need to get to that hospital."

Running on pure adrenaline, I made it to Mercy in record time, parked my Mustang in a doctor's spot, and raced through the emergency-room doors straight into a pale-blue arctic blast. The chilly ER waiting room was almost empty but for Sam, whose head shot up the minute I stormed through the sliding doors.

He grabbed my arm before I could reach the nurse standing behind the intake desk. "Dean should be out soon. They're keeping—"

"What the *hell* were you thinking?" I planted my palms in the middle of his chest and shoved as hard as I could. "Huh?"

He threw his hands up to keep me from shoving him again. "It was an acci—"

"Accident my ass," I screamed, ignoring the nurse's admonition to keep my voice down. "You could have *killed* him!"

His voice low and husky, Sam said, "My brother was in that car, too."

"And he's walking out of here tonight, isn't he?" I stalked past him to the nurse. "I need to see Cash McBride."

"Let me check." She took her sweet time, tapping the keys on her computer at an excruciatingly slow pace, her eyes on the screen in front of her. "They're moving him to a room."

"Where?" I forced myself to relax, to stop gripping the

counter so hard and leaning across the desk. "Where is he?" I asked, softer this time. My legs felt weak as the adrenaline rush petered out, and the occasional tremor still ran through me.

"If you'll take a seat, I'll let you know."

"Can I just see him for a minute, please?"

Shaking her head, she turned her attention back to the computer screen in front of her. "*Take* a *seat*, please."

Nodding, I spun around and shoved my way past Sam, then stopped and turned back around. "I'm sorry." I threw my hands up, momentarily at a loss for words. "I'm glad Dean's going to be all right."

"Thanks. And I'm really glad Cash is, too."

So was I, but I still wanted to see him. I sank into the nearest chair just as the ER doors slid open again and Reece came rushing in. She glared at Sam and collapsed in the chair next to mine.

"How is he?"

I waved a hand toward the nurse's station. "They won't tell me anything."

Her sigh echoed my own frustration. "I called Cash's cousin."

I nodded, shivering from the cold and suddenly weak with exhaustion as I searched for words to fill the silence only to fail miserably. I curled up against her, my head on her shoulder, my throat thick with tears and wrapped my arms around myself. Sam took a seat on my other side, and we all waited silently for Dean to be discharged and Cash to get settled in his room. Finally, after what seemed like hours, the nurse called us over. When she found out we weren't family, she balked because of the late hour, but Reece played the employer card and the nurse relented. We left Sam and Dean and headed up to the fourth floor, our shoes loud in the ghostly hallway.

Cash looked like he'd fought with a wall and lost. Besides his arm, which was in a sling, he had some abrasions on his face, a busted lip, and a huge goose egg above his right eye.

"He's still a little out of it, so don't stay too long." The nurse fixed his blood-pressure cuff and left us.

"Thanks," we whispered simultaneously. I don't know why we bothered to keep our voices down. It's not like he would hear us.

I stood at the foot of the bed, staring at him until Reece nudged me in the back. "What?"

"Are you gonna talk to him, or what?" she murmured.

Swallowing the lump in my throat, I pulled a chair close and sat. "Cash?"

His fingers moved, drumming a little tattoo on the blankets.

I glanced at Reece and curled my own fingers into fists in my lap. The urge to take his hand wasn't near as strong as my embarrassment over feeling so helpless.

"Do you want me to wait outside?" Reece asked.

Scrubbing at my face, I nodded, happy she wouldn't see the tears that threatened to spill over as I finally put my hand in his and squeezed. "Cash? Can you hear me?"

He groaned and smiled, but never opened his eyes. "Yeah, Boss Lady."

I racked my brain, needing to say the right thing but unsure what it was. As much as I wished I could tell him he'd taken about ten years off my life, I didn't have the right. "I'm gonna sit here with you for a while."

"Thanks," was the only reply I got before he apparently drifted off again.

Lulled by the beeping of the machinery, I settled back and tried to make myself comfortable, my hand wrapped in his as I dozed off. I only vaguely remembered Reece whispering in my ear that she was leaving, but would be back with breakfast in the morning. I slept until the hustle and bustle of a hospital coming alive woke me. My tailbone and back ached from sleeping in such an awkward position. I shifted and forced my eyes open to check my watch, only to discover Cash was awake.

"You look pretty when you sleep," he croaked.

Feeling flustered and out of sorts, I stood and stretched, forcing myself to tamp down the urge to yell at him. The last thing I needed was to get thrown out of the hospital. Since yelling wasn't an option, I settled for the next best thing. Insulting him. "You look like hell."

"I'll second that," said a voice from the doorway.

"What the *hell* are you doing here?" Cash scowled and struggled to sit up, only to turn white and fall back on the pillows.

I turned to find a tiny, gorgeous brunette standing in the doorway. "Hurts, don't it? Dumb ass," she drawled, stepping further into the room. Her scowl matched Cash's. "What the hell were *you* thinking? You ain't twenty-nine anymore, bubba."

"Shut up."

"He hates it when I poke fun at his age," she said to me as she stuck out her hand. "I'm Jessalyn Boudreaux, Cash's cousin."

If she hadn't been a relative, I would have hated her on sight, just for being so damned gorgeous. Despite the fact she must have driven all night to get here so early, she looked as if she'd stepped from the pages of a country and western fashion catalog . . . all the way down to her expensive-looking boots.

I introduced myself, uncomfortably aware of how scroungy I must have looked still dressed in my oldest jeans and T-shirt.

"You Cash's girlfriend?"

Boy, she didn't beat around the bush. "No. We work together." Shoving the chair back in the corner, I said, "I'll go rustle up some coffee. Would you like some?"

"Can't. I'm pregnant." Smiling, she patted her flat belly.

I headed for the door, wondering at Cash's indignant-sounding "Again?"

"Yeah, you should try it."

Biting my lip, I ducked across the hall to the nurses' station and asked the nurse on duty about coffee. I could smell it, but I couldn't see it.

"You'll have to go down to the cafeteria. First floor."

I wanted to protest, but decided to keep my mouth shut. At least this would give Cash and his cousin some time to talk. On the first floor, the scent of mystery meat led me to the cafeteria. Even this early in the morning, they were doing a brisk business, and I had to wait in line to pay. Reece called to tell me she was parking and would be up in a minute.

"I'm in the cafeteria."

"Then let's do breakfast. I'm starving."

I went back and got two muffins and another cup of coffee and had just settled in at a table when she joined me.

"How's Cash?" she asked, peeling the lid off her coffee cup.

"He's better." Sighing, I broke off a piece of muffin and popped it in my mouth.

Reece peered at me, her eyes slightly narrowed. "How are *you*?"

"Tired." I shrugged, then sipped at my coffee, burning my lip on the cup. Not only hot, but strong enough to stand a spoon up in. "Damn." I licked at my throbbing lip. "His cousin's up with him now."

"Good." She chuckled softly to herself. "You should have heard her on the phone last night."

I joined in, thinking of my brief encounter with her upstairs. "I can imagine!"

"You're shredding that muffin."

Glancing down, I discovered the blueberry muffin that had once sat on my plate was now in a billion crumbs. My shoulders sank as I let out a heavy breath. I picked up a large piece then threw it down on the plate. "I wasn't that hungry anyway."

"Well, I am." She broke off a huge piece and shoved it in her mouth, chewing while I sipped at my coffee. "Why don't you go get what's-her-name a muffin, and then we'll head upstairs."

I hustled back through the line, paid for the food and some decaf coffee, then met Reece at the cafeteria entrance.

"Why'd you call her?" I asked as we wound our way back to the elevators.

"He was hurt. Wouldn't you want someone to call me if you were hurt?"

"Well, sure. But it's not like he was hurt on the job."

"Doesn't matter." She jabbed at the elevator call button and stepped back. "They needed to know."

"What else do you know about him that I don't?"

The elevator doors slid open and we both waited silently for the half dozen passengers to disembark before we stepped in. "He was hurt in a rodeo in Houston back at the beginning of the year, and he has two cousins in Bluebonnet. That's it."

Filing away the information about his injury, I snorted. "Bluebonnet?"

"What?"

"I thought he was from New Mexico."

Reece never got a chance to reply as the elevator doors slid open to let us off.

"You know you can always come stay with us at the ranch," Jessalyn said as we stepped into the room.

"Did we interrupt something?" I handed her the muffin, waving off her thanks.

"Just trying to convince this idiot to come work for me." She glanced from me to Reece and back again, then Cash performed the introductions.

165

"We spoke on the phone, right?" Jessalyn set her muffin on the nightstand.

"I'm not moving in with you and all those kids."

"We only have two and you could always bunk at the big house. Robbie Jo, would you please talk some sense into him?"

Cash and I shared a long, silent moment—or as long as we could with two other people in the room. "He's gonna do what he wants to do," I finally said.

"I'm gonna go," Reece said. "Cash, can I bring you anything?"

"No, but thank you. They're supposed to spring me some time today."

"All right." She hugged me, then gave me a pointed look that probably meant "don't stay too long" and left.

"I should probably go, too." My eyes on Cash, I eased toward the door, wondering if I could catch Reece before she reached the elevator.

"Thanks . . . for staying with me."

"No problem." I exited the room on reluctant feet, Cash's next comment stopping me cold.

"I can't do this anymore."

I should have kept moving, I should have walked away; I had no business eavesdropping on their conversation.

"You've got to stop feeling sorry for yourself," Jessalyn said.

"I'm not like you. I can't just—"

"Oh, shut up!"

I bit the inside of my lip to keep from laughing. I really, *really* liked her.

"Pity party's over, Cash. You think you're the only one who ever got hurt? I mean, God, you knew it wasn't gonna last forever! Instead of crying, you should be thankful you got out with all your body parts intact!"

"I'm not you, and I have no fucking clue what to do now."

"Give it some time," she said, her voice gentler. "But stop shutting everyone out. We've been worried sick about you! Hell, if you hadn't gotten hurt, we never would have known you were still in Texas!"

The sight of the nurse with the food cart got me moving. I'd heard enough, anyway.

I fell into bed the minute I got home. Reece was gone—probably at Jack's—and I had the house to myself. Despite the drawn curtains and blinds, sleep was a long time coming, and I woke up no more rested than when I'd laid down. Finally, the sound of someone knocking on the door got me moving. I blindly groped my way downstairs, trying desperately to shake the fogginess out of my head as I opened the back door.

"Cash! What are you doing here?" Hell, was he even supposed to be driving?!

He looked about as bad as I felt with the goose egg still protruding slightly above his right eyebrow and a purplish bruise under his eye. "Can we talk?"

"Are you leaving?" Leaning against the doorjamb, I wished I was a little more alert, more prepared for this. "'Cause, if so, it's okay." It wasn't really okay, but what the hell else could I say? I tried to write off the tight twisted feeling in my gut to a lack of food, but I knew better.

"I . . . can I come in?"

I waved him in, then poured myself a glass of tea, hoping the caffeine would give me a little jump start. "Want some?"

"No. Robbie Jo . . ." He leaned against the kitchen island, his good hand shoved in his pocket. "I'm sorry for being such an ass."

"Thank you" felt inadequate and kind of lame, so I silently nodded my head.

"You've been really . . . good to me. Better than I deserved and I was a total shit. I just . . . I don't know where I'm going." His good shoulder slumped and his eyes turned suspiciously red as he struggled to look anywhere but at me. "I don't know what the hell I'm doing anymore:

"Come on." I led him outside and took a seat on the back steps, waiting until he'd joined me before I spoke again. "Tell me everything."

"After you left, Jessa said some pretty . . . well, she's not one to beat around the bush."

I laughed, but didn't speak.

"I probably should have talked to her a long time ago, but it was just easier to shut everyone out. Including you. Rodeoing *isn't* something you can do forever, and no one knows that better than her. I guess I always figured I'd be able to quit on my terms, not on some bull's terms, and after I got hurt in Houston, I laid there in that hospital bed thinking I didn't know how to do anything else—except hunt and fish and ride horses." He laughed, a harsh dry sound.

I leaned against him and pressed my lips to his shoulder, searching for something to say. I'd spent my entire life knowing what I wanted, and was damned lucky to have it. "You'll figure it out. I know you will."

"Will you help me?" he asked, running a hand through my hair.

"Of course I will, Cash." Smiling up at him, I added, "Can we start with those boxes in your living room?"

"What *is* it with you and those damned boxes?" This time when he laughed, it sounded like the real thing.

"I'm just nosy." We sat in companionable silence for a few minutes. "So, what's in them?"

"My life."

Make a Move

1

More than anything in the world I wanted out of Galveston, Texas.

To that end I now found myself sitting in the reception area of Winters, Sanbourne, and Carducci in my favorite red power suit, cooling my killer high heels while I wanted for Josh Winters to grace me with his presence.

I'd never tell a living soul this, but I'd practically jumped for joy the day my dad died. Not because he hit me or did anything gross like climb in my bed at night, but because of the family business: Cavanaugh Brothers Moving.

Sadly, the brothers Cavanaugh had both turned out to be girl-makers, but that hadn't stopped them from immersing us in the family business. I wanted out in the worst possible way. I even had my MBA, but I was reduced to spending four days a week, ten hours a day, working a moving crew, sweating my ass off summer or winter, ruining my nails, and wearing steel-toed boots, for crying out loud.

What kind of woman wanted to spend her days wearing steel-toed boots? *Which have to be the ugliest things ever cre-*

ated! Other than my cousins, I couldn't think of anyone. And really, *Galveston*? There wasn't much to recommend it for *day-*life, let alone nightlife, unless you were a tourist.

And I'm not.

Nor am I like my cousin Robbie Jo (she loves the beach and she's a bit of a tomboy, so the whole moving thing works for her).

I'm a girlie-girl, through and through. And proud of it.

Thumbing my way through an *Architectural Digest,* I drooled over homes I'd never be able to afford, tapping my high-heeled foot impatiently on the hardwood floor while the middle-aged receptionist repeatedly said, "Winters, Sanbourne, and Carducci," into the phone.

You couldn't pay me to do her job.

Lest you think I'm lazy, I assure you, I'm already hunting for a better job—in Houston—but it's hard to give an employer a start date when your future is still a bit . . . uncertain. And I wasn't 100 percent convinced I couldn't use the money from the sale of the business to invest in a better, more important project.

I looked up as the door swung open, allowing three men to enter on a shaft of bright summer sunlight. They were laughing, well dressed, and smelled like money. *I'm not sure exactly how to describe the smell of money other than to say it smells clean.* Clean like you *never* get when you sweat for a living.

Again I'm not lazy. Just . . . discriminating.

I watched discreetly as a good-looking blond with short, fashionably spiky hair and a charcoal suit collected his messages and spoke with the receptionist before turning my way. A semi-fake smile on his face, he offered me his hand. Josh Winters was the youngest of the trio, the son of my father's lawyer, also recently deceased. A thought that made me happy, in an odd way. Dealing with my father's lawyer would have been too much like dealing directly with him.

Josh led me back to his office, and we settled in—him behind a desk that stretched nearly the width of the room and me in a plush wingback in front of it. Outside the window that spanned the length of his desk was a shady, softly lit, tropical garden. Frankly, other than a half-wall of law books to my back and the smell of leather, his office didn't appear very lawyerly. I wondered, briefly, what his father would think.

"What can I do for you today, Miss Cavanaugh?"

Tucking my purse beside me, I crossed my legs and smoothed my hands down my short skirt before meeting his gaze. "I want to sell my half of the moving company."

He blinked in surprise and sort of lurched backward in his chair.

"Cavanaugh Brothers?" I prompted.

"I know what it is. I inherited your files from my father." He leaned back in his leather chair, a pad of paper balanced on one knee, a pen firmly grasped in his fingers as he scribbled notes. "Can I ask why?"

Now it was my turn to blink in surprise. "Because it's what I want."

Lips pursed, he glanced down at his paper and scribbled a few more notes. "Have you thought about the long-term—"

"I've thought about *everything*, long-term, short-term; all of it. I want out."

He nodded thoughtfully. "What about your cousins? Will you give them first option to buy?"

"It's only fair," I conceded, shrugging as regally as possible.

"You know a Realtor could probably do this for you. You don't even really need me—"

"Realtors are so . . . I'd rather you handled it, Mr. Winters."

"Josh, please." He smiled, revealing dimples that were the icing on the cake of a very handsome, very well-put-together man.

"Josh, then." I smiled back, relaxing a bit into the chair's velvety folds. "How do we do this?"

"First, I'd like to ask you something. And I want you to consider your answer carefully." He leaned forward, his deep brown eyes serious as he steeped his arms on the desk, lacing his fingers together.

My legs and gut tightened in anticipation—and not the good kind. He looked too serious and non-flirty for this to be a *good* question. "Okay."

"Why?"

"Why . . . what?"

"Why do you want to sell out? From what I can tell, it's a successful business with a good reputation and over fifty years under its belt. You can't buy that kind of advertising."

I deserve more out of life? Too vague. *I hate getting dirty?* Too shallow. "I'm a girl." *Crap-tastic.*

Both his eyebrows slowly rose, his lips twitched and then thinned as if he were trying not to laugh, and his forehead wrinkled. "Excuse me?"

Better just let that one ride. "I'm. A girl."

"So are your cousins—"

"Yes, I know, but—"

"But?" Those eyebrows hadn't come down off their furrowed peaks.

"But—" Struggling against the urge to wriggle like a five-year-old under his intense scrutiny, I scrambled for a way to make myself sound more, well, *less* crazy, "—it's just not my *thing.* Moving," I added, feeling like I needed to explain.

"Then bow out and take a paycheck. But don't sell."

"I've made up my mind."

"For what it's worth, I think you're making a mistake. There's a good solid future—"

"Mr. Winters, my future isn't with Cavanaugh Brothers Moving." As regally as possible I unfolded myself from the luxurious cradle the chair had provided and stood up. "I never wanted to be a mover, and now that my father is gone, I want out. My future lies elsewhere. Now will you help me, or not?"

He studied me for a minute, then nodded. "I'll get started on the paperwork, but I'll need to speak to your accountant and probably set up an appraisal. You might want to sit back down."

My heart chilled at the word "accountant." The sooner we got the ball rolling, the sooner I could get out. But that also meant the sooner my cousins found out what I'd been planning for the last few months, mulling over, dreaming about. If I contacted the accountant, they'd have to know. I sat back down, legs uncrossed now and purse clutched in my hands, and listened as Josh began to drone on about accountants and appraisals and capital gains and losses and taxes. Luckily the eye candy was exceptional.

My ears perked and my mind backtracked at a particularly hideous word. "*Taxes?*"

"Yes, taxes. You have to pay capital-gains tax and if you're not careful, you could lose half of what you make on the sale. There are ways around it, but they take time and a tax expert, which I'm not."

"I'd really like this over with as soon as possible." Dealing with inheritance taxes after my father's death had been enough of a pain in the ass, not to mention the tax on the sale of their house. It had taken a tidy chunk of my profit. And the ensuing shopping spree had cost me another grand before I felt better. But it had also netted me my favorite Coach purse. Smiling at the thought, I relaxed.

"I'll do my best," he said with an easy smile.

I was so proud of myself as I stepped into the bright summer sunshine forty-five minutes later. I hadn't even blinked at the retainer Josh had asked for, just whipped out my checkbook and filled in the blanks.

Sighing, I made a note to myself to transfer some funds from savings to cover the check.

I'd known going in that this would be an expensive venture, but you had to spend money to make money—right?

Saturday night I usually hit one of Houston's upscale bars, but tonight I was crashing a party. A big party. I slowly strolled across the lobby of the St. Regis as if I was in no hurry, as if I had not a care in the world, as if I wasn't about to crash a party being attended by some of Houston's wealthiest citizens—including a few possible relatives. My insides quaked at the thought.

I didn't like crashing parties, and had actually made a few friends, enough to occasionally get a legit invite, but sometimes . . . dire measures called for drastic actions and all that. Tonight's party was in one of the smaller ballrooms, a charity event and very exclusive . . . as in "you-*have*-to-show-your-invitation" exclusive. Unfortunately, I didn't have an invitation, so I discreetly scanned the area looking for a party to "cling" to and hopefully bypass security. Okay, not exactly moral or ethical or, according to my stomach, relaxing, but these were the people I needed to mix and mingle with to get where I wanted to be.

I finally spotted a crowd of seven and gently wormed my way close, smiling at the portly gentleman to my left as we flowed into the ballroom. The feel of a strong hand plucking at my elbow stopped me. I turned, my toes curling in my expensive sandals, to find a very stern-looking man frowning down at me. He could have passed for a guest, except for the earpiece he wore. "Invitation, miss."

Of its own free will my face broke into a smile and I motioned in the general direction of the soiree. "I . . . I just went to the ladies' room." I lowered my eyes, hoping he'd think I was embarrassed, and glanced up at him again before glancing at the ballroom I'd never reached. And never would at this rate. My heart sank while my stomach rolled over at the thought of being hauled out of here like a common thug, a thief, when I'd never tried to steal anything.

All I wanted was a bit of the world I should have been born to, was entitled to.

My arm clutched between his fingers, we turned and came face-to-face with Josh Winters. My cheeks were achingly hot and I could barely look at him. I didn't know whether to be relieved or embarrassed as he quickly assessed the situation.

"I was wondering where you'd gone." His eyes twinkled, as he gently took my other arm. Somehow or another, he knew exactly what I'd been up to.

"Invitation, sir." The other "guard" at the door gave him a stern look.

Josh fished it from his jacket pocket and handed it over. "We're together."

I gently tugged my arm free and moved closer to Josh, resisting the urge to rub the sore spot where the goon's fingers had gripped me so tightly. Instead, as we stepped into the packed ballroom, I focused on Josh, wondering what to say, how to explain myself. I decided to keep it simple. "Thank you."

His lush lips curved into a smile. "You're a very bad girl, Miss Cavanaugh."

Laughing, I said, "I think, under the circumstances, you can call me Carla."

"Carla, then." He grabbed two glasses of champagne from a passing waiter and handed me one, before taking a sip of his own. "So what brings you to Houston?"

I briefly considered telling him I'd left my invitation at home, but after he'd just saved my ass, lying didn't seem right. "I want to see my grandmother."

"Your . . ."

"My grandmother, Diana Wexler." And one of the honorary hosts for this evening's charity event.

I took a sip of my drink to wet my throat, but I was still so agitated over nearly *not* getting in that I could have been drinking water or straight vodka for all I cared.

"I thought Diana only had one granddaughter."

"We've . . . never actually met," I ruefully confessed.

"I see." Some of the humor had died from his eyes as one brow slowly rose. "Are you sure you want to see her?"

"Of course. Why wouldn't I be?" I discreetly scanned the room, trying to find a face to match the one I'd been snipping from newspaper clippings for months. "I was born for this," I sighed.

"You were?" He sounded surprised and . . . amused.

"I was." I met his glance head-on, feeling just as cool and decisive as I had in his office earlier today. And a wee bit defensive.

"Then how come I've never seen you around?" His hand at the small of my back, he nudged me into motion. "How come you don't know your own grandmother?"

We slowly walked, weaving through the thick, elegantly dressed crowd. It was, in a word, *daunting*. They were all laughing and talking, and for a minute, I felt like the little match girl with my face pressed up against the glass. I'd never wanted anything so badly in my entire life as I did to be Diana Wexler's *acknowledged* granddaughter.

"Earth to Carla."

Sighing, I turned to face him. "My mom married for love.

178

Which is all well and good, I suppose, but she gave *this* up to marry my dad." I waved a hand toward the upper-crust crowd.

"So you don't believe in love?" His fingers were warm and smooth as they lightly caressed my back.

"I didn't say that," I murmured, sipping my drink.

"What do you really want, Carla?"

"I want what I'm entitled to. I want this." I nodded toward the assembled crowd.

He nodded slowly, then looped my arm through his, pulling me snugly against his side. We continued to walk, silently for another minute or two, Josh nodding to this person or that. He pulled me into a corner, where we were half-hidden by a huge potted plant. "How badly do you want it?"

"What do you mean?"

"Well, this crowd isn't exactly open to outsiders." As he gave me a once-over, his heated glance warmed the silk of my dress. "They're rich and entitled; they know it, and they can smell an imposter faster than an ant can find sugar."

"So what are *you* doing here?"

"*I* was invited." He gave me a pointed look, his lips twisting in amusement.

My cheeks heated up again and I buried my face in my glass—or as much as I could a champagne flute.

"If you're a fraud, they'll know. And crashing parties is going to get you nothing but trouble."

"My grandmother—" I flicked a curl behind my ear, then immediately loosened it, not wanting to ruin the hairdo I'd spent an hour on.

"Yes, well, the only way you'll get close to her is with the right introduction."

"What makes you think I can't just walk up to her and introduce myself?"

"Care to give it a try?" One thick eyebrow arched, he nodded to a spot behind me.

Turning, all I could do was stare between the leaves of the fat tree we were hiding behind at the woman in gold. She was about my height and wore her silvery blond hair gathered in a chignon. Only a few fine lines graced her face. As if they feared her wrath and stayed away. If my mother had lived another twenty or so years, that's what she would have looked like, though probably not so . . . cold looking. Even though Diana couldn't see me, my jaw tightened and my back stiffened. Even from this distance I could tell she'd be a hard nut to crack. Something I hadn't actually thought about. Photographs snipped from the newspaper had done little to prepare me for this.

Color me a Pollyanna, but I'd wasted many an afternoon imagining a lovely reunion with us doing lunch and shopping, and her introducing me to the sons . . . er, grandsons, of all her dearest friends. In truth she seemed about as warm as an ice floe in the North Atlantic as she offered her cheek to a trim middle-aged man to kiss. "Damn."

"Still want to meet her?"

I took a deep breath, slowly let it out, and then drained the last of my champagne. Josh was right. They *would* spot an imposter; I couldn't keep going on this way, crashing parties and relying on connections that were tentative at best. I needed an inside man. "Yes," I said, up for whatever he had in mind.

"Fine, but it'll cost you."

I gave him a "you've got to be kidding" look. "After the retainer I paid you today?"

"I'm not talking money, honey." His expression could only be called lecherous, and happily so.

A tingle of excitement zipped up my spine as I met his dark smoky gaze.

"Sex?" I whispered, my lips curving into a smile. I wasn't mercenary enough to sleep with a man—*any man*—solely for personal gain. Josh was attractive, I was attracted and sleeping with him came with perks.

Nodding, he took my empty glass and handed it to a passing waiter. "In exchange I'll introduce you to Diana and take you to a few parties. Deal?"

"Just once?" I ran my hand up his tux jacket, stopping when I felt the distinctive thump of his heart against my palm.

"I guess it depends on how things go," he rumbled, his warm breath tickling my ear. "But we can work something out."

He meant, if things went bad or just so-so with my grandmother, I'd have him as a fallback.

I got Josh, I got laid, and I got my entrée into Houston society.

No matter how you spun it, this was a win-win situation.

After we'd struck our deal, I fully expected Josh to lead me over to my grandmother and introduce us. Instead, he plied me with more champagne and scrumptious hors d'oeuvres, then led me out onto the dance floor, where we swayed to something slow and slightly bluesy. I'm not sure if it was that second glass of champagne or just Josh, but dancing with him felt right, in a way that left me hot and tingly.

Josh Winters didn't *just* want to fuck me, he wanted to seduce me. And I was enjoying every minute of it.

"So what's the plan, Stan?" I teased, snuggling as close as I could get.

"Keep doing that and the plan'll involve getting a room." Despite his protest, Josh's arm tightened at my waist. His eyes seemed to warm to a chocolaty brown that drew me in, seduced me, and made the confines of the ballroom uncomfortable. "The plan is to see and be seen. Don't worry, I won't let Diana get out of here without meeting you, but I think it might be best if you didn't directly mention the family connection—for now."

"Why?" I glanced up at him in surprise.

"This isn't the time or the place, and besides, give her some credit. When I introduce you as Carla Cavanaugh, she's bound to get it."

Everything I learned about manners, I learned from my mother. Considering she'd been dead for nearly six years, I gave silent thanks for the brushup I'd gotten from a deportment teacher as we mingled, the minutes sliding by. There was definitely more to him than some small-town lawyer—not that Galveston was small in the strictest sense but it *wasn't* Houston or Dallas.

"How'd you end up in Galveston?" I finally asked as he pulled me out of the ebb and flow of people so we could catch our breath.

"Family business. Just like you." He smiled down at me, looking as cool and unruffled as he had when we'd arrived over two hours ago, while I'd started to feel frazzled and frumpy. It had nothing to do with the way I was dressed and everything to do with the way this evening had played out.

"This just doesn't seem like your scene." I discreetly wiggled my toes inside my sandals, wishing desperately that I could take them off. My feet were throbbing, my back and shoulders had begun to burn with the effort of staying tall and straight, and even my smile was beginning to wobble.

"For me, it's business," he said, leading me slowly but determinedly toward where we'd last seen Diana.

Despite being weighed down by champagne and expensive wine, the butterflies in my stomach still attempted to take flight— with nauseating results. The last thing I wanted or needed was an incident involving me and public puking. I sucked little puffs of air in through my nose, blowing them out my mouth as we drew closer to where all-powerful Diana Wexler held court.

Josh waited patiently until she looked up from the man she was laughing with. To my surprise, her polite smile morphed into something more genuine when she caught Josh's gaze.

I shored up my own smile and forced myself to stand straight and tall as we closed those last few feet, coming to stand before my grandmother much more quickly than I'd anticipated. In hindsight, I was glad we'd waited. As my fingers tightened on his arm, I pressed my knees together to keep them from shaking in anticipation.

"Mrs. Wexler—" Josh began.

"How many times have I told you to call me Diana?" If she hadn't looked so regal, so overbearing, I would have thought she was flirting with him!

"Diana."

"And who's this young lady? Are you stepping out on me?" She floated to her feet, her warm smile cooling the tiniest bit.

"Never. Miss Cavanaugh is a friend of mine."

I held out my hand, resisting the childish urge to wipe it on my dress first. "How do you do?"

"Very well," she said as we briefly shook. Her smile seemed to have tarnished a bit. "Have we met?"

"No, ma'am." A silly question, or her way of letting me know she knew who I was? To my knowledge I'd never seen her or vice versa. She'd disowned my mother for marrying Joe Cavanaugh and that had been the end of that. No contact; no Christmas cards; no birthday parties; nothing. Though I'm sure a woman like Diana had the means to see me anytime she wanted *and* without my knowledge. It never occurred to me that she might not know my name.

"Josh, when are you going to join a real law firm and take on the big time?" the man who'd been fawning over Diana asked.

Her eyes fixed on me, Diana said, "There is no greater waste of a life than failing to live up to your potential. Don't you agree, Miss Cavanaugh?"

We stared at each other, the sound of laughter, the music, a glass breaking, more laughter, all background noise as we sized each other up. My shoulders stiffened and straightened yet again. The situation was . . . daunting to say the least, but I'd be damned if I'd let some old woman (albeit one with buckets of money and social connections) intimidate me. "Yes, I do."

"See Josh, even . . . what did you say your name was, dear?" Ouch. "Carla." My chin rose a notch. "Carla Cavanaugh."

"Even Carla here thinks you should give up that small-town law practice and come to work for Henry." Diana motioned to the man she'd been speaking with when we first approached.

"I never said that. I'm sure the good folks of Galveston would hate to lose Josh. I know I would.

"Besides Josh and I have unfinished business." I smiled serenely in Henry's direction, letting him and Diana draw whatever conclusions they chose.

"What business are you in?" Henry turned to me, smiling blandly. Henry Warren was my uncle by marriage, which meant I probably had an aunt somewhere around here. To be honest, he didn't seem like a very exciting person, so the bland smile wasn't at all offensive.

"Actually that should be 'what business am I getting out of.' " Murmuring a thank-you, I accepted another glass of wine from Josh, who'd stayed relatively silent through out the entire exchange. I didn't want to drink it, but it gave my hands something to do. "And to answer your question, moving." I kept my eyes glued on Henry, even though I was dying to see Diana's reaction. "I'm getting out of the moving business."

Henry's eyes flicked from me to Diana and back again. He'd *obviously* made the connection. He might appear as exciting as oatmeal, but the man was no fool. "And you're his client." He nodded, as if satisfied. "Josh, are you sure small-time stuff like this is really what you want to waste all that talent on?"

"I'm perfectly content in Galveston." Josh's arm tightened around my waist, as if he could take the sting out of Henry's words. They hadn't really hurt—much.

"The offer's always open."

"Carla, it was a pleasure to meet you." Diana reclaimed her throne, turning her attention elsewhere in a silent signal that our visit was over.

"You, too." I nodded in my uncle's direction. "Mr. Warren."

"Well," I muttered once Josh and I had gotten far enough away, "That was fabulous."

"Regrets?"

Wishing I could look back at her one last time, I set my half-full glass on a nearby table. "None."

2

After a brief discussion on his place or mine, I followed Josh back to his house in Galveston.

"I have to warn you, it's nothing fancy," Josh said as he escorted me up the brick walkway.

"Looks pretty good in the moonlight." Though I'd expected him to reside somewhere nicer than Jamaica Beach, some folks would do anything to live on the water. And from where I stood, I could hear, and smell, the Gulf.

"I'm working on fixing her up." As we got closer to the door, the security lights popped on and I had a better idea of what Josh had meant by "fixing her up."

"I see." And what I could see *wasn't* that great. The wood siding had been scraped for repainting, the little bit of visible yard needed landscaping, and I think a few windows were missing! I clung a little tighter to his arm.

"I flip houses with a friend in my spare time."

"And you live where you flip?" Gingerly stepping through the doorway, I tried not to breathe too deeply as the scent of fresh paint and newly cut wood invaded my nose to mix with the salty tang of sea air. I didn't bother asking what "flipping" was. I didn't really care beyond hoping he had a real bed. If he didn't, I was leaving as soon as we were done, deal or no deal.

"Sometimes."

"I expected you to have a condo on the beach or something." I stumbled, my ankle twisting slightly as I came into contact with a piece of wood.

"Where's your sense of adventure?" Josh grasped my elbow and gently tugged me closer. "Watch your step."

"My sense of adventure? I think you've got enough for the both of us, sugar. Why in the world—"

"Thieves," he said, answering my question. "We've done other houses and come in to find the cabinets and even appliances missing. It gets expensive really quickly, so once we get a place structurally sound, I move in to keep an eye on things."

"You just didn't strike me as the type for manual labor."

"I've *never* shied away from getting sweaty." He pulled me close in the cramped entryway, leaning heavily on the front door as he flipped the dead bolt lock. "Wine?"

"I'm good." If he had been any other man, I might have played a little hard to get, escaped, wandered around checking out his place as another way to size him up. Josh had made that impossible with his little fixer-upper. Wandering around this place could land me in the ER!

"That remains to be seen." He laughed huskily, his mouth just scant inches from mine and moving closer with every heartbeat.

I sank against him, my pouty reply eaten by the warm sweep of his lips, his tongue colliding against mine, teasing me with promises I'd make him keep before the night was over. The lapels of his expensive jacket ended up fisted in my hands as I stood on my toes, struggling for more, working toward something deep and fierce.

Finally he pushed me away, his hands under my dress, grabbing at my panties. "You've been a very bad girl, Miss Cavanaugh."

"I have, haven't I?" I drawled, getting into the spirit of the game. My pussy, which had been damp only moments before, was now swollen and achy. The elastic of my panties cut into my thighs as he yanked them off, but I welcomed the tiny bit of pain, holding my skirt up for him and pushing my now naked hips in his direction. "What are you gonna do about it?"

"Punish you, of course." He spun me around and smacked me on the ass, the sound echoing off bare walls and concrete.

The slight sting quickly faded away, and I wanted him to do it again. As he pushed my body against the wall and leaned against me, pinning me there, his hands fumbled for his zipper. My nipples grew harder, aching for release from the lacy restraint of my bra; my forehead pressed against the wall, I closed my eyes, inhaling the chalky tang of Sheetrock in tiny shallow breaths. The naked cheeks of my ass undulated against Josh's crotch until his hand contacted sharply with my hip, causing me to squeak as my pussy clenched in response.

"Hold still."

"Sorry," I whispered, forcing my trembling legs to stop, forcing myself to take deep slow breaths. I wanted him in the worst way possible, and the waiting was killing me. Then, all of a sudden, he was inside me, his hard thick cock stretching me. A scream spilled from my lips at the sudden invasion.

My body tensed as I struggled for air and composure. Josh stayed buried deep inside me, his body lightly resting against mine, cocooning me, his face closer to mine than I'd realized until he spoke, his lips at my ear.

"Breathe."

"I am."

"Shall we continue?"

Amie Stuart

My belly muscles tightened, though now in anticipation of pleasure instead of pain, and I nodded. Josh wrapped his fingers around my wrists, drawing them close to my sides, effectively pinning me in place as he began to withdraw and thrust, each movement seductively slow—the antithesis of what I expected, standing in that ballroom earlier tonight, of what I'd expected when I'd stepped into the house. How quickly things had changed.

Behind me, he groaned, his breath hot on my neck. His pace quickened, each thrust harder than the last; hard enough to push a rough moan out of my throat every time. I struggled against his grip on my wrists, wanting to pull him to me, dig my nails in his ass, scratch him, but he wouldn't let go. Instead he stretched my arms out, spread-eagle, his fingers holding my wrists in a vise grip. The more I struggled against him, the more excited he got, the more excited I got, until I'd lost all sense of rhythm and we'd devolved into a frenzied sort of animal fucking.

"Don't you stop, Josh, don't you *fucking* stop," I babbled at him through clenched teeth.

A few more thrusts and he came, his weight pinning me to the wall as he spurted hot cum inside me. Once he'd caught his breath, he bit my neck, drawing a sobby moan from me. "Don't tell me what to do," he panted in my ear.

"Sorry." I swallowed the lump in my throat, too exhausted to figure out why the hell I wanted to cry. My legs shook like saplings in a hurricane. I realized through the sex-soaked haze of my brain that Josh had let go of my wrists and had an arm wrapped around my waist, gently holding me up.

He nuzzled the back of my hair, which probably looked nothing like the fluffy, formal do I'd left the house with earlier this evening. And I didn't even want to think about what my makeup must look like. Matter of fact, I didn't really want to think at all. It seemed I'd have to, though, as Josh moved away.

"You okay?"

I took a couple tentative steps to test my feet out and nodded. "I think so, yeah."

"Come on." His suit pants back in place, he led me through the darkened living area and up the uncarpeted stairs to a master suite that seemed to cover the entire back end of the house.

Josh drew me to the bed, pushed me down, and slid my shoes off, massaging each foot in turn. "The sunrise is amazing."

"Is that why you stay here?" I pulled off his shirt, enjoying the feel of his chest under my fingers. It was broad and smooth and surprisingly strong. I guess there was something to be said for manual labor.

I reached for his trouser snap, but his hand over mine stopped me. "We didn't use any protection. Downstairs," he added as if he needed to explain.

"Don't worry. I'm a careful girl." The last thing I needed was an unwanted pregnancy. "And I'm not exactly what you'd call promiscuous."

"Good." He leaned in sipping at my lips, slowly, teasing me, and making me want him all over again.

"Condoms?" I turned and lifted my hair so he could unzip my dress.

"Nightstand." He complied, then pulled me against him and pressed his lips to my neck. He followed with his teeth, little love-bites that hardened my nipples. His fingers were feather-soft as he slid my dress off my shoulders, his hands circling around to cup my breasts. "Nice," he whispered, his lips on my shoulder.

"Thanks." I giggled, shivering at his light touch. So different from downstairs, but he was still one hundred percent in control.

He traced his fingers down my spine, pushing me forward

onto the double bed. My hair fell around my face as I crawled higher on the silky, soft comforter. Every inch of me was taut, ready, and alert for Josh's command. I wanted to rub every naked inch of me on the comforter to relieve the ache that had invaded my skin.

"Josh—" I breathed, unable to see past my hair.

He kneaded my ass, his fingers dangerously close to my pussy. I forced myself to stay still until he nudged my knees apart and ran his index finger down my spine, down the crack of my ass, and between my pussy lips. He slid two fingers inside me, spreading my juices around my clit with his thumb. My hips thrust higher, meeting his plunging fingers, dying a little each time his thumb teasingly circled my tender, swollen clit. My pussy walls tightened, pulsating; my breath was loud, filling the room, until I came in hard rolling waves that left me screaming Josh's name.

Once the aftershocks had faded, Josh planted a soft, wet kiss on my back and slipped his fingers from me. The mattress shifted as he left the bed. Me? I collapsed, satiated, happy, and exhausted.

Unwilling to wait for the sun to rise, I slipped out of Josh's bed and left him sleeping while I quietly dressed and snuck out the front door. Josh's Audi looked silly parked in the weed-filled driveway. Of course, so did my Eclipse.

The house actually looked kind of charming in the dim morning light. Smiling to myself, I climbed in the little car and backed out of the driveway. Sex with Josh had been an incredibly pleasurable price to pay for what I'd accomplished last night. A price I'd be more than willing to pay again.

Now all I had to do was patiently wait to hear from Diana Wexler.

Unfortunately, waiting was not my forte, so the next three

days passed at an *excruciatingly* slow pace. I spent a lot of time pacing my tiny apartment, surfing the Nordstrom website and resisting the urge to call Josh and see if he wanted to kill some time. Resisting the urge to check my mailbox or cell phone every hour and almost sighing in relief when the phone finally rang.

"Carla, it's Josh."

Please God, make me an offer I can't refuse. Sex would have been a very welcome distraction right then. "Hi." Lame, I know, but it was the best I could come up with.

"The appraiser wants to go out to the moving company tomorrow."

"*Tomorrow*?!" I sank down on the couch, in a complete and utter panic. *I didn't even want to think about telling Reece and Robbie Jo.* And, for that reason, had completely put it out of my mind, confident I had plenty of time to prepare myself. And the thought of *that* confrontation made my stomach flip-flop. It was Tuesday, and Reece was expecting me to come in and help with truck maintenance this afternoon. It was a chore I had grudgingly resigned myself to doing. Glancing down at my cute Juicy lounge pants, I shuddered and made a mental note to change.

"Carla?"

"Can't we put it off until next week?" I asked weakly.

"You haven't told them, have you?"

"No." I sighed. "Not yet."

Josh's corresponding sigh filled my ear, and all I could do was roll my eyes. I was just as frustrated with myself as he obviously was with me. "The appointment is tomorrow. Nine A.M. Make it happen."

Ugh! I *so* didn't want to do this. "Okay. I'll . . . take care of it."

"Now that our business is taken care of, how about a little pleasure?"

"Pleasure?"

"Yeah. You tell your cousins what you're planning and I'll take you to a party tonight."

I felt as if my mind was chasing its own tail. I wanted to get the confrontation over with; I wanted to go with Josh tonight. I didn't want to have the confrontation with Reece and Robbie Jo. It was going to be ugly. "What kind of party?"

"I don't suppose you own a ball gown . . ."

"Ball gown?"

"Or evening gown. Whatever you women wear."

"You know, you don't have to take me out in order to sleep with me again."

I could feel him smiling through the phone.

"Not to sound arrogant, but I know. Now, go tell your cousins, and I'll take you someplace special tonight."

And then? The payoff for coming clean had better be big— and no, I wasn't thinking about the sex. Okay, maybe just a little. "Fine. I'll tell them."

"Then I'll see you at seven."

He hung up before I could ask where we were going. I disconnected and sat there thinking about calling him back, because that was much more fun than thinking of the drive I was about to make. In an effort to put it off just a little longer, I headed for my closet, where I spent thirty minutes digging around for a dress. I *had* evening gowns, though not many, and I wanted to wear something that would totally wow Josh. I just didn't have time for a shopping trip to Houston, and even hitting the local mall was out—Macy's was hit or miss for me. I settled on a dark lavender halter-style dress with rhinestones across the bodice and my silver Michael Kors pumps.

It was nearly noon, and I'd killed as much time as I could. If I didn't get moving, Reece would call. With one last glance at the disaster area that was my bedroom, I changed and headed across town to Cavanaugh Brothers Moving with only Mary J. Blige and my queasy stomach for company. Parking next to Reece's Murano, I heaved a huge sigh of relief. Robbie Jo's Mustang was nowhere in sight, and that would make this whole ordeal so much easier.

I eased open the door to Reece's office and waited for her to look up from her work. "Busy?"

"I can take a break." The smile on her face as she shifted in her seat made what I was about to do that much harder. "How was your weekend?"

"Okay . . . good." I briefly considered telling her about my grandmother, but honestly, I wasn't sure she'd understand. "You know." Standing at the door felt awkward and wrong, and I didn't want Liz to hear me, so I forced myself to step inside, close the door, and take a seat. "Where's Robbie? I thought she'd be here by now."

"She had a dentist appointment. Why?" The easy, open expression on her face morphed into her best motherly look. "What's going on, Carla?"

"It can wait." I slid out of the chair, ready to cut my losses and chicken out—evening with Josh or no, the anxiety was killing me. And I almost made it, the door cracked, freedom just inches away, but Reece was faster. She lurched out of her chair, snagging my shirt, and cutting off my escape with a click of the door.

My legs turned traitor, allowing her to propel me back to the chair I'd just vacated. She collapsed in its mate, a concerned expression on her face. "I'm not blind. I know something's up. I've known for a long time that something wasn't right with you, so you might as well spill it."

I sank lower in my seat, finally deciding there was nothing else to do but rip off the proverbial Band-Aid.

"Sweetie, whatever it is—"

"I want out." Clutching the arm rests with clammy hands, I waited for her to blow.

"Out of . . ."

Sighing, I started again. "I want out of the business, Reece. I've already talked to a lawyer—"

"What?" Suddenly, she was looming over me, white-faced but for her incredibly red cheeks. "Whoa, *what the hell*?! How? *Why*?"

It was as if a dam had broken, the words tumbled out so fast. "I'll give you first option to buy, and a fair price, but I never intended to spend my whole life as a *mover*, Reece. Do you honestly think I like hauling other people's shit around?" I knew I should have stopped, but the wiring between my brain and mouth picked that moment to go on the fritz. "Let's be frank here. I fucking hate manual labor, I hate these nasty T-shirts—" I plucked at my Cavanaugh Brothers Moving T-shirt, completely unredeemable even in pink, "—I hate sweating like a man, and I don't want to do it anymore. I'm not *going* to do it anymore. So I'm selling. The appraiser—"

"Jesus Christ, Carla, couldn't you have come and talked to me before you walked in here and yanked the fucking rug out from under me?"

As bad as I felt for her, as much as I worried what the hell I'd do if she passed out on me, I now felt as light as a balloon, and wanted out of there as fast as possible.

"I'm giving you first shot at my half." Standing, I moved toward the door, ready to make my bid for freedom. "But I can't do this anymore." I yanked it open and turned to face her one last time, silently praying she'd understand what I couldn't seem to properly say. "By the way, the appraiser will be here tomorrow with my lawyer. He'll need to go over the books and . . . everything. Sorry, Reecie."

Head down, I hustled past Liz's office, unwilling to even look at the older woman, and out the door to my car all while sucking in deep breaths of the salty summer air.

I was free.

3

Okay, so I wasn't *exactly* free, but damned close to it, and as I showered and prepped for Josh's arrival, I felt positively giddy— tinged with a wee bit of guilt. *I'm still human, after all.*

I celebrated with Kenny Chesney, or rather, my fave CD of his, while I gave myself a pedicure. I suppose I shouldn't have been surprised when Reece showed up late tht afternoon, push- ing her way inside before I could even invite her.

I followed her inside, gnashing my teeth as she fumbled with the stereo dials until she found the volume. It'd take me forever to get them properly reset!

"We need to talk."

"I'm not changing my mind, Reece."

She ignored me, prowling around my living room like a caged lion. Thank God she had no idea how fast my heart was pounding, or she probably would have come in for the kill. *Lit- erally!*

"You going to sell this place, too?"

"Maybe . . . *probably.*" Sighing, I resisted the urge to reach up and pull my own hair. I'd done what Josh asked me; I'd told them. It was over, but I suppose it was only fair Reece got a chance to vent.

"You know, Carla—" Reece turned toward the balcony, her tone motherly, "—you could have handled that better."

True, but it was all water under the bridge, wasn't it?

"You could have come to me and sat down—"

"I did. Today," I snapped, grabbing my purse and keys off the kitchen counter, prepared to run an imaginary errand. "Now you need to leave. I've got plans and I need to get going."

"Fine. But keep in mind, that even after this is all over, we're still family."

Lucky for me, Reece decided to follow. I held the door open, my keys fisted in my hand, glad she couldn't see how badly they were shaking. I was *so* having a glass of wine after she left.

"Matter of fact, last time I checked, Robbie Jo and I are the only family you've got."

"You think?" *Think again, Cuz.* The urge to smile, smugly even, was almost overwhelming, but I knew better than to pour gasoline on Reece's fire.

"Just don't forget that old saying about shitting where you eat."

I waited until Reece had stepped into the elevator before punching the button to call up the other one. No way was I dumb enough to ride down to the lobby with her and give her even more time to chew on my ear.

As for shitting where I ate, well, it wasn't a saying I was familiar with, but it didn't sound pleasant, so I put it out of my mind. I had more important things to think about, like Josh, who was picking me up in two hours. I'd be lucky to finish getting ready in time. I stepped off the elevator long enough to make sure that Reece was gone, then hopped right back on.

* * *

Josh glanced at me, his eyebrow twitching slightly as he turned his attention back to the road. "You sure don't disappoint."

"You sure know how to compliment a girl." Laughing softly to myself, I relaxed against the seats, inhaling the subtle sexy scent of expensive leather. "So where are we going?"

"Did you do what I asked?"

"Yes," I sighed, not in the mood to think about the afternoon I'd had.

"I gather it didn't go well?"

"Did you think it would?" I asked, sarcastically.

"Well, maybe a visit with your aunt and uncle will perk you up."

I turned to look at him, barely able to contain a squeal of excitement. "For real?"

"For real."

"How?"

"You heard your Uncle Henry the other night. He wants me." Josh flashed me a quick grin.

"Are you really thinking about taking him up on his offer?"

"No."

"Then why—"

"For you." He reached out and wrapped his hand around mine, giving it a squeeze.

"Thanks, Josh."

"Thank me later." Another squeeze of my hand sent tingles of anticipation up my arm. And not just about the party, but afterward too.

Josh tucked my arm in his as we stepped through the wide front doors of my uncle's mansion. "Well, was this worth the price of admission?"

Nestled in the heart of River Oaks, the older mansion was

so much more than I'd imagined. The short driveway was dotted with lights and the house was lit up like Christmas while the valets drove off in the most absolutely drool-worthy cars. The foyer was as large as my living room, with pristine marble floors and an ornate split staircase. I inhaled, breathing in the scent of pedigrees and old Houston money. They weren't the Vanderbilts, but when it came to Houston high society, it didn't get much higher than the Wexlers.

How my mother could have given all this up was beyond me.

"Still think you belong here?" Josh whispered in my ear.

Through an ornately carved doorway I watched elegantly dressed couples chatting and laughing. "Absolutely."

"Then I think it's time you met your aunt." He led me to where Paige Wexler-Warren, my aunt, stood greeting guests. From her perfectly highlighted, honey-blond hair to her tiny nose, and probably, tiny feet, the resemblance to Diana and my mother was uncanny but not terribly surprising. As we closed in on her, my fingers itched to reach up and touch my own nose.

"Paige, lovely as ever." Josh leaned down and planted a kiss on her cheek.

"Joshua, when are you going to move to the big city so we can see more of you?"

"Never. Then you can't get bored with me."

She laughed, a silly girlish sound that made me wince, then turned her attention to me—albeit reluctantly, if the stiff set of her shoulders was anything to go by. "And you must be . . . Cara."

"Carla," Josh corrected her with an easygoing smile. "This is Carla Cavanaugh."

Your niece seemed to hang in the air, unsaid. Obviously, she knew who I was. But what in the world had Diana and Henry told her about me? I was filled with the horrible, sickening urge to drag Josh out of there and call off the whole thing. But I wasn't a chicken and I wasn't going to let some snot-nosed old woman with too much plastic surgery get in my way.

Praying the heat in my cheeks would dissipate quickly, I pasted my smile firmly in place. "It's a pleasure." I held out my hand and shook the limp one she offered in return.

"I'm sure it is."

Josh nudged me away from Paige (before my temper got the better of me), and wished her a good evening. "Let's get a drink." Once, he'd secured a glass of wine for me and some Scotch for himself, we wound our way through the crowded room to the French doors at the far end. "You okay?"

"Scratched and bloodied." And feeling as if I'd walked across hot coals and somehow, managed to come out unscathed, I sipped my wine and silently congratulated myself. Hell, my run-in with Reece had been more painful than that. "But she didn't nick any major arteries."

"That's my girl." He touched his glass to mine and gave my arm a reassuring squeeze. "You do realize Paige has three children."

"Henry Junior, Peter, and Sybil. Yes, I know."

"Paige isn't going to let you get near the Wexler millions without a fight."

I nodded in understanding. "It's not just about the money, though."

"Then what is it about?"

"Don't get me wrong. I like money. I *love* money, but . . ." Here my words trailed off as I looked into Josh's eyes and wondered what he must think of me. If he thought I was as shallow as I sounded. Something that, until that moment, had never bothered me. For a brief instant, I didn't like myself very much. ". . . I'm a Wexler, too. Surely there's enough to go around," I finished weakly.

"That's not the point, sweetheart."

His endearment made my legs wobbly. "Can we sit down?"

"Not yet. We need to finish this, so you have a clear view of what you're getting yourself into with the Wexlers. To people like them, money is *everything*—their position, too. And they *don't* share. Paige will do everything in her power to make sure you get nothing. She doesn't care that you're her niece or if there's enough to go around."

"Greed." I silently studied the crowd collected in the over-sized room, thinking about how long I'd wanted to be one of them—to belong. Since childhood. My mother would tell me stories about the parties, the clothes, the rich boys she'd dated, only to give it all up for love. I didn't think it was romantic then, and I don't now. "It's about greed."

"More than that, it's about you being an interloper. And daring to want what doesn't belong to you. At least, in her eyes and possibly Diana's, too."

I nodded in understanding. As much as I loved my mother, sometimes I wondered if she'd had Swiss cheese for brains. "Because of my mother."

"Because your mother bucked the system. Paige didn't, and she views that money, as well as her status as Diana's only re-maining daughter, as her due. Same for her children, and make no mistake. She'll fight you tooth and nail for what she thinks of as hers."

"Do you think I should give up?" I scanned the room again, easily picking out Henry Junior and Peter—they were younger, more handsome versions of their father. Across the room, Diana sat in front of the unlit fireplace. She glanced in my direction once, then promptly turned her attention to the pretty young blonde sitting next to her. The family resemblance wasn't as strong, but I assumed she was Sybil.

Why did this have to be so hard?

"I think *you* need to think long and hard about what you want and what you're willing to give up to get it. But that's just my opinion, and you might see things differently."

I could see why Henry wanted Josh to come and work for him.

As evenings went the Wexler-Warren soiree was a bit of a bust—for me, not Josh. His words from the other night about outsiders being unwanted came back to haunt me every time he introduced me to someone new. I'm sure it wasn't intentional, but every inside joke, every shared event they reminisced over seemed to dig at me, and Paige and company steered clear of me while Diana slipped out early. So much for lunch and shopping.

Standing on the outside with my nose pressed against the glass, my course had seemed so clear, but now that I'd gotten a taste, I wasn't sure.

By the time we left, I had a raging headache. The last thing I felt like was sex with Josh, but a promise was a promise. Luckily, he seemed to sense my mood and the ride back to Galveston was a quiet one, with him stroking my hand the entire way. My earlier anticipation over sex with him had definitely waned in the face of this evening's sort of disasterous ending.

"You're awful quiet," he said as the car came to a stop in front of my building.

"Headache." Right behind my eyes, and a tickle in my throat. All I could think about was getting some ibuprofen down me and climbing into my favorite PJs.

"Then let's get you upstairs." He killed the engine and hopped out, circling around to my side.

The elevator seemed to crawl to the fifth floor, and I desperately needed a drink of water to clear the lump in my throat.

The feel of Josh's fingers in my hair, tucking it behind my ear, was nearly my undoing. I sniffled, trying desperately to control my watery nose as the elevator doors finally slid open. Inside, I kicked off my shoes and headed for the kitchen, the pills, and some water.

"Why don't you get ready for bed, and I'll tuck you in?"

"No sex?" I glanced up at him over the rim of my glass.

"Do I look like an insensitive bastard?" Smiling, he took the glass from me and set it on the granite countertop. He nudged me toward the hall. "Go on."

I went, scrubbing my face and brushing out my hair in record time, then sliding into a silk nightshirt. By the time I stepped out of the bathroom, Josh had kicked off his shoes, hung up his jacket, and cleared the clothes off my bed. I crawled between the covers, my eyes closing before my head hit the pillow.

"Shop much?" he asked, laughing.

"Just a little." My cheeks warmed in embarrassment as I snuggled deeper in the bed.

He tucked me in as if I were a three-year-old, and stretched out beside me. "Come here." He patted his chest, an invitation I couldn't resist, and I moved closer, sighing in relief as he gently massaged my scalp.

"Thanks," I said, my head thick with sleep.

"You're welcome."

I woke up to the sound of water running and a male voice singing, of all things, "We Are Family." I lay there, staring up at the ceiling, giving thanks that he wasn't singing Madonna instead. Though, honestly, Sister Sledge was pretty bad. And so was Josh's singing voice. What he lacked in talent, he more than made up for in kindness and well, common sense.

Something I seemed to be lacking.

Just when I was ready to shove the pillow over my head, the

water stopped and so did he. I ran my tongue over my teeth, wondering how long it'd take him to get dressed and get out of my bathroom. My mouth tasted like, well, like I'd been drinking expensive wine and my head was still stuffy. Now was not the time to be getting sick, but that seemed to be where I was headed.

Even though the clock said it wasn't even seven yet, Josh stepped out of the bathroom dressed in gym shorts and a T-shirt that looked as if it was ready for the rag bag, a smile on his handsome face.

"Morning, sunshine."

I sat up, clutching the blankets to me, and immediately flopped back on the mattress.

"Get moving, dollface. We're meeting the appraiser at nine sharp." He dried off his hair and hung his towel on the bathroom door.

Groaning, I buried my head under the pillow, but Josh wasn't having it. He yanked the covers off the bed, tossing them in a corner, and heading toward the kitchen. The chilly air got me moving. I glared at him as I headed for the shower.

A steaming cup of coffee sitting on my nightstand redeemed him—some. But I was still half asleep as he planted a kiss on my cheek.

"I'll meet you there."

" 'kay."

"Don't be late."

"I won't."

As the front door closed, I collapsed on the wrinkled sheets, thinking longingly about how nice it would be to spend the day under my goose-down comforter. Josh would kill me though. Forcing myself upright, I got some more ibuprofen, then slid into my most comfortable pair of jeans and a T-shirt. Sneering at my steel-toed work boots, I opted for a cute pair of Sketchers slides instead. After refilling my coffee, I put on my face and headed across town.

Needless to say, I was the last to arrive. I parked between Josh's Audi and the appraiser's dusty pickup. Josh just gave me a pointed look as I joined him in front of the shop.

"It's not nine yet." Ducking past him, I unlocked the door and turned off the alarm. Where the hell was everyone?

"Where's your cousins?"

"No clue." I fumbled around in the dim interior until my hand made contact with the light switches. The fluorescents flickered before gaining strength and brightening the shop's interior. I'd never understood why they had such a large building when the trucks were normally parked outside and kept behind locked gates. I'd never bothered to ask, either.

Never cared enough.

"You might ought to find out." Josh joined me and introduced me to Dick, a barrel-chested man with a full beard to combat his bald head.

His clipboard tucked under his arm, he shook my hand. "Let's start in the office. That'll be the toughest part."

While I crossed to the offices and unlocked them, I fumbled for my cell phone, discovering I had two messages—one from Reece and one from Robbie Jo. I let Dick in, and then called to listen while Josh patiently waited. Reece's message brusquely informed me they *weren't* coming in today, and I was on my own. Robbie Jo's was a deep sigh, and then a dial tone. I hung up and turned to face Josh, my shoulders slumped with the weight of my guilt.

"They're not coming." We exchanged a long look, Josh nodding slowly as it sank in a little deeper. Clicking my phone shut, I busied myself making coffee, struggling against the soggy lump in my throat that seemed to swell with each breath I took. "I can't say I'm really surprised."

I winced a bit as my words bounced off the concrete floors and corrugated metal walls to pierce my aching head.

"It's not too late to change your mind," Josh said softly, his eyes darting to the office where Dick sat working his magic.

Yesterday, before I'd told Reece, sure. But today? Definitely too late.

By the time Dick the Appraisal Guru was finally finished, so was I. My head ached, my nose was drippy, and my tummy still felt like jelly. I'd finally collapsed in Reece's office and dozed under an extra T-shirt I'd snatched from storage until Josh came and woke me up. He took me home, grabbing Chinese on the way, and tucked me into bed, where I promptly slept until he woke me up the following morning. He was the last person I'd expected to wake up next to for the second morning in a row, but I definitely wasn't complaining.

At least this time he hadn't been singing. After taking care of my most urgent problems (my teeth, my aching head, and my bladder), I crawled back in bed, glad I had nowhere to go and nothing to do all day. Too bad Josh couldn't keep me company. Smiling, I studied him through sleepy eyes. He lay on his back, both arms above his head, one tucked under the pillow. A light dusting of stubble caressed his cheeks and chin. His buff, hairless chest slowly rose and fell. If I hadn't felt so bad, I could have woken him up with some early-morning TLC. On that thought, I drifted off again, a smile on my face.

"Still feel bad?" He leaned over and pressed his lips to my forehead, his skin still damp from the shower he'd taken while I dozed.

"I'm so sick." As if to drive the point home, I sneezed and grabbed some tissues from the box on my nightstand, dabbing at my nose. I forced myself out of bed, shivering as the chilly air touched my skin. I felt worse than when I'd woke up earlier; every inch of me, from my hair follicles to the soles of my feet had ached.

"Then get back in bed."

"I need a drink."

"I'll get it."

"Your head still hurt?" Josh asked when he reappeared water in hand.

"And my throat." I took a drink and collapsed back on the mattress, clutching a tissue to my nose.

"I've got court this morning, but I'll bring you some soup for lunch."

"You don't have to—"

"I know." He fluffed the covers around me. "But just think of all the brownie points I'm earning."

Smiling, I burrowed deeper in the bed, only to wake up a few hours later feeling completely unrested after dreaming about a courtroom where my grandmother was the judge and I was found guilty. Of what, I had no clue, but I was sentenced to a lifetime of manual labor. I slugged back a couple more pills, halfheartedly watching the Food Network and dozing until Josh showed up with the promised soup.

"Feeling any better?" He set a tray with soup, crackers, and Sprite in front of me, then perched on the bed.

"A little." The taste of my restless dreams still lingered in my mouth, reminding me of the bigger question I still needed to answer.

Did I really want to fight for my spot on the Wexler family tree?

"And thank you." I smiled up at him, fully aware of how absolutely shitty I must look with dark circles under my eyes, a day's worth of bed head, and no makeup.

"I can't guarantee that soup's homemade, but the lady at Kroger's assured me it was good for what ails you." He smoothed my hair back and tightened my ponytail. "I've got to get back to the office, but I'll see you tonight."

"Tonight?" *Had I forgotten something?*

"You didn't think I was going to leave you to suffer all alone, did you?"

Feverish tears pricked my eyes and I turned my attention to my lunch, letting a bite of hot, salty chicken soup soothe my sore throat as well as my ego (bruised) and conscience (guilty). It had been a long time since someone had taken care of me—since my mom died. Dad hadn't exactly been the hugs-and-kisses type.

Once Josh was gone, I ate the rest slowly, savoring it while the annoying voice of Rachael Ray kept me company. The snot clogging my head was a perfect reflection of the thoughts cluttering up my brain. There was no denying I'd seriously screwed up with Reece, and honestly, I was surprised I hadn't had a visit from Robbie Jo yet. She wasn't one to let grass grow under her.

As for Diana and the rest of the Wexlers, by the time Rachael Ray had morphed into Paula Deen, I'd still found no answers.

I climbed from the bed and carried the cold remnants of my soup into the kitchen. Returning to the bedroom, I stood in the doorway aghast at how badly I'd let my sanctuary deteriorate. There were clothes piled in every corner of the room, along with bags and shoe boxes (most with shoes still inside), along with a trash can now overflowing with Kleenex.

Fighting the urge to crawl back in my bed, I started hanging up clothes and stacking shoes in the closet's cute little cubbies, then stripped the bed. I pulled out fresh, lime-green sheets and remade it, folding up the comforter and stuffing it in a bag so I'd remember to take it to the cleaners at some point in the week. The last of my energy went toward a shower, and drying my hair, before crawling under the crisp cool sheets with a fresh Sprite. I made a mental note to thank Josh for bringing me a twelve-pack. I was exhausted, but I felt worlds better.

He woke me up at three, breathlessly inquiring about what I wanted for dinner.

Sniffling and rubbing the sleep out of my eyes, I adjusted the phone closer to my ear. "What?"

"Dinner?"

"Where are you?"

"Late for court."

So hurry up. "Um, surprise me. I'm not picky."

"Famous last words," he laughed before promising me the most fabulous sea bass ever. His words.

Smiling, I slipped from between the sheets feeling better, if not 100 percent, and padded into the kitchen. I threw the clean sheets in the dryer and put a bottle of Chardonnay in the fridge. By the time I folded the dried sheets and put on my face and a cute pair of apple-green sweats, Josh was calling yet again.

"Do you have a grill?"

"A tiny one." I laughed. "But no charcoal. Are you *cooking*?"

"You better believe it. I promised you the best sea bass ever, didn't I?"

"Well, yeah, but I didn't know you could cook."

"I'm just full of surprises."

That had to be the understatement of the year!

By the time Josh showed up, I felt nearly human again. Three bags of groceries in hand, he nudged me out of the way, making himself completely at home in my kitchen. More at home than I'd ever been as he diced chilis and juiced limes. While the fish marinated, he put me to work fixing a salad, lit the grill, and opened the wine. He poured us both a glass and pressed one into my hand with a soft kiss on my lips. "You look better."

I laughed, my cheeks warming in embarrassment at the intimate gesture. "Like I could have looked worse?"

"Never. I'm going to change while that grill heats up." He grabbed his gym bag from the other side of the bar and disappeared into the bedroom, while I stood at the counter mulling over how easy things with Josh were. And what it all meant.

As if I needed one more thing to clutter my brain with . . . but Josh was definitely cluttering things up. While I waited, I set the table, smiling at the glimmer of pretty red Fiestaware. It wasn't fancy, but I liked the bold colors. For good measure, I lit a few of the candles on the entertainment center, then went to check on the grill.

The balcony was small—barely large enough for the single chair and tiny hibachi grill, but the early-evening breeze was too tempting. I curled up in the chair, letting the muted sound of traffic and gulls lull me while I sipped my wine and waited for Josh to rejoin me. The sun had faded to a deep reddish yellow but still gave off enough heat to warm me, and a slight breeze tickled my hair.

"You look awfully content." Josh stepped outside, the tray of marinated sea bass in one hand and his wine in the other.

"Let me take that." I reached for his glass, settling back in my chair while he put our food on the grill.

Once he was done, he silently held out his hand. I offered him the wineglass, but he grabbed my wrist, pulling me to my feet. He took my place in the chair, then pulled me down on his lap. "That's better. By the way, Reece called."

My fingers tightened around the stem of my glass.

"She got your resignation, and they're moving forward,

working on the financing. We should know something Monday."

Oddly, I didn't feel like celebrating.

"Can I ask you something?" Sighing, I leaned my head back on his shoulder and stared up at the pale, cloudless sky.

"You may."

I could practically hear him grinning, but he was so damned adorable and had been so sweet the last couple of days, I didn't have the heart to stick my elbow in his gut. "Is our . . . relationship a conflict of interest?"

"I suppose it could be viewed that way by some. But no, I don't think so. Now, if you were getting a divorce and I was your lawyer, we'd definitely have a conflict of interest."

"Have you ever been married?" *Was I getting too personal?*

"Nope."

"How old are you?"

"Thirty-two. I wear a men's large shirts, I take my coffee black, and I collect power tools."

Laughing, I asked, "Are we talking Home Depot here or the *adult* toy store?"

"To some of us, Home Depot *is* the adult toy store."

4

Curled up on the couch, I was sipping coffee and enjoying my post-date-night glow when the phone rang. My hand shook at the sight of the Houston area code. I did have some feelers out on a new job, so it could have been anyone. It might not be Diana.

It was.

And she wanted to have lunch with me. Tomorrow. For real.

I agreed on a place and time, then hung up in a complete daze.

I was having lunch with my grandmother. Squealing, I hopped off the couch and headed for my closet, where I spent ten minutes lamenting the fact I had nothing to wear. The only solution was, of course, a shopping trip.

Dressed in my favorite jeans and shopping sandals, I headed for the Galleria, where I treated myself to lunch, then descended on Nordstrom, determined not to leave until I found something absolutely stunning for our luncheon tomorrow. By the time I finally made my way to the checkout counter, I was exhausted, but triumphant. I had found the perfect two-piece suit, in the perfect shade of pink. I'd also picked up matching shoes, on sale, and a few more tops and jeans to supplement my wardrobe.

"Ready to check out?" the clerk asked.

Pasting a smile on my face, I nodded, resisting the urge to tell her I was just standing there for my health. "Yes, thank you."

She rang up my purchases, reciting the exorbitant total with a slightly arched gray eyebrow. "Will that be cash, check, or charge?"

I slid my American Express from my wallet, silently handing it and my driver's license to her. As much as I would have loved to wipe the snotty expression from her face, I refrained. It was summer, the mall was packed, and I'd spent enough years in customer service myself to cut her some slack.

On the way back through the mall, my cell phone rang. Ignoring the lure of the Coach store, I dug it out, smiling as I greeted Josh.

"I just remembered Saturday night is the Houston Bar Association dinner. Henry's the president, so he and Paige will be there."

"And?" I walked, slowly, sliding through a gaggle of teenaged girls as I wondered if the fates were laughing at me or smiling on me.

"Please say you'll go, and spare me a lonely night of boredom."

"Diana called." I came to a stop, only to have a stroller slam into the back of my legs. I stumbled forward, barely catching myself. Glaring at me, the mother wheeled to the left and disappeared while I maneuvered out of the foot traffic.

"Oh. *Oh!* Are congratulations in order?"

"Well, we're having lunch tomorrow." As good as he'd been to me, I couldn't leave him hanging. "But sure. I'd love to go."

"Bless you. I'll pick you up at seven, and good luck with Diana. And call me. Let me know how it goes."

I hung up, readjusted my shopping bags, and headed for home.

Thankful I didn't have plans with Josh that evening, I turned in early, only to spend another restless night filled with crazy dreams of my grandmother and a courtroom. But this time Reece and Robbie Jo were sitting in the jury box. I woke up before the sun had even come up, sweaty, cranky, and anxious. A long, hot shower helped some, but not much. And going back to bed was out of the question.

I'd had enough nightmares lately to last me at least a few months.

Instead, I made my way to the kitchen and poured myself a cup of coffee, then ran downstairs to get a Houston paper from the machine in the lobby, glad most of the building's inhabitants were probably still sleeping or getting ready for work.

Standing in the elevator, I breathed in the damp inky scent of the paper, anticipating opening it up to the society section, which I knew would cheer me up. Back in the apartment I settled on the couch and opened up the paper, smoothing down the crease in the middle before lifting back the pages to the right section. I skimmed quickly over the photos, excited to see they were from the party I'd crashed with Josh, then read the captions slowly, memorizing the names of people I didn't know.

I snipped out the two photos of Diana and dug out the scrapbook I kept stored under the coffee table, so I could gingerly glue them down. With my special purple gel pen, I added the date, and set the book aside to dry while I read what was left of the society pages again, letting each word sink in.

The sun was barely peeking over the horizon by the time I finished. I refilled my coffee cup and sat out on the patio, enjoying the sight of the sun breaking over the Gulf. Even though

I hadn't one hundred percent decided to sell the condo, I knew if or when I did that I'd miss this view. From my spot, the beach was almost pristine, the oil rigs in the distance so tiny I could almost pretend they were dolphins instead. Fanciful maybe, but dolphins were so much nicer to look at than oil rigs.

By the time I left for my lunch date, my bedroom was, well, less than stellar would be putting it nicely.

"I swear I'll clean you tomorrow," I whispered, darting out the door. I grabbed my keys and headed for Houston, speeding the whole way there. Honestly, not speeding in Houston traffic wasn't an option, but my excitement definitely increased the lead-foot quotient. I pulled into the parking lot of Café Karma and nearly crashed into a Mercedes, thanks to my hands, which were slippery with sweat.

I felt worse now than I had earlier this week when I'd been really sick! If this luncheon hadn't been so important, I might have turned around and driven home, holing up in my little apartment. Instead, I forced myself to wave an apology at the other driver and park.

It would take a lot more than the rustic brick exterior and cute red awning to soothe me, though.

Inside, I was greeted by the maître d' and just the mere mention, more of a mumble really, of Diana Wexler's name and he was escorting me through the crowded restaurant, winding past tables until we reached one staged between the window and the center of the room. Diana sat facing the room. The sight of her pale blond hair swept up in a chignon made me wish I'd gone for something upswept and more elegant, like a French twist, but it was too late for regrets now.

The maître d' was pulling out my chair. Nerves and nausea had me breathing through my nose, unable to thank him as I took a seat. I had to settle for a smile.

The confidence I'd felt when I put on my cute pink suit and matching Jimmy Choos not even an hour ago was long gone as I sat waiting for Diana to finish her appraisal of me.

"You look like your mother," she finally said as an effusive duo of waiters brought us menus and water and fussed over her. They took our drink orders and disappeared just as quickly as they'd come.

"Thank you." Maybe her words weren't supposed to be a compliment, but that's how I took them. I sipped my water, my smile still firmly in place, and reminded myself I had every right to be here. I was her granddaughter, after all, despite the calluses on my hands.

"What exactly is it that you want from me, Carla?"

Her directness caught me off guard, and as I set my glass down, water sloshed over the side, wetting my fingers. Honestly, even after my earlier conversation with Josh, I still had no clue. Still hadn't spent near enough time thinking about it. Beyond wanting her to acknowledge me.

"That's a good question." As discreetly as possible, I rubbed my lips together, fighting the urge to chew on them as my damp fingers curled around the napkin in my lap.

"Well then, why don't I tell you what I want?"

"All right." What was I going to do? *Say no?*

"First, decide what you'd like for lunch." Diana's congenial smile made my shoulders stiffen. Something felt . . . off. I couldn't put my finger on it, but I knew something was definitely rotten in this little French café. "It's on me."

Not that I'd been worried, but I guess that meant I could eat more than salad. And at $15.95, Café Karma was apparently damned proud of their lettuce. Despite the tempting sight of pasta and roasted Cornish hen being served at the next table and mouthwatering scent of garlic and spices, I settled on the onion soup and endive salad. That was probably all my stomach could handle anyway.

After giving the waiter my order, I turned my attention back to my grandmother. "What *do* you want?" I asked, more of my old confidence returning as I sipped at my iced tea.

Her smile never faltered, but also failed to reach her silvery eyes. They widened briefly in obvious surprise at my directness, and a triumphant tremor ran through me.

I'd been right.

I had to wait until she'd buttered a miniscule piece of bread and eaten it for her reply. "I want Josh Winters."

She could have asked for my best bra and panties and I would have been less surprised! I laughed, a loud laugh that drew stares from some of the nearby diners and a censorious frown from Diana. "And that has what to do with me?"

"Everything, dear. You see, you are in a position to deliver him to your Uncle Henry."

My Uncle Henry. No, I didn't miss that very calculated word usage.

"And?"

"And if you do, I'll not only acknowledge you as my legitimate granddaughter, I'll give you control of your mother's trust fund."

I sipped at my tea again to buy myself some time as excitement bubbled inside of me. Everything I wanted was *almost* mine for the taking. Tantalizingly so. "I appreciate your honesty and your directness."

"But?" she prompted.

"But—" Here I paused to smile, "—Josh knows his own mind."

"And you know yours, dear. I've seen you in action, and I don't doubt you can make it happen."

The rest of our lunch was anticlimactic, filled with inane chatter about the Houston heat and my Aunt Paige's annual Forth of July picnic, with broad hints dropped by Diana about a forthcoming invitation. *If I delivered Josh*, went unsaid.

I laughed all the way back to Galveston, practically gloating over the fact that *I* had what *she* wanted. Yes, of course, she had something I wanted, too. The entrée I'd dreamed about for the last nine months, if not longer. It was all so close I could taste it.

As excited as I'd been, as excited as I was at the prospect of finally attainting my goal, I knew, deep down inside, that getting Josh to go to work for Uncle Henry was a long shot at best.

Unfortunately, I didn't have time to waste thinking about it. I had to turn around and begin getting ready for tonight's dinner. Scanning my closet, I wished, in hindsight, that I'd gone back to Nordstrom and bought a new evening gown, but it was too late now. I'd have to settle for a white strapless affair I'd bought on clearance. And even that couldn't dampen my mood. I'd just gotten the last hot roller fixed in my hair when someone rang my doorbell.

Growling in frustration, I glanced at the clock, then headed down the hall. I'd learned my lesson with Reece.

I checked the peephole, not at all surprised to see Robbie Jo standing on the other side. I took the chain off and slid the door open, praying her work boots weren't too dirty as she strode past me.

"Going somewhere?"

"It's none of your business what I do, Robbie Jo." I shut the door and headed for my bedroom, hoping my rudeness would make her mad enough to leave sooner rather than later. She followed, her footsteps heavy on my pretty Berber carpet.

"It doesn't have to be . . . this . . . Carla." Her voice

seemed to trail off, but I ignored it, stepping into the bathroom and adding another coat of loose powder to my already perfect face.

"Jesus Che-rist, Carla Renée, what the hell have you been doing?"

"Shopping," I said, rejoining her in the bedroom.

"This looks more like a *raid* than a shopping trip." She scanned the room, wide-eyed.

I'll admit my bedroom looked bad, but she was totally over-reacting! But once I moved to Houston, I'd definitely get a bigger place—with more closet space!

"You wouldn't understand." Even though it was way too early, I snatched my dress off the bed and stepped into it, turning my back to Robbie Jo. "But as long as you're here, make yourself useful."

As the zipper slid up my back, she talked and I did my best to listen. "Look, things have been really weird the last couple months. But after this is over, we're still family."

"I know." I really needed to get these rollers out of my hair and do my lips.

"And we're all we've got."

"I *know*, Robbie Jo." I bit my lip to hold back a sigh of exasperation, glad she couldn't see me rolling my eyes. She *wasn't* all the family I had.

"After the way you've acted the last couple months, I *do* wonder."

My mouth open, I turned, prepared to give her an earful.

"Hear me out before you get all huffy. I respect the fact you want out—sort of—I don't really *agree* with it, but if it's what you want, then fine. I just . . . well . . . you're still my cousin and—" She faltered, her eyes skipping around the room, "— we used to be close. I just wish, you know, you'd given me some sort of warning, said something. But you've just—"

I crossed my arms over my chest. "I've *what*?"

"You—" She waved a hand my way. "—shut me out. I don't even know you anymore."

I winced as she sank down on my brand-new clothes and kicked a shoe box under the bed. "Is it a crime to want more out of life than manual labor?" The sight of her denim-clad ass on my bed was too much. I stepped into the bathroom and hurriedly took the rollers out of my hair, tossing them in the sink, talking while I worked. "I want a great job, a husband and kids, and a *nice* life." I stuck my head out the door as I continued. "A nice life where I don't have to get all grubby and work like a dog. I want more, Robbie Jo. That life's fine for you—"

"That life? *That life* put you through college and raised you and fed you." She surged to her feet and crossed the tiny bedroom to where I stood. "Do you think your parents—"

"My parents are gone! And this is *my life*, goddamn it. Now get the fuck out."

"Carla—"

"Get out!" I stepped back into the bathroom. "I have a date and he'll be here soon."

"Can you really know what you want, where you're going, if you're ashamed of where you came from?"

"Fuck you." *I wasn't ashamed, damn it!*

5

By the time I climbed in Josh's car I'd calmed down considerably, but it had taken two glasses of wine and some deep-breathing exercises. And still our confrontation kept replaying itself in my head.

"You haven't said a word about your lunch."

"It was interesting." That was the understatement of the year. I still hadn't decided how to approach Josh, but felt pretty confident that subterfuge was out. "Can I ask you something?"

"Sure."

"Why don't you want to work in Houston?"

"You know, sometimes I forget how little we really know each other." He smiled, his teeth gleaming in the car's dimly lit interior. "To answer your question, I interned in a Houston law firm. My dad had high hopes I'd move on to bigger and better. But working seventy-five-plus hours a week held no appeal for me."

"It'd be nice to have you nearby, though."

"I'm nearby now."

"But after I move, you won't be."

"Galveston isn't *that* far away."

"So we can still see each other?" I glanced at him out of the corner of my eye. This wasn't exactly how I'd meant for our conversation to go. And getting him to work for Henry was looking pretty impossible.

"I'd like to keep seeing you. Otherwise, I wouldn't have invited you to this boring-ass dinner."

"Gee, thanks." I laughed and settled deeper into the comfortable seat, watching the dusky landscape speed by. "Why do you go, if it's boring?"

"Networking. Same reason I go to all those boring-ass parties you like."

My cheeks burned, and the bottom fell out of my stomach, taking my tongue with it. No matter what I said, the probability of us ending up in a fight was high.

"Now, tell me about your lunch with Diana."

"It wasn't near as exciting as the visit I had with Robbie Jo today." How my lunch had gone really didn't matter anymore. The high I'd been on was now long gone.

"You're awfully quiet. I thought you'd be happy."

"Oh, I am. Just . . . thinking."

"About?" he prompted.

"What I'm going to do once this is all over."

"What exactly are you going to do? Besides shop and attend all those lovely parties?"

Lovely parties that he hated. I sighed, spinning my mother's engagement ring around on my finger. "I'm not sure. Maybe start a business," I said halfheartedly. "Can't let all that lovely money go to waste, now can I?"

Feeling more than a little disheartened over how our talk had gone, I spent the rest of the drive silently chewing off my lipstick. By the time we reached downtown Houston I still hadn't come up with another angle to approach Josh with about making a job change.

"Where exactly are we going?" I asked.

"The Hyatt."

I pulled down the sun visor, glad to see my French twist and my eyeliner were both still in place, and slicked on a fresh coat of lipstick, topping it off with some gloss.

He pulled out of the stream of traffic and parked. "Are you sure you still want to do this?"

I blinked in surprise. "Of course."

"You don't have to stay the night afterward . . . if you don't want to."

"Of course, I do. I've just got a lot on my mind with the sale."

"And Diana, who you've done everything to avoid talking about."

"Remember when you told me to think about what I wanted and what I was willing to give up? Well . . . I'm still thinking." I flipped the visor up with a *thunk* of finality, hoping he'd drop it.

"Good enough. Let's go eat rubber chicken." Laughing, he pulled the car back into the evening traffic.

The Hyatt's Grand Ballroom was already filled with enough noise to make the golden chandeliers shake (not literally, of course). I gave thanks for the light material of my dress as we made our way through the thick crowd, greeting Josh's associates. It didn't take much to see this was, for the most part, a different crowd than the party we'd met at. Oh, there were still the upper-crusts like Henry in attendance. We even passed my Aunt Paige, who gave me a hard once-over before turning her attention back to a handsome young man I didn't recognize.

Josh, of course, had to stop and say hello, and Paige spent ten minutes bragging on Henry's newest junior associate.

"He's quite ambitious," she said, giving me a pointed look.

Was it a jab at my own ambitiousness or a hint that she knew about Diana's offer? Before I could decide, she was speaking again.

"I understand you and Mother had lunch today."

"Yes, we did." She knew. She had to know. *Everything!*

Just then, the young blonde I'd spotted talking to Diana at Paige's party came up and slipped her arm through Mr. Junior Associate's, and Paige was forced to introduce her. No wonder she was so keen on him.

I'd been prepared to dislike Sybil on sight, especially after the insight Josh had given me at her mother's party, but the twinkle in her blue-green eyes as she hugged me, yes, *hugged me*, made that almost impossible.

"You don't know how good it is to no longer be the only girl in the family."

"I can't imagine the stress that must have caused you," Paige murmured dryly.

Josh and Sybil's escort both snorted, and Josh attempted to pull his arm from mine. "I'll get us some drinks."

"I'll come with." I smiled brightly, clutching his hand. Despite Sybil's warmth, there was no way in hell I was staying with Paige.

"Oh, no." Sybil caught my free hand in hers and squeezed my fingers. "You're staying with me."

He shrugged in the face of my pleading look. "I'll hurry."

By the time he returned I'd learned that Sybil was preparing to take the bar exam, was currently volunteering with Houston Legal Aid, and probably loved to shop as much as I did. Considering we were practically the same age, I felt like a bit of an underachiever. It's a damned good thing she was so nice.

"So you're getting out of the moving business," Paige finally asked as Josh pressed a glass of Chardonnay into my hand. "Did it not appeal to you, dear?"

I sipped and nodded, still struggling to keep her from getting to me. If being acknowledged by Diana meant putting up with my aunt, I'm not sure it was worth it. How she'd managed to raise someone as even-tempered and kind as Sybil was beyond me. "I'm ready for a change."

"What are your plans . . . for afterward?"

"I haven't really decided, other than moving here."

"Oh!" Sybil brightened. "I know some great lofts. If you want, we can go look at them."

"I'd like that."

Paige obviously didn't, if the frown on her face was anything to go by. "You have the bar to worry about."

"I've got it covered."

"And we have a wedding to plan," Mr. Junior Associate said.

"One afternoon with my cousin won't hurt." Smiling brightly at me, she added, "We'll do lunch. I know this *fabulous* hamburger place, but wear your fat jeans."

Paige, who'd apparently heard enough, excused herself.

Beside me, Josh shook as if biting back laughter, while Sybil rolled her eyes. "She's a little fussy."

Her fiancé snorted and sipped at his drink. Probably to keep from stating the obvious.

"It looks like they're getting ready to start, so we should probably find our seats."

"Oh, wait!" Sybil pulled a card out of her tiny beaded purse and handed it to me. "Call me. *Seriously!*"

Nodding, I gave her a tiny wave good-bye, reluctant to leave the first genuinely nice family member I'd met. By the time we sat down for dinner, I'd been introduced to so many people, I could barely remember my own name. The chicken *was* rubbery, but not *completely* inedible. I could imagine Sybil going out for hamburgers afterward. And through all the speechifying and clapping, I zoned out, focusing instead on what to do about Diana and Josh.

Though the solution was rather obvious. And there was no trust fund in my future.

There was no way Josh would *ever* work for Henry. Which meant there was no way I would ever get my hands on my mom's trust fund. But as long as I was dating Josh and could (possibly) count on Sybil as a friend, my days of rubbing elbows with movers and shakers were far from over.

And besides, Carla Cavanaugh had a much nicer ring to it than Carla Wexler. Not that Granny Diana had *asked* me to change my name, but you know . . . the thought had crossed my mind.

I smothered my giggles, imagining the look on Diana's face if I ever called her Granny. If I didn't stop, Josh would never take me anywhere again. "Sorry," I mouthed, giving him an apologetic smile.

Nodding, he reached up, rubbing my shoulder and eventually the back of my neck. The slow rhythmic massage hit me hard as the long day caught up with me. As much as I really wanted to be with Josh tonight, I needed sleep. Once the torturous evening was over, I pasted my numb lips into some semblance of a smile and let Josh lead me out.

Unfortunately, before we could make our escape—which apparently required a one-drink minimum—Paige and Henry stopped us.

"Will we see you at the Cabots' on Monday night?" Henry smiled genially at Josh.

"I've got court on Tuesday morning, so probably not."

Despite his own firmly fixed smile, Henry's face turned a mottled red color. "Well, that's too bad."

Apparently all the Wexlers had known about my lunch with Diana.

"Are you okay, sir?" I asked, wondering if maybe he was getting ready to have a heart attack, or stroke or whatever.

He nodded, barely acknowledging me. Paige arched an eyebrow and gave me a pointed look that told me just how worthless she thought I was, what she thought of her mother's plan, and what she thought my chance of success was all in three seconds flat. Maybe it was fatigue, maybe it was the long, stressful day I'd had, but I snapped.

"Are you always such a bitch?" I blurted out, knowing damned good and well I'd just shot myself in the foot.

Around us the noise level noticeably dropped as people strained to hear Paige's response.

"Do you eat with that mouth?" Henry blustered, finally looking at me.

"As a matter of fact, she does, sir." Josh spoke while failing miserably at holding his own laughter in. He guided me through the crowd and out of the hotel, neither of us saying a word until we'd reached the safety of his car.

He pulled the car out of the Hyatt's circular drive and parked a few blocks away, then we both exploded with laughter.

"Oh my God," I finally gasped, my sides aching. "Did you *see* the look on her face?"

"What in the hell possessed you?"

"I don't know." My face ached from laughing so hard. I sniffled and dabbed at my eyes. "But it sure felt good." While fishing for some Kleenex in my purse, my hand brushed against Sybil's card. I held it up. "I guess I can scratch lunch with Sybil off my list."

"I wouldn't be so quick to toss that. Sybil's not anything like her mother."

"Obviously, but Paige *is* her mother and that counts for something." I sighed. "How do people just walk through life thinking that whatever they want is theirs for the asking?" As soon as the question was out of my mouth, my face grew scalding hot. The shame I felt over how I'd treated Reece and Robbie Jo hit me like a punch in the solar plexus. I'd pretty much done the same thing to my cousins. I turned to look out the window, fighting tears as the enormity of what I'd done sank in.

"I don't know, but can you imagine what your life would have been like with regular visits to Auntie Paige's?" Josh snickered.

"And don't forget Granny Diana," I added, hoping he wouldn't notice how hoarse my voice was.

"How could we?"

"You know," I murmured sleepily. "She's kind of a bitch."

"So you're saying Paige comes by it honestly."

I swatted at him with the back of my hand. "Smart-ass." I turned to face him, that last glass of wine I'd drunk, and my recent revelation, giving me the courage to finally tell him what I'd been holding in all night. "Henry wants you to come to work for him."

"Haven't we already had this discussion?"

"You don't understand. He *really* wants you. He wants you so bad, Diana's willing to give me my mother's trust fund if I can make it happen."

He never took his eyes off the road, and when he finally spoke, his voice was unusually soft, "So that's what all those questions were about earlier?"

"Yeah," I drawled sleepily, "but for the record, I told her I couldn't make you do anything you didn't want."

"Smart girl." He didn't sound too pleased, but all the wine

finally caught up with me and I dozed the rest of the drive to Galveston.

I'd honestly expected to wake up in front of Josh's place, not my building. I'd also expected him to stay the night, but he didn't. He just pressed a kiss to my forehead and said he'd call me.

Bright and early Monday morning, Josh's secretary called to set an appointment to sign the paperwork for the moving company sale. As of Tuesday, life as I knew it was over. It was a bittersweet feeling.

Though I didn't go so far as to buy a new suit, I put the maximum amount of effort into preparing for our Tuesday-afternoon meeting with Robbie Jo and Reece. Everything was moving much faster than I'd expected. I sighed into my coffee cup, thinking my cousins would be glad to see the last of me. I owed them in a big way, but had no clue how to make it up to them.

After Josh didn't return any of the three messages I'd left for him, I even arrived early, hoping we'd have a chance to talk. The last thing I expected was to see him come through the door with a laughing, windblown Robbie Jo on his arm.

Talk about pouring salt on a wound! His unusual silence the last few days had left me stumped.

"Having fun?" Robbie Jo smirked down at me.

"Robbie Jo," Reece softly warned.

"I just asked if she was having fun."

"I swear, you Cavanaugh women have given me more gray hairs in the last few weeks than—"

"You don't have any gray hairs, Josh." I smiled sweetly up at him and set my magazine aside.

"How would you know?" Robbie Jo's face morphed from a smirk to deadly serious. "Let's get this over with."

I followed the trio down the hall to Josh's office, stopping in front of him and glancing at him out of the corner of my eye. "I still owe you one," I said so only he could hear.

"My place. After we're done." He gave me a gentle nudge, but his sweet brown eyes were all business.

Someone had very kindly positioned a chair near Josh's desk, and that was the seat I headed for.

"Carla, I was wondering if you'd like to come over for dinner tonight."

"Can't. Got plans." I sat and crossed my legs, waiting for Josh to begin. As much as I knew I'd done the right thing in selling out, I *did* wish now I'd handled the entire matter better.

"Let's get started, shall we?" Josh pointed the still-standing Robbie Jo toward the last empty chair in the room before taking his own seat.

"Can I say something?" She sat and crossed her legs, swinging her black, patent leather heel back and forth.

Josh looked at her sharply, and I had the oddest sensation he'd rather be anywhere else than here with us. I can't say I really blamed him.

"I'm *not* changing my mind, Roberta Jo." That I was sure of.

"She wasn't going to ask you to change your mind, Carla Renée."

"*Renée.*" Josh's lips twitched as he discreetly studied all three of us. "You ladies take care of business as you see fit, but I charge by the hour."

"That's on Carla, not us, tiger." He practically beamed at Robbie Jo, and then, as if he realized where he was, and who he was with, opted for a more lawyer-like expression.

"Carla—"

"Reece, you are not my mother!" My back and shoulders tightened while the tension among the three of us threatened to choke me. Unfortunately, now was not the time for tears and apologies.

"I never said I was."

"So quit being a bitch, and let her talk, you hag!"

"Carla, relax! Robbie Jo, you too!" Reece ran her hands through her hair and leaned forward, her fists digging into the chair's arms. "We'd like for you to come and have a celebration dinner at the house tonight. Just the three of us. This is . . . new . . . for all of us, and we just want you to know that we understand you want to go on with your life and—" she waved a hand in the air as if she were struggling to find just the right words, "—do whatever you want to do, but we want you to know that we're still your family and we're still here for you. We love you, Carla Renée."

"Yeah," Robbie Jo said even though I'm not sure she meant it.

"Robbie Jo." Reece glared at her.

"It was a sincere yeah, thank you very much."

"Carla—" Reece gave me a gentle smile that left me feeling about two inches tall, "—Will you come have dinner with us tonight? If nothing else, for old times' sake."

I glanced at Josh, sincerely wishing now that I hadn't agreed to meet him later. He was such a saint for putting up with me, while I hadn't exactly been an angel lately. Honestly, I couldn't blame him if he hated me as much as I hated myself right then.

"What's it gonna be, Carla?" Robbie Jo's eyes flickered toward Josh, then back to me, a hint of a smirk still on her face.

"I really do have plans. Sorry, guys."

She shrugged in acceptance. "Well, what about tomorrow?"

"Tomorrow's . . ." I swallowed the lump in my throat and glanced at Josh again. "Tomorrow's good."

6

I went home and changed, all ready to walk out the door and head for Josh's, when I got hit with the most brilliant idea ever! Flipping through the phone book, I called the best baker in South Texas (at least in my opinion), and ordered Reece and Robbie Jo a cake for tomorrow night, then dashed out the door.

Josh was already home when I arrived. He'd shed his suit for his ratty gym shorts and T-shirt and was lighting the grill on the back deck. I have to say the view was spectacular.

"Bring your work clothes?" A bottle of Dos Equis in one hand, he smiled at me.

"No." I slowly crossed to where he stood, unsure of what to say, if he was going to dump me, or maybe, yell at me or something. "What's on the menu?" *Me?* And I didn't mean that in a good way.

He pulled a beer from the cooler at his feet and tossed it to me. "I've got some amazing shrimp marinating and if you don't like that, there's snapper."

"Sounds good." Though I was in the mood for something stronger, I gingerly twisted the lid off my beer and took a sip.

"So." We stood there staring at each other for a few tense heart-beats before I finally spoke again. "What now?"

Josh leaned against the railing, arms crossed over his chest. "You move to Houston; celebrate your newfound wealth. Of course most of it will go toward that downtown loft that Sybil mentioned."

"I'm not moving," I blurted out, realizing as the words tripped off my tongue that I meant it. Shoving a hand in the back pocket of my jeans, I closed the small distance between us. "I'm staying here."

"Good." He reached out, tucking tiny stray hairs behind my ear. "That's real good."

"Are you mad at me?" I finally asked.

"No. I'm mad at Henry and I'm mad at Diana for using you. I know it had to hurt—"

"I kind of deserved it, though."

"That doesn't make it right. And for what it's worth, I'm glad you're going to see your cousins tomorrow."

"I ordered a cake! I know that doesn't make up for being so horrible—"

"—But it's a nice start." He leaned down and covered my mouth, his lips soft and cool as he teased and suckled at mine. Our lips still fused, he took my beer, setting both of them on the railing. One fell, and we both laughed. "Maybe we should move this inside."

Josh led me inside and up the stairs, stripping me before I had time to catch my breath. I stretched out on the bed, letting the fan wash cool air over my skin as he peeled his T-shirt off, revealing wide shoulders and washboard abs.

"Want some help?" I asked, glad when he said no. I was enjoying the show.

He hooked his thumbs in the waistband of his shorts and smiled down at me. "Have you been a good girl?"

I nodded and giggled, wishing he'd hurry up. But he didn't move. He cleared his throat and gave me a pointed look. "Yes." My muscles felt fluid; my pussy swelled in anticipation of what was coming.

"Yes what?" The grin on his face grew as he played with the waistband of his shorts.

"Yes, I've been a good girl." Propping myself up on my elbows, I spread my legs, waiting for my reward.

Josh slid his shorts off, his beautiful thick cock bobbing slightly as he knelt between my thighs. It jutted out from his pubic hair, flush with blood and so thick I didn't know if I could get my hand around it. His eyes on my face, he leaned closer and guided it between my thighs, nudging my pussy lips apart and thrusting inside me. My breath caught in my throat, and I bit my lip to hold back my shocked cry, but one escaped anyway.

"Lay back." He tucked a pillow underneath my head and cradled me while his cock seemed to pulsate with life inside of me.

I did, and the stinging, full sensation dissipated. "Oh my God."

"Open your eyes, sweetheart."

His hips gently rotated from right to left, his cock caressing the walls of my pussy.

My legs shook and all I could think was how I wanted him to do it again. A lot. "Oh. My *God.*"

He covered my mouth with his, sucking at my tongue, nipping at my lips, then plunging deeper, while his hips guided his cock in the most deliciously seductive figure-eight. It shook me to the core, tormenting me by inches until another moan slipped past my lips and my nails dug into his back.

"Is that the best you can do?" he panted, picking up the pace, circling and thrusting harder.

I looked up at him as another moan slipped past my gritted teeth.

"Come on," he panted, his cock tormenting me, teasing me. "You can do better than that."

Tears stung my eyes, and a whimper escaped. My calf muscles screamed as my hips arched off the bed; my pussy tightened, milking the orgasm I desperately wanted him to give me. I was *so* close! I could feel the first deep tremors spiraling outward.

His stubble scraped across my tender nipple, and my hands clamped down hard on the pillow he'd given me, my whole body arching off the bed. An electrical shock hit me as he wrapped his lips around my nipple and gently lapped away the sting, then suckled hard.

"Please," I begged softly, one hand fisted in his hair, holding him in place. He looked up at me, his eyes so hot and black, and I shuddered in response. "I need . . . I need . . ."

"Are you ready?" He gently nuzzled my breasts, briefly burying his face in the valley between them. His cock slowly sank deep inside me and stopped.

"Yes," I panted, nodding. *God, was I ready!*

"Close your eyes. Relax, and let it all out. Okay?"

Wetting my lips, I nodded again and did as he said, almost crying in relief when his hips slid to the right, and then the left as he set us in motion again. My thigh muscles responded, tensing in anticipation, my hips arching off the bed again as I screamed and clung to Josh. Wave after wave of white-hot pleasure devoured me; Josh kept thrusting, cleaving into me until he came inside me with a hoarse shout.

I felt . . . lethargic, like I was swimming underwater, my arms and legs refused to move. "Oh my," I breathed, relaxing underneath him, enjoying the feel of his cock still pulsating inside me, his hard sweaty body covering mine.

He shifted so his lips were close to my ear. "You're a very, *very* good girl."

I woke up the following morning, alone in Josh's bed. Pushing my hair out of my eyes, I sat up, and was wondering where he'd gone when he appeared in the bedroom door with a cup of coffee in each hand. "Come back to bed?" I was ready for what I hoped would be the first of many early-morning snuggles.

He set one down on the dresser and tossed me his favorite holey T-shirt. "Sun's coming up soon."

I slid it over my head, tugging the soft material over my naked breasts and inhaling his scent, then climbed from the bed and joined him on the deck.

Epilogue

I parked in front of the carport, terrified to climb from the car, even if Reece and Robbie Jo had invited me. Never mind that I was here to apologize . . . and grovel. My loud sigh echoed in the tiny car.

Might as well put on my big-girl panties and get it over with.

I climbed out and retrieved the cake from the car's tiny backseat. Despite the heat and humidity, it was a beautiful Sunday afternoon with just enough of a breeze to keep the humidity from feeling oppressive. How could anything horrible happen on a day like today? Juggling my purse, keys, and cake, I walked between their cars and gingerly climbed the steps. No sooner had I put my foot on the second than the screen door flew open.

"You're late." Robbie Jo held the door for me while I struggled with the last few steps.

"Sorry."

Reece glanced over her shoulder at the sound of my voice, but kept working, quickly sliding chicken bones from the fricassee and dropping them on a plate. "You didn't have to bring anything, Carla. I told you."

"I know, but I wanted to. It's from Peaches," I finished lamely, setting the cake on the island and inhaling the mouth-watering aroma of chicken, red wine, potatoes, peppers, and a mix of Mexican herbs.

"Suck-up," Robbie Jo murmured, closing the door behind me. Peaches was Reece's favorite bakery and the only time she got a cake from there was on her birthday.

"Yeah, so? And?"

Reece chuckled from her spot at the counter. "That was very sweet, Carla."

"Want a beer?" Robbie Jo pointed at the fridge.

"Sure." I shrugged, while struggling to figure out how one went about apologizing for being the Bitch of the World. And a brat, to boot. I took the bottle she handed me and twisted the lid off, a brief smile tickling my lips at the memory of last night's beer with Josh.

Reece put down her tongs, crossed the kitchen to the fridge, and nudged Robbie Jo out of the way. She ducked in the freezer and pulled out a glass. My glass. The one she always kept ready for me because I really did hate drinking out of bottles. "Thanks." My fingers curled around the glass, the heat from my body leaving marks in the frost. "I'm sorry."

"You brought cake," she said, draping her arms over my shoulders.

"You made my favorite chicken." I shrugged, giving her a watery smile.

"It's my favorite chicken, too." Robbie Jo stepped up next to us, draping an arm around both of our shoulders, and we all laughed.

Setting my glass and bottle down, I wrapped an arm around each of their waists, leaning into Robbie Jo, who'd been the closest I had to a best friend for years, and glancing across at Reece. "Can you forgive me?"

"Of course we can." Robbie Jo gave my shoulder a friendly squeeze. "Right after you tell us what's going on between you and that hot lawyer of yours."

Jodi Lynn Copeland
offers a taste of something
SWEET AND SINFUL!

On sale now!

1

She'd finally done it. Turned her porn star dreams into reality.

Freshly showered with a fluffy white robe wrapped around her, Courtney Baxter exited the hotel suite bathroom and beamed at the naked male ass asleep on the coverless bed.

Technically, it was more than an ass. A prime, hard-bodied, and excellently equipped specimen of the male species was attached to that fine backside. And she hadn't exactly become a full-fledged porn star, or ever dreamed of becoming one, for that matter. But she had enticed Mr. Hot Buns into letting her videotape their wild antics.

To think, less than two months ago she couldn't score so much as a dinner date for her average looks and behavior. Now, thanks to a little guidance from her across-the-cubicle coworker at Pinnacle Engineering, Courtney was neither average nor lacking for men to date, dine with, or just plain do.

Thanks to Candy Masterson, Courtney was a bona fide sex diva and loving every minute of it. A sex diva that was overdue to make her exit.

The secret of having fun with sex, Candy had told her, was

getting out while things were still going good. In other words, not sticking around until Mr. Hot Buns woke up from his post-orgasm slumber and Courtney had to face that awkward "I never got to know more than your sexual preference and marital status before I laid you" moment.

The beefcake in mention shifted on the bed before rolling onto his back and trapping both the top and bottom sheet beneath well-developed calves. She held her breath with the idea she'd missed her getaway opportunity. Thankfully, his eyes never opened. He just started into some serious snoring that suggested he wasn't waking anytime soon.

Releasing her breath, she took advantage of his vulnerable state and slid her gaze along his body.

Black hair covered his solid frame, thick on his head and groin, thinner on his chest and the rest of his big body. A mustache touched against his upper lip and, oh, the wickedly wonderful ways he'd used that coarse bit of hair on her.

Her pussy pulsed with the memory of his mouth down there, his tongue inside her folds, lapping at her cream. Instinctively, her gaze drifted lower, past the solid expanse of his stomach to his cock. As if he could feel her watching him, his shaft stirred, rousing to its previously solid state. This time minus the condom so she could see every inch of steely male flesh. Plump pinking head. Pre-cum oozing from the tip . . . just waiting for her tongue to reach out and lick.

Damn, it was tempting to shake the robe off her shoulders, climb back onto the bed, and let first her mouth and then her sex gobble up his erection.

It was *always* tempting.

But tempting fate by making it seem she was after more than a little harmless sex was not the point. Having fun was. Enjoying herself, her body, her twenty-six-year-old sex drive before it started petering out and she had to face the reality of an average life all over again.

That rather depressing thought got Courtney moving as it always did.

This time making her getaway meant more than chucking the robe and pulling on the red leather pants, black baby-doll top, and four-inch-heel stilettos that had taken her the better part of a week to learn to walk in without resembling a newborn foal taking its first steps. This time leaving meant gathering up her camera, tripod, and taping supplies.

She moved as soundlessly as possible through the hotel room, searching out rashly cast-aside clothing and pulling it on. She was dressed and nearly finished storing the camera and accessories in their bag when Mr. Hot Buns' snoring came to an abrupt end.

Ten feet behind her, sheets rustled. The bed gave a creak.

Courtney swore under her breath and went deadly still, silent. Pulse pounding at her throat, she felt far too much like she had when she'd gotten trapped by a wild boar on the outskirts of her parents' blueberry farm.

Cornered, and desperate for escape.

Please stay asleep.

"You should have woken me," came a sleep-roughened male voice.

She bit her lip to keep her groan inside. With the boar, she'd gotten lucky and her dad had come to her rescue. With the beefcake, her luck had run out.

Aware the only way she was going to get out of this hotel room was with action, Courtney finished stowing the tripod and zipped up the camera bag. Hooking the bag's strap over her shoulder, she pasted on her most sensual smile and turned around. Mr. Hot Buns sat in bed, his back to the plain wood headboard and his cock at full mast and calling to her from across the room. Even more than his willingness to go along with her videotaping desire, he'd been a great lay. Eager to please, again and again.

She still had to go. Now.

This sex game was about confidence, arrogance even, so she took her smile from sensual to smug. "Not on your life, buster. The way you were snoring, it was clear that I wore you out."

A frown twitched at his lips as he nodded at the camera bag. "Going somewhere?"

She'd picked him out of all the men at the bar because of the self-assured aura he gave off. Now that aura was nowhere to be found. Now he was brooding—his cocoa brown eyes reminded her of a wounded puppy—and the country girl of her roots was threatening to resurface and make her want to jump him more than ever. "It's late."

"I have this room till morning."

Yeah, and she had a personal promise to maintain. One that meant not permanently falling into the arms of the first guy who wanted her beyond an initial screw. "Sorry, but I have morning plans that require sleeping in my own bed tonight."

"I won't be getting a number, will I?"

"You said you were after a night of fun."

"I guess the whole videotaping thing made me realize you're more than a pretty face and hot body." His frown stayed in place a few more seconds, and then he shook it off and eyed the camera bag hanging from her shoulder. "Can I at least get something to remember you by?"

Something to—Oh. He wanted a copy of her tape.

Nerves ate at Courtney's belly with the thought of truly being porn material for Mr. Hot Buns, and potentially his friends as well. She considered refusing the request. But then, it was his tape, too. And it would look incredibly insecure of her to turn him down for fear he would show it to others. She'd worked way too hard at this sex-diva thing to appear timid.

"All right." Really, she would never meet his friends or probably ever see him again either. Besides, what could one little naughty videotape hurt? "I don't have an extra tape along, but if you give me your name and address, I'll mail you a copy."

"What could one little naughty videotape hurt?" Gail Taeber's voice was a cross between disbelief and outrage. Hands on her shorts-clad hips in the middle of the living room of the downtown Grand Rapids apartment they shared, she gave Courtney the evil eye. "What, are you nuts?" She waved a slim hand dismissively. "Never mind, don't answer that. It's clear what you are, what you've become. A slut."

They'd been friends since their freshman year in college eight years ago; far too long for Courtney to be offended. And truthfully, before taking control of the more pleasurable aspects of her life, she would have felt the same way.

Now Courtney knew the value of letting life's daily stresses fall to the wayside, by way of a hunk to do.

"Mmm . . . Guilty as charged." Hoping to get a laugh out of her roomie, she licked her lips exaggeratedly, then segued into a little bump and grind hip action that reminded her how tight the red leather pants were. She'd intended to come home and head straight to her bedroom to slip into something literally more comfortable, but then Gail had been up watching a movie and, from the instant Courtney stepped through the door, had started in with the grilling.

Without a hint of amusement, Gail scraped her fingers through her hair, pulling back the naturally white-blond, mid-back-length locks. "I don't get you anymore."

"You don't get 'it' at all." Courtney regretted the words the instant they left her mouth. Just because she was living her desires didn't mean she felt everyone had to do the same.

Hurt passed through Gail's eyes. Then her hands returned to her hips and her expression became one of aversion. "Is that all you think about these days? Sex?"

"Of course not!" Assuming an impish smile, Courtney gave a last attempt at humor. "I think about all the places I've yet to pick a man up."

Gail's eyes narrowed. "You're unbelievable. Not even close to the girl I used to know."

Accepting she wasn't going to get to her bedroom and comfy clothes anytime soon, Courtney dropped down on the blue and beige striped sofa. "I was kidding," she assured soberly while removing the killer stilettos and tossing them aside. "I still take plenty of things seriously. You *are* right about one thing, though. I'm not the girl you used to know. She was average. Boring. Afraid to take a chance for fear of failure." A country bumpkin who'd nearly let the best years of her sex life flash before her eyes.

"Now you're a woman who leaps into bed with every guy she meets without a thought to looking beyond if his equipment appeals to her."

"I don't do *every* guy I meet. There have been a few this month and, yeah, a handful last month. But so what? I'm happy. And I leave them happy."

"So you think. What happens when you hook up with a guy who wants more than a single night and is ready to do *anything* to see that he gets it?"

"I hook up with guys who want the same thing I want." If they changed their mind after the fact, the way Mr. Hot Buns had tonight, that was hardly her fault. Even so, Courtney was a good enough judge of character to spot a lunatic. And smart enough to know that when she did dare to walk the line, as in the case of the promised videotape, to send her package "signature required" lest it end up in the wrong hands. "That doesn't include stalkers or rapists, if that's what you're implying."

"I'm implying," Gail started sharply. Then all the bluster came out of her on a whooshing breath and a muttered, "Oh, hell."

Wearing a contrite smile, she dropped down next to Courtney on the sofa. "I don't really think you're a slut. You know me better than that. I just worry—there's always so much crap on the news about some woman being beaten, or shot to death by an ex-lover."

"Thanks for your concern," Courtney said sincerely, "but I'll be okay. We took that self-defense class in college, and I have pepper spray in my purse, if there ever comes a point when I need it. I'm not going to live in fear of such an unlikely event. This is my time for fun, for pleasure, to be more than average. No psycho man is going to ruin it for me."

Seriously, there was nothing to worry about. Courtney was behaving just like Candy, and Candy had been behaving this way for darned near a decade without incident. She would be fine. Better yet, she would be well sexed and purring like a kitten whenever the urge to get laid struck.

After spending the last two-and-a-half months in the scorching desert heat of Iraq, overseeing the first phases of construction of a multimillion-dollar wastewater treatment system, Blaine Daly was damned glad to be back to Michigan's generally mild late-June weather. Back to his role of construction manager for Pinnacle Engineering's Eastern Region. Back to an air-conditioned office building with nearly all the amenities of home, at least on those days he wasn't required to supervise in the field.

Back to Candy.

Blaine's smile was automatic as he said good morning to Sherry, the fifty-something, bottle-redhead admin working the front desk, and then breezed on past the short fogged-glass partition that separated the lobby from the two-story building's general resources and production area. He and Candy had no sexual history and too little chemistry to consider a future fling. Still, he respected her no-holds-barred approach to sex. And he enjoyed the hell out of the way she filled her scanty clothes and livened up an office otherwise occupied by mostly stoic workers.

He'd also always enjoyed her hair, dirty-blond waves that caressed her shoulders and flowed partway down her back.

The woman rifling through the double-wide filing cabinet across the room wore Candy's risqué style of clothing. A barely mid-thigh-length black skirt hugged the lush curve of her ass. Sheer thigh-high stockings, with black pinstripe, picked up where the skirt left off, and led to dark green three-inch heels that matched her off-the-shoulder, short-sleeve top.

It was her hair that was different.

This woman was a brunette. The ends of her straight, chin-length locks tipped with a lighter shade of brown, bordering on dark blond.

Had Candy gotten a cut and dye job, or who was the woman?

Blaine joined Jake Markham, one of the construction field guys he supervised, at the interoffice mail bins a few feet away. Jake's hand held open the manila mail folder with his name on it, but his attention appeared fixed on the same spot—make that babe—as Blaine's.

"New employee?" Blaine asked casually.

Jake looked over at Blaine with far too much appreciation filling his eyes for a guy still in his first year of marriage. But then, hot women had a way of screwing with a guy's best intentions, and looking wasn't really a crime. "The new Courtney."

"Baxter?" *Holy shit.*

Testosterone pumping through his system like mad and his thoughts far from work, Blaine zipped his gaze back to the woman.

To Courtney Baxter. Mindblowing, yet not a total shocker.

He'd always believed she had an inner dirty girl. Her job as a technical writer responsible for the firm's local proposal efforts meant they worked together from time to time. Each time they got close, he swore her blue-green eyes revealed naughty thoughts. He'd nearly asked her about them a time or two, and if they didn't happen to involve the two of them without a stitch of clothing. But he hadn't wanted to embarrass her, just in case he was mistaken. And nothing ever came out of her own mouth that wasn't 100-percent professional.

Until now? Or was changing the way she dressed as far as things went?

Without looking Jake's way, he mused, "Wonder what brought the transformation on?"

"Knowing how women are, she probably realized she's creeping up on thirty and figured she'd better start using it before she loses it."

Doubtful. Courtney's twenty-seventh birthday was still a month away—he recalled seeing her last one mentioned in the company newsletter and the date stuck in his mind for whatever reason. As for losing it, the raw sensuality floating off her body and sucking him in from thirty feet away made it seem unlikely there was a chance of that happening anytime in the next six or seven decades.

"I wouldn't go there," Jake said, apparently keyed into Blaine's thoughts.

Or, shit, Blaine admonished himself, maybe it was the way he was eying Courtney up like a fresh-off-the-grill porterhouse. Losing the wolfish look, he glanced at Jake. "Why's that?"

"Rumor has it she's on a pleasure quest, but that she already has a man lined up for when she decides she's had enough of the hunt."

Was that supposed to dissuade his interest in her? If so, the attempt failed miserably.

Blaine had never told Courtney that he was as attracted to her as she sometimes appeared to be to him, because he believed his player reputation could be a turnoff. Now it seemed that was exactly what she was after. A guy who knew when he was wanted and had no problem moving on when that want had run its course.

His body kicking to full awareness with the knowledge, Blaine looked back at Courtney. Only, she wound up being a whole lot closer than planned. If she were taller, he would have ended up with his nose stuck between her breasts. As it was, and with her heels on, she was almost mouth level to him and he came damned close to brushing her lips with his.

For the instant it took her to gasp and step back, he felt the warmth of her breath mingling with his own. Saw the flicker of unmistakable lust in her eyes. Caught the hitch in her breathing as her response to his nearness moved from surprise to desire.

He grinned as the truth flooded him.

He hadn't been mistaken with his wonder if her naughty thoughts were about the two of them naked. She wanted him. And the rousing of his cock spoke volumes about his want for her.

An appreciative smile curved her glistening, red-painted lips as Courtney slid past him to nod at his field guy. "Morning, Jake. Love the shirt." Slim black bracelets jangled along her suntanned arm as she fingered the open collar of Jake's polo shirt, letting the wine-colored material slip slowly from her fingertips.

Jake said something in return, but Blaine could give two shits less what it was.

Courtney was back to looking at him. Her thickly lash-fringed eyes filled with those same daring thoughts he'd been sure of seeing a hundred times before. The difference was that her expression was unguarded now. Her body inclined toward him. Her breasts inches from filling his hands. With the off-the-shoulder style of her top, it wouldn't take much effort to work the material the rest of the way down her arms and then off.

"Have a good trip?" she asked in a voice just this side of seductive.

There were a lot of ways he wanted to answer that question. Vocally. Physically. Up against the duplex printer. Preferably when the top was lifted and her bare butt cheeks pressed against the warm glass.

Since this was the office and, while he never made a secret of his reputation for getting around, he had a lot of coworkers under his employ and respecting his professionalism while on the clock, he stuck with the first. A vocal, nonsexual response. "Yeah. We got a lot accomplished. I'd love to tell you about it, but it would take a while and I'm due for a conference call in five minutes."

"That's too bad."

It for damned sure was. The department-head meeting was the reason he'd returned to work on a Friday, instead of taking the weekend to recoup. The meeting, and the fact that he felt like he'd been neglecting his local responsibilities for far too long already. The work being completed abroad was under a Pinnacle contract. Still, no one had filled the bulk of his shoes while he was away. "Drop by my place tonight."

Avid interest lit Courtney's eyes. Her smile turned wickedly playful . . . and then vanished. "I wish I could, but I have a date."

"Bring him." A little competition didn't scare him, particularly since he wasn't looking for anything serious for the time being and, clearly, neither was she. "I'm having a 'Back from Iraq' get-together."

"You are?" Jake piped in, reminding Blaine he was still standing there.

There hadn't actually been a party planned, but it appeared there was now. With Jake working in the office this morning and out in the field this afternoon, he was as good of a source for getting the news out to their coworkers as any.

Blaine nodded. "I'll shoot you an e-mail with the details."

"I'll hold you to it." Jake finished fishing the mail from his interoffice folder. After giving Courtney a too-friendly smile, he started for the stairwell that led to the construction and transportation departments on the building's second floor.

"When you said to drop by your house, I thought you meant—" Courtney stopped short, waving the words away with the clink of her bracelets. "Never mind." Her smile returned, slightly diminished but still playful enough to have Blaine eager for a taste of her lips, quickly followed by the rest of her hot body. "Maybe we'll stop by. You still live in the brownstone outside of Kentwood?"

"I do." *And those thoughts of yours were dead on.*

He wouldn't risk speaking the words where anyone could hear, but there was no reason Blaine couldn't convey what he'd intended behind the closed door of his office. "If you'd rather catch up before tonight, I should have some time after lunch. Stop by my office."

"Tempting." Perfectly arched eyebrows rose as her gaze dipped from his face to cruise intimately down his body and back up again. "Seriously, it is," she said in a thready voice when their eyes again met. "But I'll have to pass. I have a proposal going out this afternoon and you know how they have a way of dragging out till the last minute."

"I do." He also knew if his cock jerked that hard in response to her bodily assessment while he was clothed, it was going to do an entire hula when she eyed him up naked. "See you tonight."

Courtney started away from him without responding. Just when she would have rounded the corner to the hallway leading back to her cubicle, she looked back, over her sexily bared shoulder, and flashed a grin that could only be termed dirty as sin. "If you're lucky, you will."